KILLING CHRISTMAS

An absolutely addictive crime thriller with a huge twist

BILL KITSON

(DI MIKE NASH BOOK 4)

JOFFE BOOKS

Revised edition 2019
Joffe Books, London

First published as "ALTERED EGOS" in 2011
© Bill Kitson

**Please join our mailing list for free Kindle crime
thriller, detective, mystery books and new releases.**
www.joffebooks.com

ISBN: 978-1-78931-257-7

DEDICATION

For Val
Wife, lover, best friend, critic and editor

ACKNOWLEDGEMENTS

My grateful thanks to the following friends and professionals who contributed their expertise to help me in the writing of *Killing Christmas*:

Peter Billingsley MD, for his information and advice on the subject of drugs.

Judy and Arnold Smith for allowing me to nosey around their motorhome and ask awkward questions about wild camping whilst eating all Judy's cheese scones.

My 'in-house' proof-reader, copy-editor and continuity girl, Val, whose input is far greater than she will take credit for.

Steve replied first. 'I'm not happy about it. But it might save scores of lives if we can take them out.'

'Steve's got a point,' Barry agreed. 'I know Smithy's idea sounds crazy, and I take your point about the odds, but we can cut that with the element of surprise.'

'I'm still not happy about it,' Johnny grumbled.

'Go on with you,' Steve teased. 'You just don't want to get blood on your nice clean shirt.'

After three weeks without washing facilities, their faces tanned by the relentless sun, permanently dust-streaked and with sweat constantly oozing from every pore, they stank like the goats that surrounded them.

Sundown came early in those latitudes especially at that time of year. Shortly after 4.30 p.m. they began their assault on the village. By 5.15 p.m. the firefight was over. The four-man unit had succeeded in reducing the enemy forces to less than half their original strength; but had lost two of their own in the process. Barry and Steve, approaching from the south, had done most damage, getting three-quarters of the way through the village before they encountered any opposition. As Steve got to the northern outskirts he saw Barry take out three men with semi-automatic rifles, one of whom was about to fire on Steve. He turned to thank his colleague when he saw Barry stumble, fall to his knees and throw his head back, before pitching full length on the dusty street.

Steve checked for a pulse but knew by the wounds it was hopeless. He glanced around. The opposition had scattered. That assault had been their final throw. He raced out from behind the last houses to see his commanding officer despatching two more of the escaping enemy. They joined forces. 'Time to go,' Smithy said tersely. 'Where's Barry?'

'Bought it; died where he fell. What about Johnny?'

'Took one in the chest on the way in. Let's get out of here. I'm going up to that ridge to radio for a chopper. You stay here and cover my back.' The officer put his hand on Steve's shoulder. 'I couldn't ask for anyone better.'

Smithy had been gone no more than two minutes when Steve spotted a cloud of flies hovering over Johnny's corpse, first of a long queue of diners. He moved closer to say good-bye, to shoo the flies away; he wasn't really sure which. As he rounded the boulders near the body a shot whistled close to his ear. He ducked behind the nearest rock and waited.

Smithy whirled round as he heard the burst of fire behind him. He paused so briefly, he barely broke stride. Then he continued; eyes fixed on the ridge ahead. He glanced back only once. He could just make out that Steve had taken cover and was still firing. Then the gathering darkness reduced visibility. After a moment or two, the firing ceased. The night was silent.

CHAPTER ONE

'Morning, ma'am,' DI Mike Nash greeted the chief constable as he entered her office at Netherdale Police Station.

She smiled. 'Mike, let me introduce you.' She indicated her visitor, a good-looking woman in her mid thirties. 'This is Superintendent Edwards. She's here short term until Superintendent Pratt is fit to return to work. He's recovering well from the heart attack, so in three months Ruth will take up her new post with Her Majesty's Inspectorate of Constabulary; so you'd better behave yourself.'

'Don't I always, ma'am?' Nash affected a look of injured innocence as he shook hands with the newcomer.

'I hope you don't expect an honest answer to that,' Chief Constable O'Donnell retorted.

When Nash returned to his office at Helmsdale later that morning, DS Clara Mironova was waiting in the CID suite.

'What's matter?' Nash asked. 'No crime to solve?'

'I wanted to know what the new boss was like.'

'She seems very nice. Quite young for a Superintendent' – Nash kept a straight face – 'and far better looking than Tom Pratt.'

'Is Tom not coming back then?'

'Eventually. Ruth's only here until he's fit again.'

'So we're on first name terms already are we? Is she married?'

'I don't think so, why do you ask?'

'I wonder what Becky will think of you having an attractive single boss around the place.'

'I don't think she'll be at all worried.'

'What's that mean? That you're not going to tell her?'

'Of course I will. If, and when, the subject comes up.'

'Speaking of Becky, I suppose you and she will be spending Christmas together?'

Nash caught the wistful tone in Clara's voice. 'No, as a matter of fact we won't. Becky's going to visit her parents. They retired to Bournemouth and she promised she'd spend Christmas with them. Why do you ask?'

'I was hoping to get a bit of leave. David will be home for a few days and I want to see him before he goes back. It'll be his last overseas tour, at least for the foreseeable future, so I don't want to miss him.'

'That should work out fine.' Nash saw Clara's face relax. 'As I'm not doing anything special I might as well be on call. Viv can back me up; I doubt he'll be visiting his family in Antigua for Christmas. At least I won't be covering Netherdale as well now Ruth's on board.'

'Aren't you planning any holiday?'

'I might take a break after Tom gets back. Becky's trying to persuade me to go skiing, but I don't fancy sliding down an Alp on my backside.'

Mironova grinned. 'I'd have thought the après-ski would be right up your street?'

'Becky's a serious skier. She's been going since she was small and she's pretty good. I can't hope to compete with that. And I'm not into that après-ski scene.'

'Too old I suppose. A shame that. I'd have loved to see the photos. Don't you even fancy tobogganing? You can do that lying down; your favourite position.'

'Go make coffee, Sergeant. And try not to make it taste like snake venom for once.'

The house was like all the others in the row. Semi-detached, built during the 1950s, with economy as the overriding principle. The contractor had enthusiastically taken the instructions from the Ministry of Defence on board. Materials were the cheapest, appliances purely functional. Even the plot size was minimal. Profits were the only item that hadn't been cut to the bone.

It was one of the coldest nights of the winter, with temperatures well below freezing point. Bereft of adequate insulation the house was like an icebox; the central heating had been on the blink for months. It was scheduled to be replaced in spring. Reluctantly, but with two young children to keep warm, the housewife turned to the back-up heating. The gas fires were old, but at least they worked. She wasn't happy about leaving them on all night, especially as they hadn't been serviced for over twelve months, but realized she'd no choice. Anyway, the workmen would be coming to do them tomorrow.

She wished her husband was home. Steve was good with his hands. He could fix things. He'd have sorted the heating out. But he was thousands of miles away; she'd no idea how far. He wouldn't have gone if it hadn't been for the money. Or lack of it. That, and the argument. The row had been about money; what else. 'I can't manage on what we've got. How do you think I'll cope with an extra mouth to feed and no money coming in? You'll be out of work and all the bills still to pay? This place may not be up to much but at least we don't have the rent to fork out. That'd change. And all we'd have is family allowance, and a bit of money from the Social.'

Of course he'd stormed off; gone to the pub. Next morning he was up and out of the house before she woke. By the time she was dressing he'd signed on for another tour. This time it wasn't cushy. Not Gibraltar or Falklands. Not Germany. This time it was the big one. The one all the wives feared. This time it was Afghanistan. Afghanistan. Even the name struck fear into her heart, as it did with all the wives. Not knowing. That was the worst. News bulletins didn't help. "A British soldier has been killed…." Her heart lurched every time she heard the words.

A few months ago they'd lost one; Sonya's husband, from across the road. Too close for comfort. She'd seen Sonya's light on at all hours of the night. Could only guess at what she was feeling. Apart from the grief there was the worry. The MOD widow's pension wouldn't go far. The widow's mite they called it. And Sonya was what, twenty-eight and with three youngsters under seven. Sometimes she worried because she daren't face Sonya; still didn't know what to say to her. What do you say? What can you say? 'Sorry, Sonya, some bastard with an RPG has blown the rest of your life to hell and back?' You can't say it, even if you're thinking it: even if it's the truth. So you stick with meaningless platitudes.

She poured another glass of wine. It was late. Both children would be fast asleep by now. She sipped the wine as she watched TV. When the reality show ended, she drained her glass, switched the TV off. Everything done, she yawned, time for bed. Strange that doing nothing should make you so weary.

Somewhere in the early hours one of the children started to cough. In an instant, she was awake; listening. She waited for a repeat. When it didn't come she drifted back off to sleep.

The workmen arrived late. It was almost 9 a.m. when they pulled up outside the house. They rang the bell. Getting no reply they hammered on the door; still nothing. One of them went round the back. He reappeared a few minutes later, shaking his head.

'Can I help?'

They turned. The neighbour was young, young and pretty. 'We can't raise the lady of the house,' the younger workman explained. 'We're here to service her' – he paused, leered – 'appliances.'

The neighbour ignored the innuendo. 'She must be in. That's her car.'

The older workman stepped back and looked up at the bedroom windows. The curtains were still closed. Despite that, he thought he'd caught a glimpse of something glinting in the weak morning sunlight: condensation.

He'd been in the job a lot of years; realized what the condensation meant. 'Oh no,' he muttered. 'Stu, come here, quick.'

The tent was hot, dusty and uncomfortable. Unable to knock, the signals officer coughed. 'Excuse me, sir. Message from HQ.'

The colonel looked up. His signals officer, usually phlegmatic, looked distressed. 'What is it?'

He listened as the man gave him the gist. 'Oh God. Poor devil. How the hell do you tell a man that sort of thing? You never think of something like that happening, more the other way round. Better bring him in here.'

They were back in less than ten minutes. Not long enough for the officer to rehearse what he had to say. The man knew something was wrong; knew before the officer spoke; knew by the look on his face. Even if he hadn't known, the CO's opening words would have given the game away.

'Come in, Steve.'

'Where's Captain Smith?' Steve asked.

'Major Smith,' the colonel corrected him. 'Transferred back to Military Intelligence and promoted; all to do with that effort of yours last month. Now, you'd better take a seat. I'm afraid I've got some bad news for you. Very bad news.'

Memories and sadness, memories and guilt, memories and anger; they were all he had left. If it hadn't been for the row it would never have happened. He wouldn't have been here in this godforsaken hellhole. That was why he'd volunteered; agreed to go on their special assignment.

If they'd been able to afford it he wouldn't have come. If he hadn't been away, they wouldn't be dead. The 'ifs' swirled round and round in his brain, like loose ball bearings in a pinball machine. And all the time his guilt, his anger and his grief fused together like a hard knot in the pit of his stomach. He remembered his words at the time. 'If all I'm good for is a pay cheque, I might as well sign on again. That way you'll have less food to buy.'

He'd seen the hurt look on her face, ignored it. So busy with his own pride he hadn't attempted to console her. Just slammed out of the house and gone to the pub. He'd signed up again next morning, gone for the MAD assignment they'd been punting at the barracks. No one knew what it was about, but you had to be highly qualified before they'd consider you.

The officer he'd reported to was specific. Outlined what was needed. 'Special forces training, sniper grade, para qualified. Those are minimum requirements.'

'I've got those, sir. And my BELT.'

Behind enemy lines training it stood for. Hadn't had to use it in anger, but obviously worth mentioning because the officer said immediately, 'If you've got those, I reckon you stand a good chance of getting selected.'

'Can I ask what this assignment involves, sir?'

'Of course you can. Just don't hold your breath for a reply.'

That had been over eighteen months ago. Since then everything had changed. And now this.

He sat alongside the airstrip, a dusty, barren landscape bisected by the thin ribbon of tarmac. Waiting; waiting for his transport. Transport to home; that wasn't home any longer. To England, suddenly more desolate than this place. To England, and a new mission: revenge. Revenge on those who'd brought this about. He thought about Smith and his anger doubled. Promoted; he'd almost blurted it out in the colonel's tent. Promoted, for shooting one of his men in the back. Because Steve knew that's what had happened. Smith, crazed by the drug, had shot Johnny in the back for objecting to his orders. Not only that, he'd left Steve to die out there. Smith must have thought he was safe. He'd have got a hell of a shock when Steve came out of the desert. Was that the real reason Smith had been transferred?

They were here to protect the nation. That's what they were told. Protect the nation against terrorism. And because he was here, he was unable to protect his own wife, his own daughters. Protect them against what he knew was little short of murder. Well, if it was murder they wanted, they'd come to the right man.

CHAPTER TWO

Lara stared out of the window, watching the snowflakes' flickering descent, as if they were reluctant to land. The scene was a uniformity of grey, the snow beginning to shroud the lawns, the flower beds, the trees and even the countryside beyond. She sighed and turned away. Winter wasn't her favourite time of year. She was bored, needed some excitement, a new thrill. Or was it the old thrill she sought? She walked across the kitchen to the refrigerator and opened the door. Her hand hovered over the wine bottle before she picked up the milk carton alongside it. She was waiting for the kettle to boil when the phone rang, as if to ratify the good sense of her decision.

'Lara, darling, it's Caroline. Are you free tonight?'

Lara felt her pulse quickening at the familiar voice, and at the words. The question could only mean one thing. 'Caroline, I was just thinking about you. Yes, I'm all alone. Why, are you thinking of coming over?'

'If that's all right? When I've finished work, that is.'

'Of course it's all right; more than all right. You should know better than to have to ask. But what about Richard?'

'Don't tell me your husband hasn't told you his movements.' There was a mocking tone in Caroline's voice.

'He rarely tells me anything these days. I only know of a supposed Birmingham conference in January. What else is it he should have told me?'

'That he's away until tomorrow evening. Some sort of field trip.'

'Some sort of field trip? Surely you must know more than that? You're his boss, after all.'

'Yes, I do, but I can't say over an open phone line.'

'Bloody secrecy. If he's not coming back does that mean you'll be able to stay the night?'

'I can, if you want me to.'

Lara felt the blood coursing, felt the excitement rising. 'Of course I do. You know how much I miss you.'

'That's all right then. I'll see you in a couple of hours. Oh, and, Lara, one more thing.'

'What is it?'

'I'll be bringing something with me, as I promised.'

'I'll make it worth your while. You know that.'

'I do, Lara, darling. I'll be with you as quickly as I can.'

The time dragged. Lara prepared a casserole and put it in the oven. Something simple that would be ready when they were. She set the table before going upstairs for a shower where she spent a long time under the hot jet of water. She took extra care with her make-up before dressing. She was returning downstairs when she heard a car pull up outside and hurried to open the front door. The snow had stopped, the gloom dispelled by the security light. She saw Caroline climb out of the car. Lara's legs felt shaky with excitement; her pulse raced.

The two women embraced politely at the door; two old friends greeting one another. As soon as they were inside, and the door was locked against the outside world, they embraced again, but this was a totally different matter. They held each other close, their tongues exploring each other's mouths in a long, passionate kiss that left them both breathless.

Eventually they separated and walked slowly through to the kitchen, arms around each other's waist, fingers entwined and caressing, heads close together.

12

'Are you hungry?' Lara asked. 'Do you want to eat now, or later?'

Caroline walked up behind her and slipped her hands inside Lara's top. She began to massage her breasts gently as she replied, 'What do you think?'

Lara arched her back with pleasure. 'Later,' she gasped.

Caroline withdrew her hands and reached for her bag. 'Hold your hand out. Now close your eyes.'

Lara did as instructed. A second later she felt the cold metal against her palm. She smiled, dreamily.

'As I promised,' Caroline told her.

'You're a life saver.'

Caroline watched as Lara used the inhaler. Once, twice, three times. As she set the inhaler down on the worktop Caroline reached out for her and drew her close. They began touching each other intimately as their kisses grew more and more tempestuous.

They raced upstairs hand in hand and when they reached the bedroom they stopped. Observance of the next part of the ritual of their lovemaking was sacred to them. They undressed one another slowly, each movement, each garment removal accompanied by another intimate caress.

Later, as they lay, holding one another in drowsy content, Lara asked again, 'Do you want to eat?'

Caroline stretched out. 'Later,' she said. She rolled over, pushed Lara down on the bed. 'Later,' she murmured again, her voice husky with desire, 'perhaps.'

'Are you ready for off?'

Becky looked up from the open suitcase. 'Can't wait to get rid of me, I bet. Got a woman lined up for as soon as I've left? Who is it, your stunning new boss?'

Nash eyed her suspiciously. 'What do you know about her?'

'Hah! Think you're the only detective round here?'

'Anyway, the answer's no, to both questions.' Nash moved forward and took the jumper she'd been about to pack from her hand. He heaved the suitcase onto the floor and put his arms round her. 'Your train's not due for a couple of hours.' His eyes strayed to the bed.

'Why do you think I haven't showered yet?'

Later, he lay, watching her dress, admiring her figure. Thinking how much he'd miss her. 'Hey, you never answered my question.'

She swung round in the act of fastening her skirt. 'What question?'

'What do you know about Superintendent Edwards?'

'Ruth? She was three years ahead of me at school.'

'Oh Lord,' Nash groaned. 'Not another exile from St Trinians.'

He caught the shoe she hurled at him with ease. 'You throw like a wicket-keeper,' he sneered. 'So, what's she really like?'

'She's intelligent, organized, efficient and smart. You should get on well. They say opposites attract.'

'Have you been to Clara's insulting classes? You're getting to sound like her. Anything else I should know?'

Becky thought for a moment. 'Well, there was a rumour about her at school. But that's years ago, and I'm not sure if it was anything more than gossip.'

'Tell me. You know how I love a good gossip.'

'The rumour was that Ruth was of the other persuasion.'

Nash raised his eyebrows. 'A lesbian? No wonder you're so relaxed about her.'

Becky grinned. 'Come on, get dressed and take me to the station. Then you can go for that pint you're obviously pining for. When you get there, give my love to Jonas.'

'Much good that's going to do you. His heart belongs to Clara.'

'Maybe, but the vegetables from his allotment are gorgeous.'

'Ayup, Mr Nash. All alone tonight?'

'Now then, Mr Turner. Yes, I've just taken Becky to the station. She said to wish you Merry Christmas.'

''Ad enough of you then, 'as she? Found out what a bad lad you are?'

'No, she's off to spend Christmas with her parents.'

'That's a bit rough for you.'

Nash smiled ruefully. 'I'll probably not get chance to worry about it. I'm working both Christmas and the New Year.'

'No rest for the wicked, so they say. And ah suppose that means no rest for them as has to catch t' villains.'

'It's our busiest time of year, right enough. Apart from the usual suspects, there are domestic incidents to sort out. They're worst at Christmas.'

'In that case, it must be Christmas every day in our house,' Turner said gloomily. ''ave you a lot on?'

'I've a lousy job tomorrow morning. I've to escort a soldier to identify his wife and children. You remember; that carbon monoxide poisoning case in the paper.'

'Aye, that were a bad do. Poor bloke, he must be beside 'imself. It'll be hard for you, too. They call yours a bobby's job, but ah couldn't do the things you've to do, or see what you've to see at times.'

'No, but fortunately it's not always like that. And we don't have the worst of it. You should hear some of the horror stories our traffic officers tell.'

Nash waited on Netherdale station's only platform. As the passengers began to alight from the sprinter train, their arms full of shopping and parcels, he spotted the man he was waiting for. He'd have recognized him even without the uniform. The bearing, the haircut, all shouted 'soldier' louder than a sergeant major could achieve.

'Sergeant Hirst?' Something in Nash's voice must have conveyed the authority of rank, because Hirst lowered his kit bag and stood almost at attention. 'My name's Nash. Detective Inspector Nash' – he held his hand out – 'Mike Nash. I'm sorry to meet you in such sad circumstances.' As he spoke, Nash felt like screaming aloud. Such meaningless clichés, but what can you say?

15

The soldier looked down at the outstretched hand then transferred his gaze to Nash's face. Was he being assessed, Nash wondered? They shook hands briefly. 'My car's outside,' Nash told him. 'Come with me and I'll give you a lift to the …' he balked at the word mortuary, '… hospital. Then afterwards, I'll run you back to Helmsdale. If that's where you want to be.'

Hirst stared at him again before nodding. 'Helmsdale's as good as anywhere, I suppose.'

Outside the station Nash gestured towards his car. 'Listen, Sergeant Hirst, I'm not going to shove platitudes at you. You deserve better than that. What's coming isn't going to be easy. I want you to prepare yourself for the ordeal. These places are grim, believe me. And there's nothing I can say that will make it any easier. I understand, because I've been there. But if you want anything, want to talk, let me know.'

The soldier nodded again, although Nash wasn't sure how much of what he'd said had actually registered.

The identification process was bad enough for Nash and Professor Ramirez. Nash could only guess how much of an ordeal it must have been for Hirst. The soldier stared at his wife's face for a long time before transferring his gaze to his two daughters. Nash stood alongside him, could see emotion working in the man's face in the tautness of the jaw-line. Nash had expected tears, but instead all he could feel was a kind of cold, hard anger. As time dragged, Nash willed himself not to fidget, not to give any sign of his desire to get out of that ghastly place.

Eventually, Hirst stirred slightly and spoke for the first time since entering the building. 'Yes. That's my wife. Those are my daughters. Is there anything for me to sign?'

Ramirez shook his head. 'Inspector Nash will deal with it.'

Hirst looked at the bodies again and drew himself up to attention. Almost as if he was saluting comrades. He stared

16

at their faces, as if to capture the images for his memory; then turned on his heel and marched from the building.

Ramirez spread his hands in a gesture of mute helplessness. Nash nodded. 'I know. I'll be in touch.'

He located Hirst outside, facing the mortuary wall, one hand outstretched, fingers spread across the brickwork. Nash wondered if he'd been sick, or tried to be, or was about to be. 'Sergeant,' he said gently. Then, getting no response, 'Steve, are you all right?' Bloody stupid question he thought. 'I mean, do you want to go to Helmsdale now?'

Hirst looked at him. Or through him, Nash wasn't sure which. His expression desolate; the anger in his eyes so patent that Nash shivered. Hirst straightened. 'Yes, let's get away from this place.'

The journey was conducted in silence, each of them absorbed in their own thoughts. The mortuary had been bad enough. How would Hirst cope returning to the house where his wife and daughters had died a terrible death?

From the outside of the house there was little to show for what had happened. The door that had been forced to allow the emergency services to gain access had been replaced. A little piece of maintenance work; far too little and far too late, Nash thought. Even then, he knew they'd used the original locks. Cheeseparing to the very end: typical of a government department and their contractors. 'I'll come in with you, if you like.'

Hirst didn't reply, merely reached for his bag and climbed out of the car. Nash got out too. Unusually for him, the detective felt unsure what to do next. He followed the soldier as the man walked slowly towards the house. They'd almost reached the door when a voice behind them called, 'Steve, Steve.'

They turned. Nash saw a young woman standing on the pavement close to his car. He glanced sideways at Hirst, saw the momentary tension in the soldier's face relax. 'Sonya.' Hirst's voice was emotionless.

17

She walked towards them. Nash was guilty of totally inappropriate thoughts as he admired her looks, her striking figure. He shook himself mentally, ridding himself of the incongruity of his reaction, given the occasion.

'Steve, I'm so sorry. I don't know what to say.' She looked at Nash and her tone became sharp. 'Who are you?' she demanded. The sharpness was what, hostility? Nash wondered.

'This is Inspector Nash,' Hirst explained, 'he drove me here from …' Hirst was unable to use the word, 'Netherdale,' he substituted. 'This is Sonya Williams,' he told Nash. 'She's our neighbour. My neighbour,' he corrected himself. 'Her husband was killed in Helmand Province six months ago.'

'Sorry, Inspector Nash.' She held her hand out. 'I thought you were military. They're not flavour of the month round here at the moment.'

Nash took her hand and held it for a moment. 'I can understand that,' he said quietly. 'Please, call me Mike.' He released his grip before either of them became embarrassed.

'Can I get you both anything, cup of tea, or coffee? You've nothing in the house,' she told Hirst. 'I cleaned your fridge out. I thought it better than having the food go off.'

'That was thoughtful of you,' Nash spoke for Hirst, who seemed lost in his own thoughts. 'I don't know about you, Steve, but I could do with a coffee.'

'I suppose so.' Hirst glanced over his shoulder.

'I live across the road' – Sonya pointed to her house – 'directly opposite Steve.'

Nash looked at the room, decked out for Christmas, cards and tinsel everywhere. On the dresser there was a large photo of a man in uniform, the medals on his chest gleaming; her husband, obviously. Next to it was one of Sonya with two young children alongside her and an infant in her arms.

'Admiring my brood?' Sonya had come in with a tray of coffee and biscuits. She set it down on the table and passed mugs to the two men.

'I was thinking how difficult it must be for you, on your own,' Nash said.

Sonya shrugged. 'As a soldier's wife, you get used to it.'

'I didn't mean that, not exactly,' Nash smiled. 'I was thinking more about having to make all the decisions without having anyone to bounce ideas off, that sort of thing.'

She nodded, acknowledging the accuracy of his guess. 'That's the hardest part. You look round, or you think of a question to ask; then you remember. Perceptive of you to notice.'

'What did you mean?' Hirst spoke for the first time since they'd entered the house.

Nash and Sonya turned in surprise. 'Sorry?' Nash asked.

'When you said you understood. Did you mean something, or were you just saying it? It sounded like you meant it.'

Sonya looked from Hirst to Nash, saw the detective's face change; saw the mask come over his features. The easygoing, pleasant expression had vanished, replaced by a hard, almost pitiless gaze. 'I do understand,' Nash spoke slowly, reluctance obvious. 'I've been there. I know what you're going through. Not as badly, perhaps, but the feeling's the same.'

'How can you know what I'm feeling?'

Nash sighed. He realized there was nothing for it but to explain.

Later, two mugs of coffee later to be exact, Nash stood up. 'Look, I'm going to get out of your way now. But what I said earlier goes.' He passed Hirst a card. 'If you need me, give me a call. Not just official stuff. If you want somebody to sound off at, to listen, or go for a pint, anything. Don't hesitate. Pick up the phone.'

Hirst nodded. 'Thank you, Mr Nash. I might just take you up on that.' He glanced at Sonya. 'We're in the minority, the three of us. People who truly understand, I mean.'

'I'll see you out, Mike.' Sonya guided Nash from the room. 'That was kind of you,' she told him as they paused by

the front door. 'And it took a lot of courage, telling us your story. I could see that. This girl of yours, Stella, she must have been something special.'

She opened the door. 'Take care, Mike. And that offer you made to Steve, the same goes the other way.' She smiled, entrancingly, Nash thought. 'I mean, if you need to talk things over at any time. Or just feel in need of company, you know where I am. I rarely go far. I've three reasons for that,' she laughed. 'And the kettle only takes a couple of minutes to boil. It's like Steve said. Those of us who've been through it, we need to stick together.'

Nash smiled as they shook hands. 'Thank you. I might just take you up on that.'

She watched him walk back to his car. When he'd unlocked the door he turned and waved. She returned the gesture and walked back into the lounge, her expression thoughtful. 'He's nice, don't you think, Steve?'

Hirst looked up. 'I suppose so. I mean, yes, he is; very nice. He did more than necessary. Much more than....'

'I know,' she soothed him. 'But dwelling on that side of things won't help.'

'I don't want help,' his voice changed, the sadness replaced by a cold, hard anger. 'I don't need help and I don't need sympathy.'

'What do you need?'

'I need the one thing nobody else can provide. I need the one thing I can do for myself. I need revenge. And what's more,' his expression changed. All the sadness was gone. In its place was a savage kind of elation. 'I know just where to go to get it.'

CHAPTER THREE

Contrary to Nash's fears, Christmas passed relatively peace-fully. Apart from the usual crop of drink related offences, most of them dealt with by uniformed branch, there were only a couple of domestic disputes that developed into assaults. Early in the New Year when Superintendent Edwards paid him a visit, the worst he had to report was a trio of unsolved burglaries. 'The MO's the same in all three, so it looks as if we've a new kid on the block,' Nash told her. 'I reckon we've got away lightly.'

Nash had often warned DS Mironova and DC Pearce about saying things were fine. It was, he thought, a sure way to court disaster. Unfortunately, as he spoke to Ruth, he'd forgotten that.

The first part of any operation was always the hardest. In this case though, despite the elaborate and seemingly insurmountable obstacles, it was ludicrously easy. All he'd needed was to create a diversion. Then make his entry and exit before the enemy could react. Their set-up may have looked professional, but in practice, they were mere amateurs. Surveying the area, he soon found a way to divert attention. All he'd need was a saw, his tool kit and a ladder. And, to complete the job, a high-tech gadget he'd seen used a couple of times. To make detection harder and to avoid chance encounters that would make his equipment hard to explain, he'd bought a van; with a roof rack.

He watched the weather forecast each evening. He'd to wait over a week before he heard the news he was waiting for. Next evening once dark had fallen, he drove out of town to the point he'd seen on his reconnaissance trip. He parked down a farm track and climbed over a fence and crossed the field, past a flock of heavily pregnant ewes who eyed him with mild curiosity. When he reached his objective he set to work with a massive woodman's saw. He felt fleeting regret for the act of vandalism he was committing, but then thought of the cause. His resolution returned, stiffened.

After a couple of hours' hard work he judged things were as he wanted them. Now all he had to do was sit and wait for the wind to blow. The cut he'd made would ensure the tree fell in the direction he wanted. After that, there was his main task to complete.

The next morning, Nash walked into Helmsdale station to be greeted by Sergeant Binns, who was standing by reception with two harassed looking civilians. 'Mike, have you a minute?'

'Problem, Jack?'

'It's about the blackout last night.'

'Tell me about it. I was halfway through cooking my evening meal when everything went dark. I didn't fancy lasagne for breakfast.'

Binns introduced the visitors; one from the local electricity company, the other a farmer. 'The power blackout was caused by a tree falling across the power lines,' Binns told Nash.

The man from the power company added, 'Half the county was without electricity. The thing is; it wasn't accidental.'

'I thought it was a result of the gales.'

'They helped, but even with the wind as strong as it was that tree wouldn't have fallen.'

'No,' the farmer said bitterly. 'That tree was sawn through. And it was done to make sure it fell across the power lines.'

Nash stared from one to the other in astonishment. 'You mean someone went to the trouble of sabotaging the electric supply? Why would they do that?'

'Ask me another,' the engineer said. 'It wasn't kids either. It would have taken hours of work to saw through a tree trunk that width.'

'I still don't see what we can do about it. We'll investigate of course, but without some idea of the motive, I don't think we'll have much luck.'

'We've got a problem.'

'What sort of a problem?'

'I'm at the laboratory. We've had a power failure last night, just come back up. But the stand-by generators couldn't be activated by the security men.'

'Why not?'

'They'd been tampered with.'

'How did that happen?'

'I don't know, but there's worse.' He paused and took a deep breath. 'Far, far worse.'

'Go on.'

'During the blackout somebody broke into the buildings. Both the laboratory, and the offices.'

'How did they manage that?'

'I don't know how they got past the fence. I've had the guards check the perimeter and it hasn't been cut. Once they were in, all they had to do was open the doors. The electronic locks are deactivated by a power cut for safety reasons.'

'Was anything stolen? Any damage?'

'I thought of that. So I went to the laboratory first. My first thought was that it might be animal rights people. But the cages were still intact. However, a load of product had been poured into the giant blenders. All sorts of different

stuff. The blender switches had been left in the on position. As soon as the power came back up, they started working. All the contents have been rendered useless. They'll have to be incinerated. We daren't even flush them away because we don't know how toxic they are. With all the chaos, we can't even tell if anything's missing.'

'OK, that's bad, but not cataclysmic. What else? I take it there is more?'

'Oh yes, there's more all right. Our intruder went into the office block. Not only went into it, but went through it. Took a load of personnel files,' he paused before telling his boss the worst. 'And he went into your office. Your safe is electronic like the doors, isn't it?'

'Oh no! Don't say—'

'I'm not sure exactly what you had in there, but it isn't there now. The intruder even left the door open.'

'I'll tell you what was in there. All the disks. The ones with the programme details on.' His boss's voice took on a harsher note. 'And the details of everything we've done: you and I. If they were decoded and fell in to the wrong hands you know what would happen, don't you?'

'I do, but what can we do about it?'

'Let me think for a minute.'

He waited; his impatience mounting.

'As far as I see it, there's nothing we can do about the details of the programme. Nor can we abandon it, or put it on hold. We're so close to success now, and our masters are keen for results. The latest batch seems perfect, but there have to be more field trials. As for the other side of things, there are the two we've been using in our experiments. I'm afraid we can't take the chance that they might be questioned. If they talk, we're finished. So, much as I regret it, they'll have to go. And, I'm afraid, so will the third one. The one we haven't started on yet.'

'What about—?'

'No,' his boss cut in, 'definitely not. Not yet. He's too valuable. As for the others, see to it will you. As fast as you

can. No, hang on a minute. First, do the two we've been using. Get hold of the third, but don't dispose. Not yet. We might need a bargaining tool.'

Lara was bored. With Richard away at that blasted conference, and Caroline also not available, she was desperate for company. An idea struck her. She went over to the phone, dragging her filofax out of her bag. She found the number and dialled. 'Guess who?'

'Lara?'

'Got it in one. I want you. Tonight.'

'Can't do it. No car. Some berk ran into me two nights back. It's in for repair.'

'Get the bus to Helmsdale. I'll pick you up.'

'Missing me that much?' She could hear the desire in his voice.

'You'll see. Just get on that bus.'

'Okay, it'll have to be when I've finished work though.'

'Don't work too hard. You're no use to me if you're not on top form.'

'*You have to identify your target; then comes the assessment. Take your time. Observe and be patient. That's the first and one of the most important parts of the whole job. The observation; get that wrong and you've no chance. Go in sloppy, under-prepared, and you're a dead duck. Remember you've only to get it wrong once. Bollocks it up and you finish up as the target. In a war there'll always be casualties. My job's to teach you how to avoid being one. You understand me?*'

'Yes, Sarge.'

'*And your job, when you're fully trained, is to become the perfect killing machine. It's what you were picked for, soldier. So pay attention. Listen and learn.*'

He stirred slightly as if the memory had unsettled him. Even that slight movement could have been a mistake. He muttered a silent curse. '*Mind on the job, soldier.*' He could almost hear the sergeant saying it. He forced his attention back on the target; brightly lit, in the all-embracing darkness.

Here, no street lights spoilt his night vision. He looked through the window; he'd expected only one occupant, so who was the other? He didn't recognize them. So, a bit of collateral damage.

'Pick a method to suit the situation. Always remember the golden rule. In, do the job, and out. Always, before they know you're there. And, wherever possible, leave no trace. If you can make it look like an accident, so much the better.'

His hand strayed to the kit by his side. Mentally, he ran through his equipment. Tools to effect entry, hypodermics and the equipment to disguise the kill. Had to disguise it, in a war zone it wouldn't matter as much. But this wasn't a war zone. This was rural England.

He'd wait until they settled for the night. No risk of being disturbed anyway, the cottage was miles from anywhere. Silent entry, quick kill, then sit and watch: away before dawn. No point in taking unnecessary risks.

Time to move. The locks were easy, easier than anticipated; no bolts. That helped. Inside he moved slowly. He knew the layout perfectly. He'd been inside before; several times. But then the cottage had been empty, and it had been daylight. Up the stairs, one, two, three. Careful, the fifth step creaks.

At the bedroom door. Listening. Nothing at first; then the gentle sound of breathing. Good. They were asleep. The door had creaked but butter from the fridge had cured it last time he was there. Edge it open. No wind tonight; nothing to cause a draught. Ease your way inside. Wait for your night vision to adjust. Hypodermics at the ready. Strike once, twice. Done.

He moved swiftly across the room out of range, but after the first involuntary movements neither of them stirred. Nevertheless, no point in taking chances. His hand hovered over the light switch, but that same sense of caution stopped him from switching it on. Better get on with finishing the job. He trotted down the stairs, ignored the one that creaked. The occupants of the house weren't going to hear

him: ever. He went to locate the fuse box then flicked the trip switch and went into the kitchen. He unrolled his tool kit, placed his torch where its beam would light his working area. Working methodically without need for haste, he stripped bare a length of wire and left the contacts exposed. He crossed to the sink and opened the cupboard below. His search yielded four promising items. He could hear his sergeant again. *'All houses contain a selection of highly inflammable substances. All you've to do is put them close to a heat source. Whoosh! The lot will go up. Best of all, unless you do it wrong, it'll look accidental.'*

He waited outside until the house was well ablaze then walked unhurriedly towards the main road. He was struck by a horrible thought. Something he'd forgotten. What was it? Then he remembered. Something he'd meant to remove from the house. He glanced back, saw the blaze and relaxed. The fire would be all-consuming. Every scrap of evidence would be destroyed. The first of his targets had been identified and eliminated. Now he had to start on the next.

Superintendent Edwards was about to leave an early morning meeting with Nash when his phone rang. 'Hold on a second, Ruth.' He listened. 'OK, where?' She saw him scribble a couple of notes on his pad. 'Right, give me time to arrange things at this end then we'll be with you. Have you told Mexican Pete? No, OK, I'll see to that.'

'What's happened?'

'A house fire. That was CFO Curran. It happened overnight in a remote spot towards the top end of the dale. The nearest village is Gorton, but that's a couple of miles away. The alarm was raised by a local gamekeeper. He saw the smoke, but by then it was a smouldering ruin. Almost completely gutted, by all accounts.'

'We'll have to get out there. Anything to do first?'

'We need Jack Binns to organize some uniforms to be on site.'

'I'll deal with that.'

'That'll help. In the meantime, I'll get hold of Mexican Pete.'

'Who?'

'Sorry, I mean Professor Ramirez. Our pathologist.'

'Fine, and whilst we're travelling you can explain the nickname.'

Nash introduced Superintendent Edwards to Curran and Mexican Pete. 'Doug's based in Helmsdale, but his area covers Netherdale as well. And this is our pathologist, Professor Ramirez, of York University.'

Ramirez inclined his head in a bow of acknowledgment. Pathologists rarely shake hands. And police officers never shake hands with pathologists. 'What Nash means is, I attend the university occasionally,' he told Ruth, 'when Nash is on holiday, or when he's having an off day and hasn't found any bodies for me to examine.'

'What's the score here?' Nash directed his question to both men.

Curran spoke first. 'There are two victims, both badly burned. Professor Ramirez has had a preliminary look; he'll be able to tell you more.'

'On the face of it, they appear to be typical fire or smoke inhalation victims,' Ramirez told them. 'We should be able to get identifiable material, either by DNA or dental records.'

'Why do you say, "on the face of it," have you any reason to suppose otherwise?' Edwards asked.

The pathologist gave a sour smile. 'I'd have little doubt, but for him turning up,' he indicated Nash. 'He sniffs out dead meat and foul play even better than a bloodhound in a butcher's shop.'

Nash hid a smile and turned to Curran. 'Any idea of the cause?'

'Nothing I'd like to be quoted on, but at the moment I'm inclined to think it was some sort of electrical fault. It looks like the sort of place that hasn't been re-wired since the first electrics were installed. As to why it blazed so well, that's down to the fact that it was half timbered. A lot of these Tudor style cottages have far too much inflammable material in them.'

'Nothing suspicious then?'

'Not that I can see, although it's early days yet.'

'Who owns the house?'

'No idea. There's nobody registered on the voters roll.'

Edwards looked at Curran for a moment before turning to Nash. 'Better check them out, Mike. The locals might know something. Try credit reference agencies, and get onto the DVLA.' She pointed to the car alongside the ruined building. 'That should give us an ID.'

She paused and looked at him; saw his frown. 'What is it? Something wrong?'

Nash hesitated. 'No, at least, I don't think so. I just have this feeling.' He grinned as he heard Ramirez groan.

'Tell me,' Ruth encouraged him.

'It's probably nothing.'

The Superintendent arched an eyebrow. 'Go on, share it, Mike. Have you had a flash of your famous intuition?'

'It's just an impression, well, that there's something more to this fire than meets the eye. It's probably my imagination working overtime.'

'Nothing tangible to back it up?'

'Maybe I'm reading more into it than I should, but there seems no apparent reason why anyone living in this sort of a house wouldn't register for voting.'

'Maybe they haven't lived here long, or they're not interested in politics.'

'If they've not been here long the previous occupiers would be on the roll. And where's the other car?'

Ruth looked up in surprise. 'The other car? What do you mean?'

'This house is two miles from the nearest village. Gorton only has three buses a week into Helmsdale. If the owners were man and wife, they'd need two cars. Unless they were hermits practicing *The Good Life*.'

'I see what you mean. Definitely worth looking into. I can see why you're so successful. Can I leave it to you to follow up? I'd better get back to civilization. I'll stop off in Helmsdale; make sure nothing else has happened.'

'That's OK; I'll get a lift back with Ramirez.'

Nash and Curran watched Ruth pick her way carefully through the tangle of hoses and past the trio of fire appliances. 'I'll tell you something, Mike,' Curran said thoughtfully. 'Mexican Pete may have mentioned bloodhounds, but that new boss of yours is as fit as a butcher's dog.'

Nash grinned. 'I'll be sure and tell your wife you said that next time I see her, shall I? Anyway, from what I've been told, your opinion and mine might not be of any interest to Ruth.'

'Really? That's not the impression I got every time she looked at you.'

Nash changed the subject hastily. 'Is it safe for me to have a look inside?'

'Yes, as long as you wear a condom.'

Nash grimaced. The hazmat suits, referred to as 'condoms', were as universally unpopular as they were necessary. Although they protected the scene from contamination and the wearer from potentially dangerous chemicals and gases, they were also extremely uncomfortable, caused the wearer to sweat profusely in even the coldest weather and rustled alarmingly at the slightest movement.

It was ten minutes before he was ready. As he approached the building, Nash felt an overwhelming sense of sadness. No matter what happened, this blackened shell could never be returned to what he felt sure was its former glory. He wondered about the occupants. Had they died unmourned, or would there be grieving relatives to deal with? It looked like more of a family home than a dwelling for a couple on their own. In which case, where were the others?

As they picked their way carefully through the debris, Curran gestured towards the kitchen. 'Seat of the blaze,' he explained.

Although Nash knew the fire officer was shouting, the sound was muffled by the suits they were wearing, reaching him as little more than a whisper. He nodded to signify understanding; it was simpler than attempting a spoken reply.

When they entered the room, Nash paused and looked around, assessing the scene, trying to visualize what the place had looked like before fire turned it into a reeking, blackened heap of twisted metal and charred timber. As he moved forward towards the part where the damage was most severe, something on the floor caught his eye. If the winter sun hadn't been streaming in through the hole where a picture window had once been he'd never have spotted it. He bent forward, peering down.

Curran joined him. 'What is it?' The fire officer roared as he knelt on the floor, careful to avoid the sharp edges of a chunk of fallen plaster. Several small strips of rubber, or plastic, he wasn't sure which, had escaped the blaze. 'Looks like insulation from around electrical cable.'

Nash shouted back. 'What do you reckon; DIY disaster?'

Curran straightened up. His face, or what little of it Nash could see through the visor, was grim, 'Either that,' he screamed, 'or we're looking at arson.'

As Curran spoke, Nash felt a familiar prickly sensation, as the hairs on the back of his neck stood on end. 'Which means we've got a double murder on our hands,' he yelled.

Upstairs, the damage was nothing like as severe. The bedroom, where Ramirez was supervising the removal of the corpses, had suffered worst. Through the hazmat suit, Nash could still smell the all too familiar aroma of burnt flesh. He suppressed a shudder and turned his attention to the other rooms until the pathologist and his team had completed their macabre task.

When Ramirez signalled that they'd finished, Nash and Curran re-entered the bedchamber of death. They found little of significance, until Curran's foot caught a small object on the floor and sent it spinning into the corner of the room.

Nash followed it and picked it up, not without difficulty because of the gloves he was wearing. He examined the object for a moment, turning it over in his hand, before removing an evidence bag from one of the pockets on the suit. He placed the item inside, sealed the bag and pointed towards the stairs.

Outside, both men removed their helmets and spent a few moments breathing in the clear, cold winter air. 'What is it? What did you pick up?' Curran asked eventually, glad not to have to shout.

Nash held up the clear plastic bag. 'It's an inhaler.'

Curran shrugged. 'I don't see the significance.'

'I just thought it was curious. The inhaler isn't damaged. Despite that, there are no markings on it. No manufacturer's name, no retailer or chemist's label. Don't get me wrong. There may be a perfectly innocent explanation. But I thought something like an inhaler ought to have some sort of label. If it was prescribed by a doctor, the chemist has to label it, for legal reasons. And the makers would have put their own label on. So, if it wasn't a prescription medicine, or a proprietary brand, where did it come from?'

'Perhaps whoever used it removed the label.'

'Even then, there would be a batch number or code stamped onto the casing to cover just such eventualities.'

'As you say, there's probably a perfectly innocent explanation.' Curran was clearly less than impressed.

'I'll give it to Mexican Pete, get it checked out anyway.'

When they reached Helmsdale, Ramirez dropped Nash outside the station. 'Thanks, Professor, let me know what develops,' Nash said.

'I'll do the PM the day after tomorrow, the examination of that inhaler might have to wait a day or two longer.'

CHAPTER FOUR

Viv Pearce was sitting at the computer. 'Morning, boss. You were away early.'

'Is that a way of trying to cover up the fact that you were late?' He saw Pearce's expression cloud over. 'I was only kidding,' he reassured him. 'Speaking of late comers, where's Clara?'

Pearce grinned. 'She phoned about an hour ago. She and David have been in Scotland. They've been delayed. She'll be back in about an hour. Apparently, they've had a bit of snow.'

Nash had seen news footage of the blizzards that had swept across the Grampian and Highland regions. 'I'm not sure we should let her get away with that, Viv. It's a bit like you going back to Antigua and ringing to say it's too hot for you to get home on time.'

Having been assured that Clara would get a good ragging from Pearce, in addition to what he could dish out himself, Nash turned to business. 'Viv, do me a favour.' He passed Pearce a sheet of paper. 'Run that registration number for me, will you? It's from the car parked at the fire scene out near Gorton.'

'I heard about that on Dales Radio as I was driving in. Have they found out if anyone was inside yet?'

Nash nodded. 'There are two dead. We need to try and establish identities, so we can find and inform next of kin.'

'What about the voters roll?'

'Curran's already checked it. Said there was nothing shown for that address.'

'How about the council? They must have paid council tax.'

'I'm going to do that whilst you're on the computer, seeing as Clara isn't here.'

His call to the local council took about ten minutes. When he put the phone down, Pearce was standing by his desk. 'Well,' Nash asked, 'what did the DVLA come up with?'

'The vehicle is registered to a firm of solicitors in Leeds, their name is—'

'Richardson, Grace and Parsons,' Nash finished off for him.

They stared at each other in surprise. 'OK, I'll ring them; see if one of their partners lived out Gorton way.'

'It's a hell of a trek into Leeds every day; must take over an hour and a half. Unless you've got a Ferrari.'

'This isn't a Ferrari, nothing like it. When did you last see a solicitor driving a Ford Focus?'

His call to the solicitors yielded nothing. 'The house doesn't belong to any of their staff, nor would they confirm that it belongs to one of their clients. All they would say is, "they're aware of the situation", heaven knows what that means. This client confidentiality lark is bloody frustrating.'

'I reckon it means the owner is one of their clients, which doesn't help us one little bit.'

'When Clara eventually poles up, I'm going to send her across to Gorton. She can talk to the villagers, and check at the post office. There must be mail for the occupiers. Somebody must know who lives there.'

The group standing in the hotel conference room were deep in conversation as the receptionist approached. 'Excuse me, Dr Richards?'

'That's me.' One of them acknowledged.

'I've a message for you, sir. You've to phone your office. They said it was urgent.'

'Thanks.' He waited until the woman left. 'Excuse me a moment.' He plucked his mobile phone from his pocket as he walked a few yards from the others and pressed the speed dial number. 'Dr Richards here. You wanted me?'

He listened for a moment. 'I understand. Any idea why? I mean I was supposed to be going straight home tonight.' He waited, then continued, 'All right.' He looked up as the door opened; tension apparent in his expression. He saw who the newcomer was and relaxed. 'OK, not to worry. I'll be there.'

He disconnected and smiled faintly at the woman who was strolling across the stage towards him.

'Is anything wrong?' she asked.

'I've just had an odd message from the office. They want me to go back there tonight instead of going home. The secretary wouldn't say any more than that, and I can't understand why, but she was most insistent.'

'Probably something and nothing. Concentrate on getting this lecture out of the way; then we'll have the whole afternoon to ourselves.'

He smiled, the thought made his pulse race. 'How would you like to spend the spare time? Admiring the beautiful architecture of this fine city?'

She laid her hand on his arm, caressing it gently. She glanced round, saw no one was watching and slid it lower. 'I thought we could take it in turns admiring the paintwork on your bedroom ceiling.'

His heartbeat went into overdrive. 'Caroline, you get some great ideas. After all people spend lots of money to look at the ceiling in the Sistine Chapel.'

'In that case, I'll try and remember to open my eyes now and again.'

It was early afternoon before Mironova arrived. Nash and Pearce were standing in the CID office, mugs of coffee in hand. 'Nothing changes, I see,' she remarked.

Nash turned to Pearce. 'The face looks familiar, and I think I recognize the voice. How about you?'

'Vaguely, Mike, only vaguely.'

'All right, all right. I might have known I'd get some stick. The thing is—'

Nash cut in. 'She's going to tell us about the atrocious weather, Viv. About the fifteen-feet high snowdrifts, the impassable roads, the drifting pack ice in the Firth of Forth.'

'Polar bears sighted near Stonehaven.' Pearce's imagination was beginning to work.

'And near Ullapool.' Nash lowered his voice dramatically. 'Out in the snow, a footprint is found. Human, or not? Surely it is too large to be human. Could it be the tracks of that mythical beast, "The Abominable Scotsman"?'

Clara stared at them, stony-faced. 'I might have known better than to expect any sympathy from you two morons,' she stated in exasperation. 'Anyway'– she indicated the mugs – 'it doesn't look as if you've exactly been rushed off your feet.'

'We have been busy,' Pearce protested, 'this is our break.'

'What she's trying to say,' Nash corrected him, 'is, have we missed her? The answer's no, but now she's condescended to join us, I think I can find something for her to do.'

Luck was on Clara's side when she reached the village. Not only was the small post office-cum-village shop quiet, but the postman had just arrived to empty the post box. After interviewing him and talking to the postmaster, Clara learned that mail delivered to the house had been addressed to R and S Richards. 'What can you tell me about them? How old were they, for instance? Do you know if they had any children?' Clara asked the shopkeeper.

'I guess they'd be in their early forties,' the man thought for a minute. 'But I'm no good on people's ages. I think there are a couple of children. The boy would be grown up now. The girl's away at school, I think. She'll be about seventeen

36

or eighteen. Not that I know too much about them. They didn't socialize in the village, that's for sure.'

'Any idea what Mr Richards did for a living? Or where he worked?'

The man shook his head. 'Like I said, they didn't mix much.'

Despite asking round, even to the extent of visiting the pub, Clara gleaned no further information.

By the time Clara got back to Helmsdale it was late afternoon. The street lights were reflecting from the road, made shiny by the sleet showers that had been falling most of the day. She pulled into the station yard and hurried across to the building, as a fresh burst of stinging sleet, driven by the wind, hurled itself into her face.

There was no sign of Pearce, but Nash's door was open. Mironova paused in the doorway, staring at her boss with concern. The expression on his face was one she'd not seen for a long time. It was one she hoped she'd never see again. A sad, defeated look. A look of hopelessness.

'What's matter, Mike? Has something happened? Something gone wrong?'

Nash roused himself, with an obvious effort. 'Why do you say that?'

'The look on your face, that's all.'

'I started thinking about the fire at Gorton, wondering if there'd be any relatives to face. I've seen my share lately. Just after Christmas I'd to escort Sergeant Hirst; the soldier whose family was killed by that carbon monoxide leak, to do the identifications.'

'That must have been an ordeal. For you, I mean. I can't even begin to imagine what it was like for him.'

Nash acknowledged the truth of this with a nod. 'After we left the mortuary, I brought him back to Helmsdale and met one of his neighbours, a young woman with three children whose husband was killed in action recently. Anyway, before I knew it, I was telling them about Stella, and how she died.'

Clara grimaced. 'I can see why you did it, establishing a common bond, but I was beginning to hope you'd got over that.'

'I'm not sure you ever do, not completely. You go on for ages without thinking about it; then something happens that brings it all back. In this case it was the senseless waste of young lives. And something else; in a way I was trying to use it as a distraction because of the look on Hirst's face. Only at times, but it was a look I didn't like. To be honest, it scared me.'

'Scared you? What sort of a look was it?'

'A sort of latent violence and hatred: a promise of what he could do. More than that, that he isn't just capable; that he will do it, as soon as he allows himself off the leash. Maybe I'm wrong. Maybe it was just my imagination working overtime.'

'I certainly hope so by what you've said.' Clara didn't voice her other thought, the one that really concerned her: the fact that Mike was rarely wrong when it came to reading people's thoughts and emotions.

Their concern would have multiplied into alarm, had they known that Hirst had already slipped the leash.

Nash seemed anxious to change the subject. 'How did you go on?'

'Gorton is one of those villages where the houses either belong to people who commute or they're holiday homes, so there were very few people about. The village shop was the only place I got any joy. I don't think, from what the sub-postmaster told me, that we'll have much luck even when we do catch up with the house owners in the village. He told me the couple's name, but said they're hardly ever seen, and never socialize, or attend local functions. He thinks they're in their early forties, with two children.'

'Names?'

'Mr and Mrs Richards. No Christian names, or for the kids. Boy would be a young adult, girl about eighteen. Now you know as much as me.'

'OK, Clara. Get Viv to contact the Registrar's office in the morning, and check the PNC as well. Even a driving conviction would be a help.'

The next day brought more frustration. Pearce reported to Nash and Mironova. 'The problem is there are no births registered to a couple named Richards that tally with the age groups Clara suggested. Nor is there a record of a couple with those initials marrying in the sort of timescale we need.'

'Forensics reckon they'll have some fingerprints from the parts of the house that were least damaged,' Nash told him. 'When they send me them, try for a match through our computer. Failing that, Richards must be an assumed name.'

'Why do you think they'd not be using their real names?' Clara asked.

'Could be one of several reasons. One or other of them might be a convicted offender trying for a fresh start. Or they might be on the run. They could be political refugees, although that seems unlikely, or they may have been relocated in a witness protection programme.'

'Any idea how long they've lived there?' Pearce asked.

'The locals reckon about seven years. They couldn't tell us much.'

'As you say, it seems a bit fishy. We'll have to wait for the post-mortem results and try to get a match to those fingerprints. I'm going through to Netherdale to watch Mexican Pete at work,' Nash told them.

He was still out when the fingerprints arrived. He returned, to find Pearce studying the results, his brow furrowed. He looked up. 'There were three set of fingerprints identified by the SOCO boys,' Pearce told him.

'Did you get any matches?'

'Just one,' Pearce paused.

'So, who is it?'

'That's the problem. I can't tell you. One set got a positive match, but instead of the name, I got an error message.'

'What sort of a message?'

'It just said "access denied".'

'Denied, by whom?'

'That's another problem. I don't know. Someone wants the person whose prints are in that house to remain anonymous.'

'This is getting weirder by the minute.'

Two days later Nash got the post-mortem findings. He set off through the offices to the far side of the building, part of a complex built to house all the emergency services, taking the file through to Curran's office. 'Listen to this,' he began. 'Mexican Pete's report is like everything else in this case. It doesn't answer any questions, just raises a whole load more.

'"Analysis of the victims' blood reveals oxygen depletion, together with concentrations of carbon monoxide and cyanide. Carbon monoxide is also present in the lungs, suggesting the victims were alive when the fire started. The reduction in oxygen levels, together with the amounts of carboxyhemoglobin and cyanide, point to the fact that death would have occurred very rapidly. It is difficult to say whether the cause of death was a natural outcome of the fire, or whether it was induced. The reasons I cannot state the cause with any degree of certainty are as follows:

1. I understand the building dates from the early or middle of the nineteenth century.
2. That being the case, I cannot understand how cyanide came to be present in the victims' bloodstreams.
3. The reason I am querying this is that hydrogen cyanide is a product of fires where the buildings concerned are of relatively recent construction. This is due to the introduction, in significant quantities, of synthetic polymers into building materials over the last fifty years.
4. Given that this house is much older, that issue remains unresolved. Without samples of the building materials and/or the fixtures and fittings, this issue remains unresolved.

5. I would recommend close consultation with the forensic officers of the fire service regarding this, and other aspects connected with the cause of the fire.
6. Identification of the victims via dental records has not been possible. The NHS dental database contains no records matching either of the victims. The quality of the dental work on one of the victims, the male, tends to suggest private practice, in all probability overseas. I will return to the condition of the female victim's teeth in paragraph 8. For identification to be possible, the best remaining option would be via familial DNA. If close relatives of the deceased can be found, or their DNA matched with that already on the national database, there is every chance of obtaining the requisite information. I have posted the results from the DNA test, but have not had any match. Failing that, the victims' identities, as with the cause of death, must remain unresolved.
7. There is one other, highly significant fact that came from analysis of the blood sample taken from the female victim. This revealed a significant amount of a variant of methylamphetamine, together with a masking agent and another, at present unidentified substance.
8. The poor condition of the female victim's teeth suggests that ingestion of the drug referred to in the previous paragraph had been taking place over a prolonged period."'

Curran looked confused. 'What do you make of all that? And what was that drug business about? Mexican Pete didn't give an explanation, so presumably he thought you'd know all about that methyl-whatsitsname stuff.'

'Methylamphetamine is a recreational drug that's widely used by people seeking high levels of sexual pleasure. Its more common name is crystal meth.'

'Ah, I've heard of that.'

off because of our Kirsty's accident. That's how insurance companies are.'

Clara nodded sympathetically. 'That suspect list, I know you were being flippant, but have you noticed anyone hanging around recently? Someone you might not have seen before, or somebody you don't usually expect to see in this part of town.'

Lee shook his head. 'The problem is, with it being such a small town, and us being in the market place, everybody passes here from time to time.'

Lee's brother, Simon, had just finished serving a customer and joined them in time to hear the last part of the conversation.

'There was that young lad,' he volunteered.

'Young lad?' Clara looked at him questioningly.

'I'd forgotten about him,' Lee confessed.

'He was around yesterday and the day before. Surprised me, because he looked as if he hadn't eaten meat in his life,' Simon commented.

'Aye, skinny little runt he was. I served him,' Lee told her. 'Not over keen on the personal hygiene either. You wouldn't stand down wind of him for long. Looked as if he'd been sleeping rough. Had to dig around in every pocket to come up with enough for a sausage roll. I was on the point of taking what he had in his hand just to get rid of him. I'd a shop full and the other customers were beginning to look sideways.'

'The thing was,' Simon chipped in, 'he'd been about all morning. Didn't notice him the first time or two, but when he kept passing, I started looking out for him. It was the same yesterday. We didn't want him coming in again, in case it upset other customers.'

'Can you describe him?'

'About five feet eight inches tall, skinny, painfully thin. I'd be surprised if he topped eight stone,' Lee told her. The butcher's reputation for being able to gauge the weight of beasts at auction mart was a local legend.

'Any distinguishing marks?' Pearce was writing the details down.

'None I can bring to mind,' Lee looked at his brother for confirmation.

'There was a mole. On the right side of his chin,' Simon said after a moment's thought.

'Hair colour, length, style?' Clara asked.

'Black and greasy, lank, down to his shoulders; looked as if it hadn't been washed for months. He must have shaved recently though. He'd stubble, but only a few days' growth.'

'What about clothing?'

'Jeans, some sort of dark top, maybe a sweatshirt, anorak with a hood on. One of those padded ones. And trainers: none of it looked new, or clean.'

'Anything else?'

'If I'd to guess I'd say he might be on drugs,' Lee said. 'His eyes were odd. Glassy looking, small pupils.'

'Did our forensics people say if they'd found anything useful?' As Clara was speaking she noticed Pearce had closed his notebook and was buying what looked like a small mountain of sausage rolls from Simon.

'They weren't sure. They said they'd collected a fair number of samples, but they couldn't be sure if they were relevant or not.'

CHAPTER FIVE

Wonderful. Better than fantastic. Words can't describe how good 'trips' are; but waking from them is hell. The better the 'trip', the worse the reaction. He knew he'd gone too far. But he had the money, so he bought the gear and took it. Now it was time to wake up, to work out where he was. How long he'd been there.

The first thing he noticed was the smell. As he opened his eyes, he realized he was in a barn and that the smell wasn't from animals. It was him. Sometime, during the 'trip', he'd soiled himself. As if that wasn't bad enough, his jeans felt wet. He looked down, moving his head slowly, painfully. Yes, he'd pissed his pants as well.

Hatred and self-loathing swept over him. How could he have got to this state? How could he allow the stuff to take over, to rule his life? But it had, it did and it would continue to do so. He knew that, just as he was hating himself. He knew at the next opportunity he'd have to get a fix. He began to tremble, to shiver, with a sort of cold, like he'd never experienced before. He sat up and felt nauseous as a fresh wave of stink, his own stink, wafted over him.

'You need help.'

He jumped in alarm, hadn't noticed the man before, couldn't see him properly now. There wasn't much light in the barn, and his face was in shadow.

'What? Who are you? What are you doing here? Where am I?'

The man ignored the questions. 'This is a small town. How long do you think you can continue getting away with it?'

'Away with what?'

'Oh, come off it. I've been watching you. You did the filling station a couple of weeks back, then it was the pub, and two nights ago you did the butcher's.'

Panic. 'What's it to you? You a copper?'

'No.' The man laughed as if this was some very funny joke. 'I'm definitely not a copper. Here,' his hand came forward.

North squinted at what the stranger offered. A small case. Easily recognizable. 'What's that?' Like he didn't know only too well.

'The makings. Don't worry, everything's clean. The best gear and the needles are brand new.'

'Are you giving me this? Why? Are you a homo, or what?'

'You don't for one moment imagine I'd go near your arse, the state you're in.' There was no mistaking the tone of the man's voice. Anger: and disgust. 'Let's just say I'm a friend of the family.'

'I don't know you.'

'Your mother and father did. I was quite close to them, before they died. That was tragic. I'm sure you must miss them terribly.'

'What do you mean? They're not dead.'

The stranger took out a copy of *The Gazette*. 'I'm sorry, I assumed you knew.'

Adam scanned the headline. He didn't need the photo to recognize the house. Even as a smoking shell. 'Oh God,

no,' he reached for the kit. For refuge; for an escape away from reality.

'That's it.' The stranger encouraged him. 'I'm sure it's going to make the pain easier to bear.'

Adam scrabbled with the case, removed the contents and filled the syringe from the phial. He pressed the plunger and waited for the drug to take effect. He looked up. 'I still don't know your name.'

'Barry, you can call me Barry. Shall we go?'

'Go, go where?'

'Away from here. I've got a special place lined up for you. I'm going to take care of you.'

'It's not a rehab clinic is it? Because it won't work.'

The stranger burst out laughing. It was some moments before he stopped. 'No, it's definitely not rehab, Adam.' Another chuckle escaped him. 'You'll be the death of me, you will.' He paused and added under his breath, 'But that's only fair. Because I'm going to be the death of you.'

'Forensics has come back with results from the butcher's,' Nash told Clara and Viv as he examined the internal mail. 'There was nothing inside the shop, but they found a mucus sample immediately outside the back door. The DNA extracted matches a known drug user.' He paused as he read further details from the report.

'He's listed as Adam North, aged twenty-one. No recent address. Three convictions for possession; the last of them a short custodial.' Nash stopped.

He was silent for so long that Clara asked, 'What is it, Mike?'

'The DNA also gives a familial match to that of the female victim from the Gorton house fire. According to the forensic evidence, the woman who was killed there was Adam North's mother.'

'What about the male?'

'Apparently, he was no relation.'

'What are we supposed to make of that?'

'Two choices. North's mother had an affair with some-one else from which Adam was conceived, or, the man who was killed in the fire wasn't her husband. Either way we have to find Adam North. Both to question him about the robbery at the butcher's, and to find out what he knows about the fire that killed his mother.'

It took the local vicar more than half an hour to drive from Bishop's Cross to Gorton. Not that he resented the journey. In fact he quite enjoyed it. The time spent behind the wheel on the lonely country roads gave him time to ponder his sermon. He just felt sad that it was necessary. Time was when each of the villages had its own minister. Now he had to divide his time between Bishop's Cross, Gorton and Kirk Bolton.

Even so, he was aware that he'd be lucky if there was more than a handful of parishioners prepared to rise so early in order to receive The Sacrament from him. And those few that were present would be well into their pensioner years, concerned principally, as his bishop had cynically remarked, with 'paying their after-life insurance premiums'.

When they shuffled off the mortal coil what would become of the churches in those villages? Turned into sec-ond homes, holiday cottages and the like. Or craft cen-tres. Certainly something secular. The vicar sighed, he was approaching the village now, and this was no state of mind in which to approach an act of worship.

When he rounded a couple more bends the village would come into view, and that would cheer him up. It always did, Gorton was that sort of place, what he thought of as a proper village – built around the green that doubled as a cricket field, despite the slope, and the presence of an ancient oak tree at deep-long-leg. Despite the fact that the road ran inside the boundary, and that the boundary on one side was the pub wall.

The green was fringed by the pub, the church and a pleasing mix of old stone cottages and newer bungalows designed to blend with their older neighbours. If Hollywood ever wanted to find a traditional English village location, Gorton must surely come high on their list. It even had a pair of stocks, one of the last remaining sets in the county, to remind visitors of a time when punishment was more direct, community led. He smiled at the thought. The positioning of the stocks close to the church gate was an obvious inducement to the wrongdoer to repent their evil ways.

He ditched his reverie and parked close to the church gate and got out, avoiding the light dusting of snow covering the icy puddles. He began searching in his cassock for the keys. Another sign of worsening times, once, the church would have remained open, service or no, without fear of theft or vandalism. He sighed, locked his car and made to walk through the lychgate into the churchyard.

One hand on the gate, he paused: something was wrong; something he'd noticed out of his peripheral vision. Slowly, unwilling to acknowledge what his brain was telling him his eyes had seen, he turned and looked again, directly this time. He let out a long, whistling breath of horror and disbelief. 'Oh dear Lord, no,' he muttered. He went slowly forward to check what his heart told him he didn't need to.

One or two of his parishioners were making their way along the road towards the church. He had to stop them. He had to get to them before they saw the horrible sight that was behind him. The vicar strode to intercept them, his footsteps urgent.

Celebration of Holy Communion was deferred. When the screens had been erected to shield the crime scene, one or two villagers went into the church to join the minister in praying for the soul of the victim who had been placed in the midst of their community.

Outside, forensics officers were examining the remains and the surrounding area, supervised by Professor Ramirez. Alongside the pathologist, DS Mironova watched, averting her eyes occasionally from the corpse.

'It's a long time since the stocks had an occupant, I'll bet.'

They turned in surprise. Mike Nash was standing only a couple of yards behind them outside the screen. At his side was Becky Pollard. 'Mike, what are you doing here?' Clara demanded. 'You're supposed to be having three days off.'

Ramirez snorted. 'You don't imagine a minor detail like that's going to keep him away, do you? It's clear you've no understanding of the power of necrophilia. Nash probably scented the corpse from twenty miles away.'

'Actually, I didn't. We were going to the pub for lunch' – Nash gestured to The Buck Inn – 'and saw you lot over here.'

'And of course Mike couldn't keep away,' Becky contributed. 'The fastest I've seen him move for weeks is when he legged it across the village green to get here.'

'What's the story?' Nash asked.

'The stocks are kept padlocked. The killer probably picked them, placed the corpse inside and secured the padlocks again. Then the man was pelted with tomatoes, eggs and a variety of less pleasant substances.'

Nash raised an enquiring eyebrow.

'Some form of excrement,' the pathologist explained.

Nash looked round at the meadows surrounding the village. 'Probably cow shit' – he pointed – 'there must be a fair amount available. How was he killed?'

'In a very unpleasant manner,' Ramirez told him as he led him inside the tent. 'He was alive when he was put in the stocks. I know that because his wrists and ankles are bruised and bled a considerable amount, as he struggled to free himself.'

Nash looked at the corpse. 'Why didn't he cry out for help? A place as quiet as this, someone would be bound to hear him.'

'He couldn't,' Ramirez told him, his tone grim. 'See the bloated appearance of the body, the way the cheeks are distended? The killer glued his eyes closed, squirted glue into

each nostril and down his throat. As the glue set, breathing would have become more and more difficult, and eventually, impossible. He would have choked to death. It would have been a slow, painful and extremely unpleasant way to die.'

'Very nasty,' Nash agreed. They stepped back outside to the girls who were discussing their respective Christmases. 'What do we know about the dead man?'

'Mike, you're not at work,' Becky protested. 'Leave Clara to get on with it.'

Nash stared at his sergeant. After a moment, she shrugged. 'Early twenties, I guess. No identification on the body. There are needle marks that suggest long and sustained drug abuse. He's in a disgusting state; appearance suggests he'd been living rough.'

She paused, and Nash asked, 'So, who do you think he is? Someone we're looking for with regard to a string of burglaries perhaps?'

Ramirez and Becky stared at him curiously. Clara smiled. 'That obvious was it?'

'The description of the suspect from the robbery at the butcher's shop matches the victim almost perfectly.'

'I agree,' Clara nodded. 'But we'll have to wait on DNA to confirm it.'

'The method of killing's interesting.' Nash's voice was thoughtful, almost as if he was talking to himself.

'Why do you say that?' Clara asked.

'Placing someone in the stocks was a traditional form of punishment. The fact that the killer chose them suggests he knew the dead man was a criminal. Although in this case the punishment is harsh in the extreme. So perhaps there's more to the motive than mere retribution.'

'Come on, Sherlock, that's enough.' Becky tugged at Nash's arm. 'I'm starving. Let's go eat. Sorry to disturb you, Clara. I'll try and keep him out of your hair, but whether he'll eat anything's a different matter. Probably spend all his time staring out of the window wondering if you're doing things right.'

A phone call from forensics next day confirmed the dead man's identity. Clara thought for a few moments. On impulse she reached for the phone.

'Mike, it's Clara. Are you busy?'

'Bored rigid. Do you know how turgid daytime telly is? Is there a problem?'

'It's about that corpse; the one in the stocks. Something's come up, and I don't quite know what to make of it.'

Clara explained the development. 'I know you're not a great believer in coincidence, so I wondered what you thought.'

'My first suggestion would be to try the Registrar's office. See if you can locate North's birth certificate. You might get the parents' details that way. Always supposing Adam North is his right name. And that the birth was registered in this country.'

'Thanks, Mike. I'll try that. Hopefully, I'll see you in a couple of days.'

The man known as Dr Richards had been driving home from Birmingham when the crash happened. The resulting injuries had not only caused him over a week's stay in hospital but had left him frail. He walked slowly out of the entrance. Apart from the police officers who'd questioned him about the crash he'd had only one visitor; the woman who now came to greet him. He smiled at her, a gesture she didn't return. 'I've my car in the car park,' she told him. 'Do you think you can make it, or would you prefer to wait here and I'll bring it round?'

'I'll make it,' his voice sounded pitifully weak.

During the journey, they were silent for the most part. Once they'd cleared Leeds however, he stirred in his seat. 'Where are we going? You're not taking me home, surely?'

If he'd been watching her he'd have seen the tension in her face, noticed her hands gripping the wheel until the knuckles whitened. 'No, I'm not taking you home,' she said after a moment. 'You wouldn't have expected me to, would you?'

'I suppose not. Why didn't anyone else come to see me? I mean, I know things have been bad, but I'd have expected....' His voice trailed off.

It was no good; she couldn't dodge the issue any longer. 'Look, there's a motorway café just up the road. Why don't we stop for a cup of tea? We need to talk.'

He looked across at her. It was unusual for her to be so reticent. 'All right,' he agreed.

When they were seated in the café she reached across the table and put her hand on his. 'Do you remember anything about the day of the crash?'

'Bits and pieces, that's all. I remember the lecture, and us being together. That's about it.'

'Don't you remember the phone call you got? From the office?' she prompted him.

Memory stirred, but not vigorously enough. 'Vaguely, but I can't remember what it was about.'

'You were asked to go straight to the laboratory. Not to go home first.'

'That's it. I wondered why. It seemed such a strange thing to ask.'

'Well it wasn't.' Her grip on his hand tightened. 'The reason they didn't want you to go home was,' she paused, 'there was a fire the previous night. Your house was destroyed. There were two people inside, a man and a woman. Both died in the fire. The police haven't been able to identify them yet, but they're assuming them to be man and wife.'

She noticed his jaw tighten, felt his hand tremble slightly, his voice was calm. Unnaturally calm? 'Presumably Lara and her lover.'

'I'm afraid that's not all.'

He looked up and she saw what she'd taken for calm was shock. Shock and distress. 'What else?'

'There was a body found last week, in what the police are describing as suspicious circumstances. I'm afraid it was Adam.'

'Oh dear God, no. What was it? A drugs overdose?'

'No, at least I don't think so. I mean, he might have been drugged, but from what little we could find out, that wasn't how he died.' She took a deep breath. 'Richard, I'm sorry. The police think Adam was murdered.'

She saw the bright glint of tears in his eyes. It was a long time before he spoke. Again, his voice had a calmness she knew was a shell, one that was almost at cracking point. 'I gave up on Adam a long time ago. I tried everything. Rehab clinics, therapy, hypnotism, the lot. I gave him money, it didn't work. Denied him money, he stole it. Kicked him out of the house, time after time. Took him back, time after time. I thought one day I'd get the news. A visitor, a phone call, whatever. Thought it would be an overdose. But not murder. Do you know what it was about? Was it over drugs?'

'I don't think the police know for certain. They don't think it was drugs related, not directly, even though Adam had a lot of it in his system.'

He looked up in sudden alarm. More than that: panic. 'What about Jessica?'

'She's all right. Our people have her safe. She doesn't know what's happened yet.'

'What do you mean "our people have her safe"?'

'They've taken a house near the laboratory. All she knows is she's to wait there until you arrive. They didn't tell her anything, but they reassured her you were fine.'

'I don't understand. Why the need for all this security?'

'They're concerned for your safety. Yours and Jessica's. They weren't too worried about Lara, but after Adam was killed, somebody hit the panic button.'

'You mean they reckon Lara's death might not have been accidental?'

'They're not sure, but you know what they're like. They won't take the chance. There was a security breach at the lab just before all this kicked off.'

'I thought the place was watertight.'

She grimaced. 'So did they. Whoever got in was cleverer than they thought. They sawed through a tree close to the main power lines, caused a power blackout over the county for several hours. Long enough for an intruder to get over the fence. By the time the guards realized, he'd long gone. He made a bit of a mess in the labs before he got into the office block.'

'What on earth was he doing in the office block? Why not just the lab?'

'That's the bit that got our spooks spooked. He went through all the personnel records. Not only went through them, but took a portable, battery operated copier with him. Cheeky swine left it behind when he'd finished.'

'Do they know what the records he copied were?'

'Personal details; family, home address, all the things they're supposed to be keeping out of the public domain.'

'Any idea who might be behind it?'

'The official line is it might be down to one of the more violent animal rights groups. Given what we do at the lab, I suppose they're the most natural suspects.'

'Caroline, will you do me a very great favour? Will you go with me when I tell Jessica? I'm not sure I can do it on my own.'

She thought about it. 'Very well, but I don't think she should learn about us. Not now, and probably not for a long time.'

CHAPTER SIX

'Morning, Mike. Couldn't keep away?' Clara reached the CID suite next morning to find Nash was already in his office. She heard movement and peered in.

'Becky got called in by *The Gazette*, so I thought I might as well come to work as well. I've been reading the file on the Adam North murder. Have you made any progress tracing the rest of the family?'

'I have the paperwork on my desk, I'll go get it.' She returned seconds later. 'I had a lot of trouble finding anything, but eventually I managed to locate details of a passport application for Adam North. It was made about six years ago. On the same date there was another application, for a Jessica North, aged twelve. The parents' details are the same, so I assume they are brother and sister. The reason there's no registration for them in the UK is they were born abroad. In the United States, to be precise. The parents are listed as Richard and Lara North, nee Matthews. The father's occupation is given as university lecturer, mother is shown as housewife. I was going to try contacting universities round here today, see if North's been engaged by any of them. Even if he hasn't, they might know of him.'

'It would be useful to find out what subject he specializes in. I take it North senior is a British citizen?'

'Yes, both he and his wife are, or were. We're still not sure if he's alive or dead.'

'I think we have to assume he's dead. Why else hasn't he been in contact?'

'I traced their birth certificates once I'd the details from The Passport Office. He was born in Leeds, forty-five years ago. Interestingly, his mother's maiden name was Richards. That was the surname on the mail sent to the Gorton address. That was what the locals knew him as.'

'I wonder why they needed to use assumed names? What were they hiding from? Or who? Did you make enquiries with the authorities in America?'

'I did, I sent an e-mail to the FBI, but as yet I haven't had a reply, unless something came in overnight. Mind you, I'm not sure I want to know what they find out. The problem with this case is, every bit of new information we get throws up more questions.'

'If you're going to be tied up ringing universities this morning, why not get Viv to do an internet search on Richard North? It may give us something. I realize it could be historical, if he's been living under a false name for a while, but it could shed some light on what the elusive Mr North was up to, before he found it necessary to disguise his identity.'

Nash paused, as a random thought struck him. 'Whilst he's doing that, get him to enter Dr Richard North as well. If he's a lecturer, we could safely assume him to be well qualified.'

'OK, I'll get him onto it as soon as he gets here.' Clara turned to leave; then looked over her shoulder. 'By the way, Mike, it is good to have you back.'

Nash looked at her suspiciously; then realized she was being serious, not lining him up for another insult.

By mid-afternoon, Nash was beginning to wonder whether he'd have been better off at home watching *Cash in the Attic*,

Bargain Hunt or *Loose Women*. The first intimation that all might not be as it should came via a reply from the FBI. Sent from their Quantico headquarters, it was phrased in terms that could be diplomatically described as curt, but more accurately, downright rude. The message was to the effect that even had the American law enforcement agency been in possession of any information about Richard North they were either unable or unwilling to share such knowledge with their British counterparts.

Nash was still trying to work out whether the FBI actually knew anything and were being deliberately obstructive, or they didn't and weren't prepared to admit their ignorance when Clara entered his office. 'I've tried all the universities in the north of England,' she told him, 'including those Metropolitan ones.'

Nash smiled. 'They used to be called Technical Colleges in my day.'

'I'd no idea there were so many. Not that it did me any good. None of them have a Richard North on their teaching faculty. There's a Helen North at Newcastle, but she's six-ty-three, comes from Northumberland and teaches Eastern history. I think we can count her out.'

Nash's phone rang. It was Superintendent Edwards. 'How are things going?'

'How did you know I was here?'

'Guesswork!'

'I've a few difficulties to sort out.'

'They wouldn't be about the Adam North murder by any chance, would they?'

Nash's eyes opened wide with surprise. 'How did you guess that?'

'That wasn't a guess. To be honest, I had a phone call about half an hour ago, some captain from Military Intelligence. He informed me that inquiries into this mat-ter were out of our jurisdiction and that I should instruct my officers to refrain from asking any questions that were unconnected with the actual killing. He went on to suggest we concentrate on the drugs connection, and that he felt sure we'd find that was the motive behind the crime. On no account were we to attempt to involve other members of North's family in our investigation.'

'Really? And what did you say to that?'

Her reply left Nash grinning. 'I apologized for missing the announcement of his appointment as Chief Constable. And I followed that up by explaining that the Chief Constable was the only person I take orders from. I certainly don't instruct my detectives to follow lines of inquiry based on vague assertions from a junior army officer.'

'What was his reaction to that?'

'He said he was going to ring God and tell her what he'd told me. Said he felt sure she'd be more cooperative. So I told him to go ahead, but I nipped in to see her before he had chance. My instructions from Gloria are, "Continue to pursue the investigation and don't let anything or anybody get in your way". I don't think she likes being threatened any more than I do.'

'That's the best news I've had today, and it confirms my suspicion that there's more to this case than meets the eye: much more.' He went on to tell her about the message from the FBI. 'As a result of what we've learned, I'm going to treat the Gorton house fire as a suspicious death, and accordingly we'll be investigating three murders instead of one.'

'Any ideas how you're going to proceed, given that you've so little hard evidence?'

'I've a couple of thoughts that I'm going to get Clara and Viv working on.' He explained them before adding, 'I know it's a long shot, but that's about all we have.'

'Go to it. Keep me posted. And if you get any further attempts to obstruct your investigation I expect you to take a hard line.'

Nash put the phone down. It seemed as if the attempt to block their inquiry had only succeeded in putting Ruth's back up, which suited him fine. He looked up to see Pearce hovering in the doorway. 'I've trawled the internet,' Viv told

him. 'I couldn't find anything relating to Richard North, not our Richard North anyway. There's a Canadian novelist and a New Zealand academic whose speciality is Maori culture, but that's all. Oh, and I've a message for you. Doug Curran wants a word. He said it's about the Gorton fire.'

'OK, I'll ring him. You'd better come in. We'll go about finding North another way.'

Nash picked up the phone. 'Doug, you wanted a word?' He listened for a few moments. 'That's interesting, very interesting indeed. Does it mean what I think it means?'

Nash stared at the file on his desk. He looked up. 'Curran's just told me their forensics people had another look at the seat of the blaze at the house near Gorton. They found several more pieces of tubular plastic on the kitchen floor, some of them melted, some of them intact. Somebody wasn't as careful about covering their tracks as they should have been.'

Pearce frowned. 'What do you mean, tubular plastic?'

'The outer layer that insulates electric cables. Somebody stripped down the cables, leaving the wiring exposed. Then they located it close to a collection of highly inflammable cleaning products; they'd been placed on a worktop next to the cooker. Tell me who in their right mind stacks cleaning stuff next to a heat source as powerful as an electric range cooker. All the killer had to do was switch the mains power back on and leave the building. Now, as to Dr North,' Nash explained what he wanted. 'Let's hope we meet with more success doing it this way round.' He paused and added, 'Let's face it, we couldn't have any less.'

The course of action Nash had set in motion yielded fruit next day. Pearce was first to report. 'I found details of a Richard North, who was a student at Leeds Grammar School. He meets all our criteria regarding age. The dates he was at the school and the timing of his examination results fit our man perfectly.' He passed Nash the information.

Clara came in with more news. 'Following up on what Viv found, I discovered he went on to Leeds University, was

there four years, graduated with honours; then went on to do postgraduate studies. He was sponsored by an American company. He got his doctorate and went to work for them in California.'

'Doing what, precisely?'

'His degree and doctorate were in chemistry and micro-biology. I checked the firm he worked for, the one that paid for his postgrad work. They're listed as defence contractors by the US government.'

'Good work, the pair of you. At least we now know something about him. All we need to do now, is work out what brought him back to the UK.'

'One thing for sure, it wasn't to lecture at university,' Clara pointed out.

'No, I'm beginning to think the job description on the children's passport application is a massive red herring. So, has either of you got any idea what Dr Richard North might be doing in this neck of the woods, if he isn't teaching?'

There was no reply. Both Clara and Viv struggled with the problem for a few moments before Clara said, 'Beats me. Do you know, Mike?'

'I've a theory, yes. But it's only guesswork at the moment.'

Clara and Viv looked at one another. Pearce shrugged.

'Go on then, mastermind,' Clara encouraged. 'Give your undeserving acolytes the benefit of your wisdom.'

Nash grinned. 'How about Helm Pharm?'

Clara thought about the chemical company situated on a green field site just out of town. 'Of course,' she breathed, 'it's obvious really.'

'That's what they always say after a magician discloses his secrets,' Nash told her smugly.

'That still doesn't explain why the military were getting so hot under the collar about our inquiries,' Pearce pointed out.

'It does if North was working on something secret. Which, come to think of it, is the only reason the military

would become involved. Helm Pharm is just the sort of establishment they'd choose. A small, discreet company, tucked away in the countryside. Out of sight, out of mind. Absolutely perfect as a cover.'

'But a cover for what?'

'I've no idea, Clara. And I'm not sure I want to know, unless it's relevant to our investigation. But if we assume Dr North is working on some secret project, there must be grounds for concern that what's happened to his wife and son might be a way of getting at him. If he's still alive, that is. For all we know, he might have died in the fire.'

'You're not convinced about that, are you?'

'I might have been, but for the attempt to block our inquiry. Why would that officer be so concerned about what we might discover about a dead man? But if North is still alive, all the more reason to want to protect him. Let's assume that North wasn't the man in the fire. We now have two problems, apart from the question of who killed Adam North, Lara North and the unknown victim.'

'What?'

'Problem one, where is Dr Richard North? Problem two, where is Jessica North?'

'Just when I thought everything was becoming easy.'

Nash grinned at Clara's sarcasm. 'Resolve those problems and it might well do.'

With a good idea of how to contact Dr North, Nash phoned Helm Pharm, the pharmaceuticals company that had opened six years previously. He identified himself to the receptionist, stressing his rank. 'I'd like to speak to Dr North, please. Dr Richard North.'

The reply was instantaneous. Too quick? Nash wondered.

'I'm sorry, we have no one here of that name.'

'I see; in that case would you please put me through to your director or personnel officer.'

'I'm afraid neither our director or personnel officer is available.'

'Either of their assistants then.'

'There is no one available to talk to you.'

'Can you tell me when someone will be available?'

'No, I can't.' Nash blinked at the curtness of the reply.

'Can't or won't?'

'My instructions are that no one will be free to speak to you or anyone else from outside the company for the foreseeable future.'

'Very well,' Nash's tone was gentle. 'Can I have your name please?'

The dialling tone told Nash the receptionist had put the phone down on him.

Nash met with a similar lack of cooperation when he tried the Leeds firm of solicitors handling North's affairs. The stonewalling tactics were beginning to annoy him. He thought for a while, before picking up the phone again and explained what had happened to Ruth Edwards, seeking her approval for his next course of action. As soon as she'd sanctioned it, Nash called Mironova and Pearce into his office. 'Go find Jack Binns,' he instructed Pearce. 'Tell him I want him to round up whatever uniforms will be available' – he glanced at the clock – 'in an hour's time.' He then explained what he intended to do.

Clara looked at him dubiously. 'Mike, have I ever told you that you're a devious bastard?'

Nash grinned. 'I believe it may have cropped up in conversation once or twice.'

Pearce pulled in opposite the entrance to the company premises. Clara parked behind. The three detectives got out of the cars and surveyed the site. The two buildings were set well back from the road; the perimeter of the property was protected by a ten foot high wire fence, topped with evilly efficient looking razor wire.

The sturdy looking steel double gates directly in front of the watchers had a gatehouse to one side. From his viewpoint, Nash could see two uniformed security guards inside.

The business part of the property comprised two brick buildings. Nash guessed the larger, two storey building, would be the laboratory, the smaller an office block. Under the eaves of both, surveillance cameras were mounted on the facia boards. As they watched, the detectives saw the cameras swivel slowly, scanning the terrain. 'There's something almost sinister about them,' Clara observed.

Nash nodded. 'They obviously feel they've something inside that's worth protecting, but as to what it is, and who they're protecting it from is another question altogether.'

'The fact that military intelligence has become involved in trying to block our investigation might give some clue,' Clara suggested.

'True, although it could equally be industrial espionage they're concerned about.' As Nash was speaking, a white Transit minibus pulled in behind their car. 'Here we go.' Nash signalled to the others to follow him.

One of the guards stepped out of the gatehouse as they approached. 'What do you want?' he demanded.

Nash turned to Mironova. 'That's what I like, good old fashioned courtesy.'

The guard was either immune to sarcasm or failed to recognize it. He stared at the police officers with thinly disguised hostility.

'I'd like to speak to Dr North please, Dr Richard North.' Nash's tone was polite.

'Nobody here of that name.' The guard's reply was as quick and as curt as the receptionist's had been.

Nash took out his warrant card and held it up in front of the man's eyes. 'I'll ask you again. May I speak to Dr North?'

'And I told you, there's nobody here of that name.'

'Very well, in that case I'd like to speak to the director.'

'You may want to, but that doesn't mean you're going to.'

'Couldn't you at least ask?'

'No, I couldn't. Clear off.'

Nash sighed. 'That is very disappointing.' He nodded to Binns, who'd joined them. 'OK, sergeant.'

Binns pulled a pair of handcuffs from his uniform pocket and began to administer the caution. As he reached the phrase, 'Anything you say', he snapped one cuff over the guard's wrist. At the same time, one of the uniformed constables, who Nash knew to be a rugby player, took hold of the guard's other hand and pulled it behind his back.

'Hey, what are you doing? You can't arrest me. I'm only doing my job. What's the charge?'

'Obstruction.' Nash watched as they started to lead the man towards the Transit.

The gatehouse door opened and the second guard stepped out. 'What's going on?'

'Your colleague's been arrested. He's to be charged with obstruction. Now, do I get to speak to someone in authority, or not?'

'There's nobody here wants to speak to the police. And you can't arrest him.'

Nash smiled sweetly. 'Yes, I can. Jack,' he called.

Binns pulled a second pair of handcuffs from his pocket. Causing Clara to wonder how many sets he carried. As he stepped forward beginning a second recital of the caution, the guard swung his fist and aimed a punch at Binns. The sergeant swayed out of the way and clipped a cuff over the man's wrist.

'Make this one obstruction, assaulting a police officer and resisting arrest,' Nash told him.

He watched as the uniformed men led their prisoner away to join his colleague.

Clara nudged him. 'Look there, Mike.'

Nash followed her pointing finger. Four more security men had emerged from the office block and were walking towards the gates. 'This should be fun,' Nash said dryly. 'You know what you've to do, Jack?'

'On my way.'

Nash waited until the Transit, complete with prisoners, had pulled away. He turned to look at the approaching guards who formed themselves into a line inside the gates. 'What's going on here?' one of them asked.

'Your colleagues have been arrested for obstruction and assault. I've asked, quite civilly, to speak to someone in regard to a murder investigation I'm in charge of. Nobody seems to want to talk to me. If you want your men back, I suggest someone starts doing a bit of a rethink.'

'You can't do that,' the man protested.

'I'm getting a bit tired of people telling me what I can and can't do,' Nash said quietly.

'We'll get our solicitor onto this. They'll be free within the hour.'

Nash smiled. 'Well, good luck to you.'

He swung round to Pearce. 'Viv, will you drop me off at home please? Then, you go off too. I don't want you back at the station tonight. We're off duty as of now. Clara, you OK?'

Clara nodded, then watched as Nash and Pearce drove off. She wandered over to her car and drove a discreet distance from the laboratory. She turned the car so it was facing the main gates and parked.

On the journey back into town, Nash told Pearce what he wanted. 'Go straight home, or go for a meal, whatever you want, as long as you don't go near the station. I'm going for something to eat. Later, I'll take over from Clara. Tomorrow morning, I want you both to go straight out to Gorton. I want you to do another search of Dr North's house and the grounds. See if there's anything that got missed in the first place. We were only looking at it as an accidental death then. Now it's probably murder.'

'You'll be in the office, will you?'

'No, I'll be out all morning, things to do. Your search will take at least as long. That means there will be nobody available to order the release of those men until tomorrow afternoon. Perhaps the people in charge of Helm Pharm will have had time to think things over by then.'

'Clara said earlier that you're a devious bastard,' Pearce smiled. 'Now I see what she meant.'

CHAPTER SEVEN

It was almost dark when Caroline and Dr North reached the house, a semi-detached in a row of similar properties, but there were no lights showing. 'That's strange,' she said. 'I'd have thought they'd have switched on by now.'

Across the road, hidden in a dense shrubbery alongside a path leading to a park, a figure watched with interest as they emerged from the car. The watcher raised a powerful pair of binoculars and studied the new arrivals. He couldn't see their faces in the half-light.

North stretched, easing his back after the journey. Although the worst of his injuries had been to the head, the force of the collision had caused severe bruising – stiffness was a natural after-effect. They walked the short distance to the front door where Caroline knocked on the glass panel. The door swung open. 'Something's wrong.' She pushed the door wide.

They went through the ground floor. There was no sign of life. 'There were two of our men guarding her. I can't understand what's happened. Let's check upstairs.' In the largest of the three bedrooms they found the two men. Both were alive, both unconscious. They were bound, hand and foot with duct tape. They checked the other bedrooms. The second double room showed signs of female occupancy. But

Jessica was missing. 'I'll have to ring our people,' Caroline told him.

She looked across the room. Richard North was standing by the dressing table. He was clutching a teddy bear and staring at a photograph. It was a family group, mother, father and two young children. His family in happier days. Now, two of them were dead, a third missing.

Caroline went downstairs and began phoning. When she returned, North was still staring at the photograph. 'Security are on their way,' she told him briskly. 'Give me a hand to cut the guards free.'

He gave no indication that he'd heard. 'Richard,' she said sharply.

'Sorry,' he put the photo down and followed her from the room. At the door she saw him turn and look back. As if it was the last time he'd see them.

Both men were beginning to regain consciousness. When they were fit enough to speak, they told their tale. 'I heard a knock at the door and went to answer it. I looked out first; thought it was you, Dr Dunning.'

Caroline blinked in surprise.

'The car was similar to yours,' the guard explained. 'When I opened the door there was a man standing there. I remember thinking, I know you, then I felt a pain in my arm and that's the last thing I knew, until just now.'

They looked at the second man, who took up the tale. 'I heard a voice, thought it was him,' he gestured to his colleague. 'I can't be sure, but I thought he said, "Are you there, Frank?" So I came out of the lounge. That's the last I knew.'

They were interrupted by the sound of vehicles pulling up outside. Caroline crossed to the window. She turned to the guards. 'Your boss has arrived. This should be fun.' The expression on their faces told Richard her idea of fun and theirs differed greatly.

When they'd re-told their tale, the head of security questioned the second man. 'How certain are you that he used your name?'

'I'm not really sure,' the man admitted. 'But I thought he did.'

North watched with increasing bewilderment as the team of security men went from room to room. Quite what they were searching for, he wasn't certain. Outside, more men were using ladders to ascend a street lamp and nearby tree. The security chief drew him to one side and explained. 'Don't worry, Dr North. The man who abducted your daughter won't be aware that we had every room in the house bugged, and that we positioned surveillance cameras to cover every aspect of the building. Between them there'll be plenty of evidence to identify him. We'll be able to get a recognizable likeness of the kidnapper, plus the cameras outside the front will tell us what car he's using and the registration number. We'll have a name and address within half an hour and have your daughter back safe and sound in no time.'

'Shouldn't we inform the police? Isn't that what usually happens?'

'Hardly,' the man's scorn was apparent. 'A bunch of country bobbies would have no chance of any success compared to the resources we can command. Leave it to us. We're the experts. We'll sort it.'

A man appeared at the door. 'There's nothing from the room bugs. Just one sentence, when the man called out. Frank was wrong. He didn't use a name. After that, nothing but vague muttering, then rustling noises, and the sound of the duct tape being pulled out. But we've retrieved the tapes from the CCTV cameras. The ones at the back are blank, but there's some footage from those at the front. It's all set up, ready to view.'

The leader beckoned to Richard and Caroline to follow. In the lounge they stood in a semi-circle in front of the TV. The tape started, showing an excellent image of the drive. After a few seconds a car pulled in. Caroline frowned. 'That's my car.'

'I don't think so, Dr Dunning,' the security chief stated. He pointed to the screen. 'Look at the time. That's a couple

of hours before you got here.' He turned to the other security man. 'Stop the tape and zoom in on the number plate, will you?'

The man operating the remote control pressed a couple of buttons. Gradually the image enlarged and centred on the rear of the vehicle. As he adjusted the focus, the letters and numbers became clearly visible. 'I told you that was my car,' Caroline exclaimed. 'That's my registration number. You must have the time set wrong on the camera. If you run the tape on I bet you'll see Richard and me getting out.'

The assistant pressed 'play'. As the tape moved forward, they saw a man climb out of the driver's seat and close the door. 'Who's that? And what's he doing with my car? That's impossible. The time must be wrong. I was in Sheffield collecting Richard then.' Caroline was mystified.

There was no reply; although North noticed the security man's lips tighten as if he was in pain. They watched as the man knocked on the door. One of the guards opened it. After what seemed only an instant, they saw the guard collapse across the threshold. The intruder glanced round. 'Stop it there,' the chief ordered. 'Zoom in on his face.'

The close-up image was frustratingly unable to pick up little more than a silhouette. 'I'm sure I know that face from somewhere,' the head of security muttered. 'No matter; let the tape run on. We're sure to get a better image when he leaves, he'll be head on to the camera then.'

The intruder scooped the guard up, seemingly without effort, before carrying him indoors. There was a long pause, whilst the screen showed nothing more action-packed than an image of the house door. Eventually it opened, and the intruder emerged, carrying a large bundle, wrapped in a blanket. 'Now we'll get something,' they heard the security chief mutter.

The kidnapper walked to the rear of the car. He shifted the bundle effortlessly over his shoulder into a fireman's lift, then opened the car boot. He placed his burden gently inside, before closing the boot lid. 'That must be Jessica,' North said in a low tone.

They watched the man walk to the driver's door and open it. Before getting into the car he turned, directly facing the camera. He made no effort to avoid recognition. They watched as the man raised two fingers in an unmistakeable gesture of contempt and defiance. 'Cheeky bastard. Zoom in. Let's see who he is.'

All four viewers stared at the close-up image in astonishment. 'I don't fucking believe it,' the security man said. North continued to gaze at the screen. If the camera was to be believed, his daughter had been abducted by the late American President, Ronald Reagan.

'Now, will you involve the police?' North demanded.

'We can't. Believe me, I know. We'll just have to sit tight. See what this guy's demands are.'

'My wife's dead. My son's been murdered. My daughter's been kidnapped. And you're asking me to sit around and wait. Wait for what? Wait until Jessica's body's found? Wait, while in the meantime that lunatic could be doing God knows what to her?'

'What makes you think the police will have any more success than we'll have?'

'They couldn't have any less. Could it be that you've an ulterior motive for not involving them?'

'If I have a motive, apart from your daughter's safety, you know what it is, Dr North. The work you're involved with makes you a prize target for potential enemies of this country. If they're behind this, how powerful a bargaining tool do you think your daughter is? Apart from that, as you should know, my course of action is limited by the need for secrecy. I simply cannot allow the police to become involved.'

The car drove into a disused quarry. The driver pulled up close to a van. He sat for a few minutes, deep in thought. He got out, walked to the rear of the car and opened the boot. The blanket had slipped, revealing the unconscious girl's face. He looked at her closely for the first time, struck by her good looks. Better not to go there. Better to concentrate

on the job. He lifted her gently clear and carried her easily across to the van. He put her inside and drove the van to a safe distance before he stopped and removed three petrol cans. After dousing the car liberally, both inside and out with petrol, he tossed the empty cans in through the open car window; then pulled the mask off. He threw that into the car, lit a match and flicked it through the window, turning immediately to shield his face from the blast.

There was a soft whoosh of sound and he felt the heat on the back of his neck. He turned and watched the burning vehicle for a few minutes before he was satisfied destruction would be total. Then returned to the van and drove away.

'One thing you must be prepared for is the unexpected. Be prepared for it, because you can't plan for it. When it happens, and believe me, soldier, it will happen, you've two possible courses of action. Either you continue your mission as you set out in the first place, which will be highly risky, or you find a safe place, go to ground and think out a new plan to cope with the changed circumstances. That's the wise choice. That's the choice that marks out a good soldier, places him above the average, understand? You have to be better than good; you have to be brilliant. And that means showing the ability to react to sudden changes in battle conditions. Got it, soldier?'

As he drove, he pondered events. What was that saying he'd heard once? Something about hearts and minds? That was it. 'When you've got them by the balls, the hearts and minds automatically follow.' Well, he'd got the girl; all that was left of North's family. North might not regret his wife's death too much, as she was obviously sleeping with somebody else. He spared a fleeting thought to wonder who the man killed in the fire was; then shrugged it off. A casualty of war, that was all. And North wouldn't spend too long grieving over his son. A dropout, petty criminal and junkie. No one would miss him. The girl though, that was a different matter. But what should he do with her? That question wasn't as easy to answer.

Shortly before lunchtime, Mironova's mobile rang. She and Pearce had almost completed their search of the area

surrounding the burnt-out cottage. She glanced at the screen, 'Hello, Mike.'

'How's the treasure hunt going?'

'Absolutely zilch.'

'Pack it in when you've finished the outside. I doubt if the house itself will yield anything the fire service couldn't find. I'm on my way to the office. I just switched my mobile on. I've got nine missed calls, all from the same number. No idea who it is. Has anyone called you?'

'Ruth Edwards rang. Apparently that solicitor from Leeds has been bending her ear. She referred him to Helmsdale. She said he wasn't happy.'

'The day I start worrying about a solicitor's peace of mind is when I know it's time to retire. Particularly if it's one that's been messing us about. I'm going to pick up a sandwich. See you later.'

When Nash walked into the reception area at Helmsdale station, Binns was talking to a fresh-faced young man. Or rather, listening to the visitor, who appeared to be delivering a speech. Nash waved to the sergeant as he headed for the door to the CID suite. The young man swung round. 'Detective Inspector Nash?'

Nash turned. 'Richardson, Grace and Parsons,' the visitor announced.

Nash blinked. 'What, all three?'

The joke appeared to throw the man. 'Er … no, actually, my name is Drew. Theodore Drew. Richardson, Grace and Parsons is the name of our practice.'

'And what can I do for Richardson, Grace, Parsons and Theodore Drew?'

'I represent two men you arrested yesterday evening. Two men employed as security guards by Helm Pharm Laboratories. I'm here to secure their release.'

'You are, are you? Well, when I've interviewed them, I'll make a decision as to whether to release them or not.' With that the young solicitor was left watching the door close behind the detective.

After Nash had checked his mail and spent a short while reviewing the sparse facts he had regarding the Adam North murder, he relented. He owed as much to Jack Binns, who he guessed by now must he heartily sick of the solicitor's voice. He rang through and asked the sergeant to escort Drew to his office.

'I've decided not to press charges,' he told the young man. 'Your clients are free to go. Before you leave, however, I must warn you I'm far from happy about your firm's conduct. I appreciate you are bound by client confidentiality, but you must appreciate that I have responsibilities also.

'Two members of Dr North's family are dead. His son was definitely murdered and we are now treating Mrs North's death as murder. For some time my colleagues believed that Dr North also perished in the house fire at Gorton, but we now believe that was not the case. Can you confirm whether Dr North is alive or dead?'

'I'm afraid I can't, Inspector.' He saw Nash's expression change. 'I'm not being obstructive, but Dr North isn't one of my clients. I was only asked to represent the two men you're holding in your cells.'

'In that case, can I ask you to talk to the partner who looks after Dr North's interests? Tell him I have serious concerns, not only over Dr North's safety and whereabouts, but those of his daughter. Now, I'll sign the release forms for the two guards from Helm Pharm, but I expect contact from someone with news of where Dr North and his daughter are, together with some way of contacting them. Apart from my concerns about their well-being, either one or both of them may have information that would give some clue as to who killed Adam North and his mother.'

When Mironova and Pearce returned they were anxious to learn what had happened the previous night. Nash explained. 'About an hour after I took over from you, Clara, a car with two security men in it left the laboratory. I followed them to a house on the other side of town. After they'd been inside, two more emerged, got into the same car and drove off. It looked like a shift change. After that it got really weird. A car arrived with one man in it. I took a note of the plate. He went inside, came out again about ten minutes later. I couldn't see his face, but he was carrying a bundle. He put that in the boot and drove off. A couple of hours later, just about nightfall, the same car came back. This time there was a man and a woman in it. They'd been inside about a quarter of an hour when a load more cars turned up. There were security guards and other types, about a dozen of them. And get this, judging from the haircuts I'd say they were all military. A couple of the blokes started fiddling with something across the road from the house; more of them disappeared round the back. When they'd all gone inside I took a look at what they'd been messing about with. Guess what? There was a surveillance camera pointing towards the house, and another one round the back. What the hell's going on, I've no idea. But I got Jack Binns to check that registration number. The owner is Dr Caroline Dunning, Chief Scientific Officer at Helm Pharm Laboratory.'

Nash's phone rang. 'Yes, Professor,' he listened. As he was waiting, Nash drew a sombrero on his pad. Clara grinned. 'Don't worry about it,' Nash told Ramirez. 'Easy to miss, I guess, with all the other damage.'

He put the phone down. 'Mexican Pete revisited his toxicology findings on the two Gorton victims. There are minute traces of a sedative in their bloodstream. You could mistake them for a prescription drug, but for one of the ingredients. The fact that it's there means it had to be injected, not ingested. The choices are a suicide pact, or murder. There were no traces of a syringe or phials in or around the house. Together with the Fire Service evidence, I reckon that definitely makes it murder.'

CHAPTER EIGHT

Waking up was slow. It was gradual. And it was painful. Her first conscious impression was of sound, muted, as of traffic in the far distance. Next, she became aware that she wasn't comfortable; far from it. She was lying on her back on something soft. A bed? The discomfort was in her wrists and ankles. It was dark. Where was she? This wasn't her room at school or the room at the house they'd taken her to. So, what had happened? She struggled to quell the growing feeling of panic. She failed.

Gradually, her vision adjusted. She could just make out that she was in a bedroom, that there was light behind the curtains, that there were articles of furniture. Her next sensation was the smell. The aroma wasn't unpleasant. On the contrary, it was light, fragrant but not overpowering. Comforting, reassuring in the way a pleasant memory is. It was a clean scent, such as she'd used when she was younger. That was it. She was in a girl's room. Or a room that had recently had a young girl in it.

Her mouth felt dry, her tongue wooden, unable to introduce any moisture, to work the saliva glands. She tried to move; to roll onto her side. She couldn't. Her hands were in front of her, close together. And with a shock that brought her totally awake, she realized why she couldn't move. She was tied up – wrists and ankles bound tightly. Alarm increased tenfold. Worse still were the implications. What had been done to her whilst she was unconscious? What was going to be done to her, now she was awake? Who was holding her prisoner? And why? She shied away from the last question. One reason came to mind, and try as she might she couldn't dismiss it.

Memory. Concentrate on that instead. She'd been taken from school. That was the first part. The men from her father's work had come for her. Security, that was how they described themselves. Said they were acting on her father's orders. They'd driven her to a house in Helmsdale. She remembered that. One of them had carried her belongings to the room she'd be using. They'd called the house something. What was it? A safe house; that was it. Like they refer to in films, or on the telly. She'd asked why. Not once, but over and over. All they'd said was, she'd find out why when her father arrived.

But he hadn't arrived. A boring week had passed, with her as a virtual prisoner. Safe perhaps, but still a prisoner. She'd been at screaming point when one of her guards finally announced her father would be coming the next day.

So, if she wasn't there now, where was she? The last thing she remembered had been as she waited for her father to arrive. A man had come to the house. She'd only caught a brief glimpse, but there'd been something weird about him. Something about his appearance? Now she remembered. He'd been wearing a mask. Not a frightener, like the junior school wore on Halloween, or a clown, or an ape or anything like that. It had been a mask of someone famous. She couldn't remember who, and it didn't matter.

He'd spoken to her, said something about her father. 'I'm going to keep you for your father.' Such a strange thing to say. Even stranger; during all this no one had mentioned her mother. Not that Jessica minded that much. She'd more or less cut ties with her mother after the way she'd treated Dad.

She heard a voice, startling her to fresh levels of panic. Had he been there all along? In the darkness? Watching her?

'Jessica. Would you like a drink? Or something else? What do you need?'

She needed to be able to see. She needed to be untied. She needed to be able to move. She needed her father. She needed to know what was happening. She needed to know why she was being held prisoner. She needed to be free. She needed answers to a whole string of questions. Weakly, she said, 'Yes please. My mouth's dry. I would like a drink.' Her voice was barely audible, a croak at best.

'That'll be the effect of the injections. I'm sorry, but I had to keep you sedated. Now, let me lift you up, so you can take a drink without choking yourself. Be careful though, just sip the water; roll it round your mouth like a gargle before you swallow it. Whatever you do, don't try to gulp it. That'll make you sick. When you've had a drink I'll untie you.'

Not an unpleasant voice. Not threatening, or sinister, or creepy. Neither young nor old. She felt herself being lifted, her shoulders supported. In the gloom she could just about discern his outline, dark against the faint light from behind the curtains. Next, she felt the rim of a bottle placed against her lips. She sipped at the ice-cold water as he'd instructed.

The change in position brought another discomfort. 'I'm sorry,' her voice was a little less of a croak, more her normal speaking voice, but still husky. 'I need the toilet.'

There was, not laughter, but certainly amusement in his voice as he replied. 'That's all right. We'll attend to that as soon as I've untied you.'

Her arms were raised slightly. Then something cold touched the back of her hand. 'Stay still. Absolutely still. Whatever you do, don't move your hands.'

There was a slight tug at her restraints, and the pressure on her wrists eased immediately. 'Hang on, this might sting a bit.' She felt her captor's hand touch hers, feeling for her wrist; followed by a sharp tugging sensation. The tape binding her hands together was removed. The pain from the

adhesive being removed was nothing compared to the sensation of release, of relief. She felt his hand touch her again, this time on her leg as he groped for the bonds around her ankles. He sliced through the tape, pulled it away and she was free.

'Steady now. Don't try to get up. You'll feel dizzy to start with. That's only to be expected. It'll soon wear off, but in the meantime I'm going to carry you.'

Before she realized what was happening he lifted her clear of the bed. He walked across the room, three quick strides, without seeming to notice the burden he was carrying. Then he opened the door and she blinked against the light. She looked at the man who was holding her prisoner. She guessed him to be about thirty years old. Tall, well built. Obviously strong, the way he was carrying her so effortlessly. She concentrated on his face. She needed to know what sort of a man her captor was. It wasn't a bad face. Not evil, or sinister. In fact, although she searched for signs of wickedness, she could only see sadness. Or was that her imagination? Or wishful thinking?

He carried her a few more steps before opening another door to a bathroom. He set her down next to the toilet and retreated to the far side of the room. 'I'm afraid I can't leave you alone.'

She felt her face go hot with embarrassment. At school she'd been used to performing private functions in the semi-public of a communal bathroom, but that had been different. Those around her had been girls. Not a man, and not in plain sight, no more than eight or ten feet away.

Eventually the need overcame her reserve. When she'd finished, she zipped up her jeans and reached for the handle. As she flushed the toilet, she looked round the room. There was an old lady sitting on top of the cistern tank, knitting. A disguise for the spare toilet roll. Over the wash basin she saw a collection of bottles, shampoos and toiletries, together with a ladies depilatory cream that was advertised nightly on TV. All unmistakeable signs of a woman's presence. The idea that a woman lived here comforted her. She felt the fear subside.

On the side of the bath were plastic ducks. Not only a woman; a family. This was his home. Or was it? If that was so, where was his wife? Where were his children? Could it be that this wasn't his house at all? Or, Jessica shivered involuntarily at the thought, was there a more sinister reason for their absence? Question after question crowded her mind; unasked, unanswered.

'Ready now?'

He was looking at her. Not staring. Not like, well, Jessica was used to the way some men stared at her, aware of what their thoughts were. This wasn't like that at all.

'I must wash my hands.'

She turned away from the basin and immediately the room began to see-saw as he'd predicted. As she swayed, he was alongside her immediately, his arm about her waist. Supporting, not gripping her. In other circumstances she'd have been comforted, might even have enjoyed the experience. Here, she was confused. What she found strangest was that the panic, the fear had retreated. They were still there, but in abeyance. 'Come on; let's get you to somewhere you can sit down. Then, I'll make you something to eat. It's no wonder you're dizzy, you haven't eaten for two days.'

Had she been out of it for two days? That meant he must have drugged her a second time. Why? Once he'd captured her, what was the need to keep her sedated? An obvious reason came to mind, but she was able to discount that immediately. She hadn't been assaulted. She'd have known. Even if it had happened whilst she was drugged, she'd have been aware of it. Other questions followed, questions she couldn't ask. Dare not ask; not yet. And probably not at all. As she watched him the fear that had temporarily left her returned. Not unabated, but amplified. A strap over his shoulder was attached to a squat, black, ugly chunk of metal: a gun. A big, efficient looking gun. She didn't know what make or calibre or anything like that. All she knew was the terror it inspired.

She was sure she wouldn't be able to eat. But as he started to grill sausages and bacon, she realized how hungry she was. She watched him prepare the food, the evil looking gun still in the shoulder holster. She broke the silence at last. 'Do you ever take that off?'

He swung round, saw where she was looking. A smile that might have had traces of humour in it passed across his face, fleetingly. He lifted it, watching her face as he did so, noticing the alarm. 'Not often,' was his sole reply.

'Not even to sleep?' She was aghast. At the situation, at the gun, at her daring to ask such a question.

'Sometimes, not always. Depends.'

What did that mean? 'Aren't you afraid it'll go off accidentally?'

He hefted the weapon in his hand, looked at it; almost lovingly. 'This only goes off when I want it to.' As he was speaking he swung the barrel towards her; watched the terror multiply. He held it pointing directly at her before lowering it. 'Don't worry. I'm not going to shoot you. Not yet, and possibly not at all. Do as you're told and you'll not come to any harm.'

The food was simple, but good. He watched her eat, picking at it at first; then, as her appetite returned, she wolfed it down. He poured her a second mug of tea. She pushed the plate away and cradled the mug in her hands. 'What happens now?'

'Now, we have to move. That means I have to tape and gag you.'

'Please don't do that.'

He looked at her for a long time in silence. 'I need your word that you won't try to escape, or call for help.'

'I promise.'

She was looking at him as she spoke. He couldn't see any sign she was lying, but still. 'I can't take that chance. It'll only be for a few minutes. Just till we get to where we're going.'

Meekly, reassured by his tone as much as his words, Jessica held out her hands. He strapped them with the duct tape, then her ankles, before tying a handkerchief over her mouth. Then he scooped her up and carried her effortlessly outside. The night air was cold, but before they'd gone more than a few yards he stopped. Jessica couldn't see clearly, the handkerchief was flapping over her eyes. She heard him open another door, before carrying her up a step and sliding through. He put her down, on a couch she guessed. 'I'll be back in a minute. Got to lock up.'

He was no longer than he'd said. 'Promise to behave? Not try anything stupid?'

She nodded furiously.

He released the gag, and she looked round. They were in some sort of caravan.

'I promised before, but you took no notice.' Her tone was cutting. She wasn't sure, but she thought he smiled.

He sliced through the tape and pulled it off. 'OK, up front,' he ordered.

'Up front where?'

He pointed towards a curtain. He pulled it back and Jessica realized she'd only been half right. It was in fact a motorhome. He helped her to her feet then guided her into the passenger seat, which had been swivelled towards the living quarters. When she was sitting down he turned the seat to face forwards. When he heard it click into place he got into the driver's seat. 'Where are we going? Where are you taking me?'

'We're going on a little journey. When we get to the place I have in mind, I'll tell you why you're here. Don't worry. You're not going to come to any harm. Not as long as you're with me. That's the reason I took you away from that house. To keep you safe.'

'What do you mean?'

'I'll explain later. Just sit back, put your seat belt on and relax. There's a bottle of water in the glove compartment in front of you. We've about an hour's journey ahead of us.'

For the most part, the journey was completed in silence. 'What did you mean?' she said at last. 'About keeping me safe?'

'You were in danger. At that house. Leave it at that. I'll explain when we get there. It won't be long now.'

Paul Farley was a mild-mannered young man, who worked in the Helmsdale branch of Three Shires Building Society. As such, he was a normal, law-abiding citizen. In his alter ego however, he had several convictions all for minor public order offences. Whether his employers disapproved of the actions that led to his various arrests or not, Paul had never been reprimanded by them.

He returned from work, went to his room and switched on his computer. He glanced round as he waited for it to boot up. The walls were plastered with posters and photographs relating to Paul's two abiding passions, the environment and welfare of animals.

He clicked open one of his e-mail folders where his username was 'Eco Sounder'. Paul, as leader of the local branch of an environmental action group, was also heavily involved with animal rights activists – a group who favoured a direct, not to say confrontational approach with those who, as they saw it, exploited animals. Paul, or Eco Sounder, was one of the leading lights. The one exploiters least wanted on their doorstep.

He was so engrossed in the contents of a new e-mail that his mother had to call him three times to tell him his tea was ready before he responded. If the information he'd received was correct, there was a company right on his doorstep that was conducting experiments on animals. How come he'd missed that? His failure to pick up on the exploitation added to his sense of outrage. Something would have to be done. What's more, it would have to be done soon. And it would have to be strong, direct action. Nothing less would serve to put a halt to this cruelty and bring the perpetrators to the notice of the public.

During his deliberations, Paul never stopped to think about the sender of the e-mail. Never stopped to wonder why a complete stranger should pick him, to inform him of these facts. Or to question the sender's motives. None of these questions crossed Paul's mind. It's doubtful if they'd have influenced his course of action even if they had. Eco

Sounder had been roused: he had a mission to fulfil, a crusade to organize.

His mother wasn't sure if her son actually enjoyed his tea, or even if he tasted it. She was about to ask if he wanted a dessert when he stood up. She supposed she should have been grateful for the 'Thanks, Ma,' delivered over his shoulder as he left the dining room. He was too preoccupied with the task before him to be concerned with such trivial matters as food. He had to get back to his computer. He needed to mobilize his troops for their best demonstration yet. More than that, he would do his level best to gain access to the place where he now knew they were torturing helpless animals. He felt his gut twist in agony. This was no reflection on his mother's excellent cooking, but the thought of the suffering those poor creatures had endured – were still enduring.

Well, if he'd anything to do with it, that suffering would soon be over. Next weekend would be the best time for what he had planned. The movement could always count on greater support at weekends. In addition, he reckoned the target for their activities would have less staff on hand to raise the alarm.

Paul ran down a mental list of some of their most radical minded activists. Ones who, like Paul himself, would have no qualms in breaking the law, breaking a whole raft of laws to achieve their ends. And, he'd send a copy to the guy who'd e-mailed him. Only fair he should be kept in the loop.

He began composing the e-mail he would circulate to all like-minded individuals who he knew would possibly be available. No point in sending it to those in Cornwall or Essex. They had to be within striking distance of Helmsdale. They'd need to arrange a meeting place as well. And they'd need directions to their target: Helm Pharm.

CHAPTER NINE

Eventually, after what seemed an age, the motorhome turned off the main road and onto a narrow, winding lane. In the beam of the headlights, Jessica could see grass growing through the tarmac in the middle of the single track. What she could make out of their surroundings through the windscreen looked wild, moorland country, with no houses, or barns even. They hadn't passed a village or a signpost for several miles until, as her captor slowed the vehicle, the headlights picked out a sign. There was only one destination shown on the board. It read: 'Stark Ghyll 8 miles'. Jessica gave an involuntary shiver. Her fear returned, amplified. She knew she was at this man's mercy. A chaotic jumble of thoughts crowded her mind. He'd said he was keeping her safe. Safe for herself, or safe for him? Why had he taken her? Certainly not for her money. She had none, her father had very little. If not money, there could only be one other explanation, but it horrified her. The fear became terror. Subconsciously she shrank away, pressing close to the passenger door. She was miles from the nearest human habitation. Alone, with a man who'd kidnapped her. And her only explanation for her abduction was that she was now at the mercy of a rapist.

'You don't have to worry,' his words broke a silence that had become oppressive.

'What do you mean?' Jessica was proud of the calm tone of her voice.

'I mean that I haven't kidnapped you for the reason you're thinking about.'

'How did you know what I was thinking?' The moment she blurted it out she regretted it.

In the darkness she saw his teeth. He was laughing. At her? 'You're not an heiress. You're not a famous film star. You're not a millionaire's daughter. You haven't got a map of a mine where there's buried treasure in your possession. So the only other logical explanation is that I'm a sex maniac after your, admittedly, highly attractive body. And that I've brought you out here to this remote spot to have my evil way with you. Until I get tired of you that is, when I slit your throat and drop you down a disused mine shaft. Is that close enough to what you were thinking?'

'You're not? A sex maniac I mean?'

'Oh yes.' Although she barely knew the man, Jessica recognized the sarcasm in his voice. 'You'll be the tenth this week. If it continues like this I'll have to find another mine shaft. This one will be full by the end of the month.'

As he spoke he swung the vehicle off the track. They were now on the open moor, bumping over the uneven ground. 'Not long now. Bit bouncy for a while, but you're quite safe.'

They'd only travelled a couple of hundred yards when the ground before them opened up. They drove slowly down a long slope until they were in some sort of a natural bowl. 'Where are we?' Jessica asked as he stopped the vehicle. 'What is this place?'

'Old quarry,' he told her as he unbuckled his seat belt. 'Disused for centuries. Come on.'

He opened the curtain leading to the back of the van and gestured to her to go inside. 'Better sit down,' he told her. 'Before I tell you why I've brought you here, I want you to tell me about your family.'

He pressed a switch and warm, subdued lighting lit the small living space. He pulled the curtains across the windows behind the couches, then the longer one separating them from the driving area.

'My family, why do you want to know about my family?'

'Tell me what they're like. Do you love them? All the normal things. What's home life like? Anything that comes into your mind.'

She laughed, but he saw no humour in her expression, in her eyes. When she spoke, her voice was bitter. 'That's a joke for a start. Calling them my family, I mean. I don't have a family. I just have a set of relatives. My mother's a lush and a nymphomaniac. My brother's a thief and a junkie. And I hardly ever see my father. You call that a family?'

This was going to be easy. Easier than he'd imagined. 'Doesn't sound as if you'd miss your mother much. Or your brother for that matter. Now why's that I wonder?'

She hesitated; decided she owed her mother no loyalty. Or Adam either. 'When I was fifteen years old I was sent home from school, because I'd been sick. I walked in the house and heard noises from the bedroom. The one she shared with my father. But at that time she was sharing it with two other men. Complete strangers. The moment I saw what she was doing with them, saw the look on her face, at that moment I ceased to have a mother.'

'Not a pleasant thing for a young girl to find out. Especially about her mother,' he agreed. 'And what about your brother? What about Adam?'

'You know Adam?'

He nodded. 'Know of him,' he corrected her.

'That's the best way to know Adam. I wasn't granted that luxury. My grandmother died when I was five. I only met her a few times because we were in America. She came to visit us, but not often. She left me a beautiful necklace. It was made up of diamonds and rubies. Father had it valued for insurance. They said it was worth ten thousand pounds. Four years ago, before I'd even had chance to wear it, my brother stole it. He sold my necklace to buy drugs. I found out later he only got seven hundred pounds.' Her tone took on a new level of bitterness. 'He couldn't even get a decent price for it. If my father hadn't pleaded with me, I'd have reported him to the police. I think that says everything about my relationship with my mother and brother. So, what would you like to talk about next?'

'Your father. Tell me about your father?'

'What is this all about?'

He shook his head. 'Later. First I'm going to make us a drink. What would you like? I've tea, coffee or drinking chocolate. Whilst the kettle's boiling you can tell me about your father.'

'Hot chocolate please.' Was there no understanding this man?

There was a long silence. So long he thought he was going to need to prompt her. Then, at last she spoke. Her tone changed, the bitterness vanished, to be replaced with a gentler, more protective air. 'It hasn't been easy for him. Dad isn't strong, you see. He's not able to face up to things. That's why people feel they can bully him, take advantage of the fact he's so easygoing. When he was at university he got headhunted. It must have seemed like a great deal at the time. The opportunity of a lifetime, especially for someone so young: so naive. He was sponsored to do research. That was fine; it was what he enjoyed doing most anyway. But then they wanted payback; big style. By then, he and my mother were married and Adam was on the way. They called on Dad, wanted him to go to America, wouldn't take no for an answer. They wanted him at their headquarters in California, to head up some research project they'd just started.'

'Do you know what that was?'

She shook her head. 'Dad's never been allowed to talk about his work. Anyway, all this was way before I was old enough to understand what was going on. Then, one day, out of the blue, he told us we were all moving back to England.

'Until then, we'd been fairly happy. But after we got to England, everything went wrong. Mother started her antics;

then Adam started on drugs. Dad always seemed so unhappy. A lot of the time I put it down to Mother's behaviour, or Adam's problems, sometimes I even wondered if I'd caused it, but eventually I came to understand there was far more to it than that.'

'Did he say why he decided to come back? Was his work in America over?'

'I don't think so.' Jessica screwed her face up in an effort to remember. 'He said it was because he'd been transferred. That was it. That was the word he used, transferred. As time went on, things got worse and worse. Mother's behaviour got more outrageous. Adam was totally out of control. And Dad, well, I hardly ever saw him. When I did, he was either too upset to talk, or simply too exhausted. Or sometimes both.'

She looked at him, sudden realization came to her. Something he'd said. 'You asked me if I'd miss Mother or Adam. Why did you ask that? Has something happened to them?'

He thought for a moment before replying. 'They're dead,' he told her laconically.

Shock flared in her eyes. Shock, but no distress. 'Dead?' she repeated. 'How did they die?'

'I killed them.'

He said it in so matter of fact a tone she didn't realize what he'd said for some time. When realization came, she began to shake. 'Don't worry. I said I wouldn't harm you, and I won't, as long as you do as you're told. As I tell you. Understand? Behave, and you live. Misbehave, and all bets are off.'

'I understand.'

'Say it properly. Say, "I promise to do everything you ask of me. I promise to obey you at all times."'

She repeated the words. He wasn't bothered about what she said. It was the voice he was interested in. As she spoke it was getting more and more slurred. The effect of the sedative in her drink.

'That's enough. No more talking for tonight.' He watched her eyes glaze over as the drug took effect. He fielded her empty mug and swung her legs onto the couch. He reached into the stowage compartment underneath the bunk and took out a duvet. He covered her and tucked a pillow under her head. 'Good night, Jessica,' he said softly. But she was already fast asleep.

He slid open a drawer and took out a laptop, plugged it in and switched on. Fortunately the area was close enough to several military establishments, so signal wasn't going to be a problem. When the internet connection was made, he located the cursor over the space bar and began to type the word 'STOCKHOLM'.

When time had passed with no contact, Nash had all but given up hope of getting a positive response to his request for information regarding Dr North. The phone call came as a considerable surprise, not the least part of which was due to its source.

'Detective Inspector Nash? Major Smith, Military Intelligence.'

'Another one?'

'I'm sorry?'

'A colleague of mine had a phone call from a Captain Smith. I wondered if you'd been promoted? Or if you're all called Smith, like in *The Matrix*?'

'Coincidence,' the major told him. 'I understand you're concerned about Dr North?'

'That's certainly no exaggeration.'

'I'm happy to tell you Dr North is both alive and well. Unfortunately I'm not in a position to tell you much more.'

'That's certainly good news, although it's of very little help in my investigation.'

'I understand that, and believe me, I am sympathetic. However, I may be able to be of some limited assistance, as far as I'm allowed. I can tell you that Dr North was at a meeting in Birmingham on the night his wife died. Over twenty people can vouch for that fact. They include several eminent scientists and half a dozen high-ranking army officers. As for when his son was killed, Dr North was in hospital at the time, having suffered head injuries in a car smash. And before you ask, my people have conducted a thorough investigation into the accident and there are no suspicious circumstances surrounding it.'

'It would have been useful to speak with Dr North, if only to ask him if he has any idea of a motive for either murder, or even a possible suspect.'

'I'm sorry to disappoint you, Inspector, but my superiors will not allow that. Dr North's work is highly sensitive, and I understand it to be at a critical stage in development. Please believe me, though, we have questioned him ourselves as to who might be behind these deaths and he has absolutely no idea. I can also assure you that he is being extremely well protected. Without wishing to denigrate your officers, I believe we can offer him far better protection than you would be able to.'

'And what about Jessica?'

There was a pause. 'To the best of my knowledge, Miss North is also alive and well. I'm sorry, but that's all I'm allowed to say.'

After the man rang off, Nash stared at the phone for a few moments. That pause worried him. That, and the sentence that had followed it. Reading between the lines, he wondered if the military actually knew where Jessica was.

He called Clara into his office. 'Go back to Gorton. Talk to anybody and everybody you can. Find out anything you can about Jessica North. If nothing else, ask if anyone's ever seen her in school uniform, and if so, see if they can describe it. If they could, it might be a help, especially if the logo or badge is distinctive.'

'Damn it, Mike, why didn't I think of that?'

'How do you mean?'

'One of the forensics guys unearthed something from beneath a huge chunk of broken plaster. It had come off the wall of the smallest bedroom. It was a plaque in the shape of a shield.'

'Can you remember what it looked like?'

'No, but I'm sure the fire service collected a lot of the smaller items such as that.'

It took an hour of searching through a series of black plastic bags before they located the shield. Clara held it up; then stared as Nash began laughing. 'Drive over to Harrogate this afternoon. I'll give you directions.'

Clara blinked. 'You recognize this?' She looked at the shield. Despite the smoke damage she could make out a griffin's head, an oak tree and two white roses. 'How come you know it?'

'Because I went to the same school.'

Clara stared at him. 'But Jessica's a girl. How come? Is it a mixed school?'

'It is now. It wasn't when I went.'

'I bet a lot of mothers would be glad about that, if they knew.'

It was mid-afternoon when Mironova rang him. 'I spoke to the headmaster. Jessica was taken out of school a couple of weeks ago. The men who came for her had Military Intelligence warrant cards. The headmaster told me he wouldn't have accepted the cards on their own, but that they also brought a letter explaining that Jessica's mother and brother were dead, and that Dr North was in a hospital, unconscious, and that there were fears for Jessica's safety on grounds of national security. The letterhead was Helm Pharm, who Jessica confirmed as her father's employers. The headmaster didn't pass the contents on to Jessica but kept the letter. I've brought it away with me.'

'Who signed it?'

'Dr Caroline Dunning. Her title is given as "Head of Scientific Research". The headmaster asked Jessica if she knew Dr Dunning. She told him Dr Dunning worked closely with her father.' Clara paused. 'He got the impression Jessica didn't like Dr Dunning much.'

Nash sat pondering the news. Jessica had been taken from the school by Military Intelligence, on the strength of a letter signed by Dr Dunning. So, where had they taken her? Presumably to the same house where Dr Dunning had arrived. So, what had the panic been about after her arrival? What was it Major Smith had said? 'To the best of our knowledge Jessica is alive and well'. Or in other words, we don't know where she is. Nash had a mental image of a man carrying a bundle out to a car. A man whose face he hadn't recognized, although it was familiar. Not just to a car, but to Dr Dunning's car.

The connections came, thick and fast. It was the front page of the newspaper visible on Mironova's desk that did it. It carried the picture of the new, charismatic American president. Nash realized whose face he'd seen. The man carrying the bundle had been wearing a Ronald Reagan mask. And he'd posed for the surveillance camera. But why use Dr Dunning's car? Of course; to allay suspicion. The guards would be expecting Dr Dunning. He picked the phone up. 'Jack, do me a favour. That car you checked out. See if any others of the same make, model and colour have been reported stolen in the last seven days, will you?'

The reply came back within minutes. An identical car had been taken from Netherdale the day before the incident at the laboratory. Nash was convinced he was right. So what had been in the bundle? With a jolt that was almost physical, Nash realized he'd used the wrong word. Not 'what' but 'who'. Someone light enough to be carried by a fit young man. A soldier perhaps? Now he knew why Smith had hedged when asked the question. Of course they didn't know where Jessica was. That was what the panic had been about. She'd been kidnapped. Right from under their noses.

Jessica hadn't expected to get any sleep. Not after what he'd told her. But then, she didn't know she'd been drugged. Then, memory returned. He'd said that her mother and brother were dead. He'd told her that he'd killed them. Was that true? Or had he been feeding her a line? Thinking about the gun he wore she doubted that. If it was the case, if what he'd told her was true, why didn't she feel terrified? Or distraught?

Two of her three closest relatives were dead. They'd been killed by the man who was holding her prisoner. Surely she should be in tears. More than that; hysterics. But then again, she'd told him how much she despised her mother, how little she cared for her brother. That had been true, but it didn't mean she shouldn't be upset to hear they were dead. Did that make her unnatural? A cold-hearted monster? As unfeeling as, she paused in her thought process, as, well, as *he* was?

He'd shown no emotion as he'd told her of the killings. No remorse, no regret. Neither had he glorified in it, or tried to explain or justify his actions. He'd just told her. As a fact; like telling the time. And what was all that about her father? Why had he wanted to know so much? About him: all her family? What was his agenda?

She heard a noise. Slight, the merest whisper of sound. She looked across the room. He was standing in the doorway, staring at her. Assessing her. Suddenly, she felt afraid. A level of fear greater than any so far.

'So, you're awake.' His voice was remote, distant, cold even.

'Yes, I've just woken up. Do you want me?' Silly question. Worse, a dangerously leading question.

His expression changed, relaxed. 'Time to get up,' he told her, obscurely.

Slowly she swung her legs off the couch. 'I need the loo.'

He helped her to her feet, guided her to the tiny compartment that served as toilet and shower combined. As she was unbuttoning her jeans, she looked up. He hadn't closed the door, hadn't turned his back. He was standing watching her. She waited for him to avert his gaze. When he didn't she asked, 'Can I have some privacy.'

'No,' his tone was neutral. 'You have no privacy. Not from me. And when you've finished I want you to take a shower. I have some clean clothes for you.'

'Clothes? Where from?'

'I bought them, when you were out of it. Took the sizes from what you were wearing.'

He slid the shower curtain across in front of the toilet. 'The controls are self-explanatory, bath towel's hanging there.' He pointed to the pegs on the wall.

She turned her back on him and started to undress, slowly, unwillingly. As her fingers fumbled with the bra strap, she wondered, was this it? Was he going to rape her? She looked round for somewhere to put her clothing. A hand reached over her shoulder and took the garments from her. He was standing close to her now, really close. So close she could smell him. A clean, soapy smell. She turned slowly to face him, taunting, striking a deliberately provocative pose, head to one side. He looked her up and down, slowly. She felt the blood rush to her cheeks. After what seemed an age, he smiled. 'Very nice,' he pointed to the cubicle. 'Now get your shower. You need it.'

In the shower she felt her fear recede marginally. He didn't want her. Not that way. Although, when he'd looked at her, standing naked in front of him, she thought she'd seen a glimmer of something in his eyes. Not lust, something she was unable to place. Was it sadness?

She groped for the towel. It was placed in her hand. So he'd been there all along. She stepped out onto the mat. He continued to watch her, standing no more than a couple of feet in front of her as she dried herself. When she'd finished he reached out for the towel. She stared into his eyes. Had she been wrong? Had he been waiting until she was clean?

He took the towel from her trembling hands. 'Turn round.'

She obeyed, moving slowly, reluctantly. Didn't he want her to look at him whilst he was raping her? The towel flopped over her face, over her head. He began to rub, vigorously.

Jessica realized she was as far as ever from understanding this man, or gauging his emotions or motives. She stood still as he dried her hair; not even flinching when he felt it to make sure it was dry. He hung the towel back on its peg. 'Come on,' he took her hand.

Jessica sat down on the couch, knees primly together, hands across her breasts. He ignored her and walked across to the wardrobe compartment. He took out a pair of jeans and tossed them on the bed. From a drawer he took out a top, bra and pants, then stood watching as she dressed.

When she'd tied her trainers, he helped her to her feet. 'Breakfast time.' He kept hold of her hand as they went across to the kitchenette. Why? she wondered. He'd not attempted to assault her, had given no sign that was in his plans. There'd been nothing lecherous in the way he'd looked at her, even when she'd been naked, tempting him. She felt comforted by that, and by the warmth of this human contact. And then she realized, with a fresh degree of shock, that she was holding hands with a self-confessed killer. With the man who'd murdered her mother and brother. It should have repelled her. Oddly, it didn't.

He asked her what she wanted to eat. She opted for toast. Jessica looked round. The closed curtains reminded her of the house. 'That place we were in, before you brought me here. Was that your home?'

He nodded, preoccupied.

'Don't you ever draw the curtains or blinds? They were closed all the time I was there, now you've done the same here.'

'It wasn't safe at the house. You never know who might be watching.'

'The police, you mean? Is that who you're afraid of?'

He swung round in surprise. 'No, not the police.' He laughed. 'And I'm not afraid.'

She waited for him to explain, but it appeared he wasn't ready to.

'But won't people think it's odd? The curtains being closed when it's broad daylight?'

That expression was back in his eyes, a kind of sadness, sadness and anger combined. 'They won't think it's strange. Not in the circumstances. Not round there.'

When they'd finished eating, he stood up. 'Come on.'

'Where to?'

'We're going to watch TV.'

'Television? What's on television at this time of day that you're so keen to watch?'

'Nothing on TV, we're going to watch home movies.'

He walked over to the portable TV/DVD player and switched it on. He sat alongside her and pressed the remote control. What followed was a collection of film clips obviously taken with a camcorder. Almost all of these featured a young woman with two small girls, presumably her daughters, Jessica guessed.

The setting for the clips varied. Some had been taken in the garden of a house. His house? Some were on beaches, some at theme parks and a few taken in and around a motorhome, this one she guessed. From time to time Jessica glanced sideways at her captor. His eyes were fixed on the screen, his expression a compound of rage and sadness.

The last clip was taken indoors, and from the furnishings, Jessica recognized it as the house she'd been kept in. On this occasion the camera was being operated by someone else, the woman perhaps. It had obviously been shot on a Christmas morning, for there was the tree, in front of the window, with the two girls squatting on the carpet, opening present after present. The camcorder microphone picked up their squeals of delight.

Watching them with obvious pride was a man. As the girls jumped on him and hugged him with gratitude, he turned to face the camera. It was the man sitting alongside her, but for a moment Jessica failed to recognize him. He looked so much younger, little more than a boy, his expression happy and carefree. Jessica was still trying to come to terms with this when the screen went blank.

She looked at him. He was staring at the screen, as if willing it to show more.

'What happened to them? Where are they?'

He turned away, his reluctance obvious. When he faced her his expression was of hatred. 'They died,' he told her, teeth gritted, each word a fresh torture. 'There, in that house.'

'How? When?'

'Carbon monoxide poisoning is what they called it. Murder is what I call it. They died because the MOD didn't maintain the appliances. They died because I wasn't there to protect them. They died because we were so short of money I volunteered for a special tour of duty. A tour that involved me in something I found out was horrific. Something the intelligence creeps dreamed up using your father and others like him. Taking his skills and corrupting them for their own perverted ends.'

'But my father isn't involved in weapons or anything to do with warfare. He's not an engineer, he's a chemist. What on earth could he provide that would be useful to the military?'

Jessica listened as he told her. Listened, and learned for the first time the dreadful nature of what her father's work produced. What she was unaware of was that her captor was in the process of brainwashing her. The solitary nature of her captivity, the lack of contact with anyone apart from her captor were the first stages in a process designed to bend her will to that of her abductor. The real reason behind the closing of the curtains and blinds was not to avoid detection, but to heighten the sense of isolation. Showing the film clips was calculated to engage her sympathy.

The next stage would involve increasing her dependency on him. Over the next few days and weeks, aided by the drugs he was feeding into her system, Jessica would come to realize that every action she took would need his blessing. Everything, from eating, drinking, sleeping, washing, using the toilet, dressing and undressing, could only be done with his involvement and approval.

It mattered little to him whether Jessica was aware of what was being done to her or not. His objective would be unaffected. He was going to use Jessica in the same way as he had been used. And in doing so, he would create a weapon as potent as he had become. He'd used the short time they'd been together to study the girl closely. He already knew far more about her, both physically and mentally, than she could have guessed. Her physique was ideal – tall, with a good fig-ure and a suitable level of fitness. That would be honed by the training regime he would introduce until she was as strong as he could make her. Mentally, she was tough, with all the strength of character her father lacked. She'd not once cried, or had hysterics, even when she'd been certain he was going to rape her. He smiled inwardly at the thought. It wasn't that he hadn't been tempted. She was attractive enough. He couldn't be sure quite what had stopped him. Perhaps it was down to respect. His respect for her courage; the unconscious display of spirit that showed in a refusal to break down. He knew he would never be able to break that spirit. So his only option was to bend it to his will, pervert all those qualities she possessed for his own use.

CHAPTER TEN

The bar of The Horse and Jockey was crowded when Nash and Becky walked in. Busier than usual for a Friday night. Nash fought his way to the bar and got their drinks. He found Becky in the corner, where she was sharing a table with Jonas Turner. 'Evening, Jonas, what's the crush for? Not another darts tournament?'

Turner grinned. 'Not likely, most of this lot couldn't hit double top if they were standing next to t' board. There's a load of regulars from out of t' tap room come in here because they don't like the company in there.'

'It's a bit early for tourists, isn't it?'

'They're not tourists,' Turner snorted. 'It's a load of those animal rights activists.'

'What are they doing round here? Helmsdale's a bit off the beaten track for anything like that.'

'Nobody knows for sure. Although somebody started a rumour the Bishopton Hunt were starting up again and might be holding a meet this weekend. I happen to know that's nonsense though, 'cos 'ave a couple of friends who are followers.'

'So, if it isn't the hunt they're interested in, what do you think is the real reason they're here?'

'T' other whisper ah heard were that they're planning to break into that laboratory out on t' Bishop's Cross road. The bloke who told me said they've found out the company have been experimenting on animals.'

Becky saw the change in Nash's expression. 'That'll be Helm Pharm you're talking about, I take it?' she questioned Turner. 'Do you know anything about them, Mike?'

'Let's just say they interest me,' he said, 'and leave it at that.'

Later, as they were walking back to Nash's flat, Becky took up the subject again. 'What's your interest in Helm Pharm?'

Nash thought for a moment. 'They employ the father of that man found murdered in the stocks. They do a lot of work for the military. Everything there is so hush-hush I'm surprised the animal rights people got to know anything about them. I think I ought to warn our uniform people and put the company's security on alert that there might be trouble over the weekend.'

Becky slipped her hand through his arm. 'Mike, I need to talk to you.'

Nash looked at her, remembering how they'd met. He'd thought she looked beautiful then. She looked even lovelier now. 'What about?'

'There was a meeting at *The Gazette* today. My uncle's decided to retire later next year. That means they've to find a new editor and they're reluctant to let it go out of the family. So they've asked me to consider taking over when he goes. The thing is,' she hesitated, 'they want me to go to London for twelve months, to work on one of the nationals to get experience.'

'Oh, I see. What was your answer?'

'I said I'd have to ask you before I made any decision.'

He stopped and turned her to face him. 'Look, Becky, if it's a question of your career, don't let me stand in your way. I'll miss you like hell, but twelve months isn't forever.'

'Are you sure, Mike? It'd mean we'd have very little time together. They made it pretty clear when I got down there the work would be fairly hectic. We might go months without seeing one another.'

'I understand.' He took her hand. 'I really do, Becks. It's just come as a bit of a shock.' He smiled at her. 'When do you start?'

'If I say yes, they'll want me down there in a month's time. The arrangements will have to be finalized before then.'

'A month? That doesn't give us much time.' He slipped his arm round her waist. 'So we'd better make the most of what we've got.'

What Jessica had seen from those film clips made her even more bewildered. All right, the tragedy he'd suffered would knock any man sideways. But what she'd seen pointed to him being a decent, caring family man. So what was it turned him into a self-confessed murderer? One who'd killed two of her family, and had been within an ace of killing her. What made a human being into a monster? The thought of what he might be capable of made her shiver. He'd been restrained, so far. Would that end? Would something trigger off another blood lust? And what would it be? A word? A gesture? An unthinking remark?

He switched the TV off. 'Lunch,' he explained curtly.

She watched him making sandwiches. It was hardly lunchtime. She risked a glance at the clock: 11.30 a.m. If she'd been less afraid of him she might have questioned the timing. He put a plate containing chicken salad sandwiches in front of her and turned to brew tea. She ate, slowly at first; then realized in spite of the hour, in spite of her fear, she was hungry. When she'd finished he took her plate and replaced it with a mug. She was three quarters of the way down the tea when she felt a sudden cramp in her stomach. She almost gasped aloud with the pain. She waited for a moment until it eased. She looked up to find him watching her. 'I'm sorry,' she muttered. 'It's just, there's something I need.'

How could she explain? To a stranger, to someone she was in fear of? His expression didn't change, but he crossed to one of the wall units. He opened the door and rummaged inside. Without a word he took out a small cardboard box and passed it to her. She stared from the box, with its distinctive logo, to her captor. He gestured towards the toilet. If his understanding of what was wrong had led her to hope for privacy to do what was needed, that was soon dashed as he followed her.

She completed the operation, scarlet with embarrassment and shame, and turned to wash her hands. The room went dizzy. He caught her as she fell, hoisted her up and carried her to the couch.

When she started to regain consciousness she was aware something had changed. She could feel the soft cotton of the duvet covering her, against her skin, and realized she was naked. He'd undressed her; that much was obvious. Why? If he'd assaulted her, she felt sure she'd be aware of it. Besides, he wouldn't, surely, knowing what he knew of her state.

She turned onto one side. In the semi-darkness she could just discern another figure, on a bed similar to hers, only two feet away. Her captor? Or another victim?

The figure stirred, stood up. A second later he pulled back the curtain and a small amount of light filtered into the compartment. She turned her head away. There was enough light for her to see that he too was undressed. She heard movement and risked a sideways glance. He was pulling a shirt over his head. A second later and he was dressed. 'Come on, time to get up.' He switched a light on. He was wearing a camouflage shirt and combat trousers. He held out a small bundle of clothing. She swung her legs off the bed, keeping the duvet wrapped round her body. He laughed. 'No false modesty. I said before, you have nothing to hide from me.'

He pulled the duvet from her and hoisted her to her feet. She swayed slightly, knew he must have drugged her again.

He held on to her for a moment, watching her face. 'All right now?'

She nodded and turned to get dressed. She looked at the clothes, questions racing through her mind, tumbling over each other. The sports bra and Lycra leggings were similar to those she used in gymnastics class at school, but why did he want her to wear them? And where had he got them? She straightened up and he held out a pair of trainers and sweatshirt. 'Come on, no time to waste. Training starts in five minutes.'

He walked a couple of paces to the rear of the compartment and opened a door. He steadied her as she stepped out. She took a deep breath. The air felt clean and cold. She looked around; there was snow on the hilltops. Dawn was just breaking, which explained why it had been so gloomy inside. The moorland stretched as far as she could see.

'Let's get started. See that peg?'

She followed the line of his pointing finger. She could just make out a stake driven into the ground about two hundred yards away. She nodded.

'You sprint as fast as you can to the peg. You touch down, count to fifteen slowly; then run back here as fast as you can. Got it?'

'How do you know I won't run away?'

'Three reasons. One, you've nowhere to run to. There's no human habitation within ten miles of here. That's why I've chosen this spot. Added to that, I doubt if your time for two hundred metres is within three seconds of mine, and I can maintain that pace, or close to it for almost three miles. More when I'm in peak condition. And finally, most important of all, you want to know what this is all about, who's behind it and what I intend to do, with you and everything else. If you did manage to get away, you wouldn't get to find that out. If you come back to the van, I'll tell you after breakfast.'

When he was like this, as she'd seen him on the film he'd shown her, she wasn't one bit scared of him. She even found herself questioning his claim that he'd killed her mother and brother. After all, she'd no proof they were dead, only his word.

As if he'd read her thoughts, he said, 'They didn't tell you, did they?'

'Tell me what? Who didn't tell me?'

'The people who took you away from school. They didn't tell you that your mother and brother were dead, did they?'

She stared in confusion.

'Like I said, eventually you'll start to think and act as I do. That's part of it.'

Part of what, she wondered. She wasn't to know that the reason she was so relaxed was the drugs in her system. This was the first stage of the treatment. And that was why he was able to gauge her thoughts and emotions so accurately. Because he'd been through the same process. Not once, but many times. Indeed, he was going through it again. Because it was pointless feeding her the drugs that would turn her into a warrior, such as him, if he was unable to match her aggression when the time came.

At first she enjoyed the sprints, whilst trying to avoid the small patches of ice. He'd made her go through a rigorous fifteen minute warm up programme of exercises before she started. He stood alongside the van, stopwatch in hand and shouted, 'Go.' She ran, reached the peg and stopped, one hand resting on the top. She counted to fifteen, turned and ran back. 'Again,' he told her. 'And this time run as if you mean it. As if you're late for a bus. Not out for an afternoon stroll.'

So, she tried again. And again. After five laps, she turned on him. 'Let's see you do it faster.'

He reached out and grabbed her hand. Before she was properly aware, she was running, half-towed along by her captor. She was running faster than she thought she was capable of. They reached the peg, quicker than she'd managed alone. He kept hold of her hand, and together they raced back to the van. Again and again they ran, until her muscles ached and her chest heaved as she fought to get air into her lungs.

Eventually he stopped, and she was pleased to see he too was a little short of breath. Surely now they'd rest?

'Right, now we're going for a bit of stamina training. Your muscles are like jelly. They need toning up.'

Toning up, in his terminology, involved a seemingly endless long distance run, over patches of snow interspersed with moorland turf; through peat, that came over the tops of her trainers and squelched uncomfortably against her toes. She was by now in a haze of exhaustion. Unable to see, she knew she'd have fallen several times were it not for his hand, steadying her, guiding her, pulling her with him. She wasn't aware they'd turned round, and it was a shock when he slowed them to a halt outside the motorhome. He glanced at his watch. 'Not bad for a beginner,' he commented.

Was that praise? And would she have some rest now? Seemingly not, for he opened a small compartment on the side of the vehicle and took out some objects she recognized, her heart sinking. 'You need building up,' he told her, 'and this is the quickest way, short of steroids.'

The weights weren't too bad. Not at first. But as the exercises got repeated time after time, the strain on her already tired muscles got worse and worse. His insistence on adding weight to the bars didn't help. Eventually he called a halt. 'That's enough for this morning. We'll go through the same routine this afternoon.'

'Oh good,' she panted. 'Something to look forward to.'

He ushered her inside and opened the door opposite the tiny kitchenette. 'Get your clothes off. I'll rinse them through whilst you're showering.'

The water was hot. As she was soaping herself down, she realized she'd stripped naked in front of him without even thinking about it. She was puzzled, but accepted it. When she got out of the shower, he was standing outside the door. He too was naked.

He smiled at her. 'Clean clothes on the bed.'

From inside the cubicle she could hear the water running. She had the opportunity to escape if she wanted to. She hesitated, before sitting down. The clothes he'd put out for her were a T-shirt and jeans, bra and pants, alongside which was a clean pair of trainers. In fact they looked brand new. Everything did. She dressed slowly, thoughtfully. Why hadn't she taken the chance to make a run for it? She knew the answer even as she asked the question. He'd promised to tell her what it was all about. She was keen to know. He'd also promised to tell her what was going to happen to her. She wasn't as desperately keen to hear that, but she knew her curiosity would keep her here until she'd found out.

He emerged from the shower and strode across to the bed next to hers. Without glancing at her he dressed, in much the same outfit as he'd given her. Minus the bra, she thought, and realized with a shock that she'd made a joke. He turned and smiled, she wished he wouldn't. It confused her. She knew she should be scared, but she wasn't. She knew she shouldn't sympathize with this man, but she did.

He stood directly in front of her. He lifted her chin until she was looking into his eyes. 'The training is part of the process. Part of your new life. How long this will take I don't know. But whilst it lasts, you belong to me. To do with as I think fit. Spoils of war. And this is what I've chosen for you. You will become like me. You will think and act like me. You will eat when I eat, drink when I drink, sleep when I sleep. Every action of yours will mirror mine. Don't try to fight against it. There's no point. That isn't a threat. It's a natural result of what's happening to us. Now, breakfast. Then I'll tell you what this is all about. I'm afraid you're in for some shocks.'

Despite Paul Farley's careful planning, the raid on Helm Pharm was a disaster. He wasn't sure quite how their plans had been blown, but the police were there before them. When he saw the line of officers waiting in front of the gates to the laboratory, Paul noticed they were reinforced by a strong contingent of security guards inside the pharmaceutical company grounds.

Security lights blazed from the roof of each building, flooding the area in harsh detail. Any attempt to enter the laboratory by stealth was obviously going to be doomed to failure. If he'd any remaining doubt that their plans had been leaked, these were dispelled when he spotted cameras from two local TV stations set up ready to record the action. Alongside one of these he noticed a photographer from *The Netherdale Gazette*.

Paul had a quick word with a couple of his most trusted comrades. 'Spread the message round everyone. The entry's a bust. Stick to a peaceful demo outside the gates. If anyone wants to go for a sit down protest it's up to them. I'm going to try and find out how we've been rumbled.'

He headed for the place where the press photographer was standing, her camera already snapping stills of the developing protest. He knew her, slightly. Becky Pollard was a customer of the building society where Paul worked. Alongside her was another of their customers. He greeted them with a cheerfulness he was far from feeling. 'How did you get to hear about this?'

He addressed the question to Becky, but it was Detective Inspector Nash who answered. 'I hope you weren't considering anything more radical than this?'

Nash gestured to the lines of chanting, banner waving protesters. 'Of course not,' Paul lied. 'Even if we had been, it wouldn't have been much good. How did you know we'd be here?'

Nash smiled. 'You should choose a different pub to meet in. Or pick a night when I'm not in the other bar. I saw your lot last night and guessed this place would be the object of your attention.'

'We only wanted to draw attention to what they're doing in there.' Paul jerked a thumb in the direction of the laboratory. 'To put them on notice that we're aware of the cruelty they're inflicting on poor defenceless animals. And I suppose I'd better get on with it.' He stepped away to join the rest of the demonstrators. 'But we'll be back, make no mistake,' he muttered – to himself.

Later, as Nash and Becky were dining in their favourite Italian restaurant, Nash fell into an abstracted silence. Becky watched him and waited, knowing he was trying to work something out. It was some time before he came out of his reverie. So long in fact that Gino, the proprietor of La Giaconda, was beginning to wonder if there was something wrong with the seafood salad Nash had ordered.

As her companion lifted his head from contemplating his food, Becky grinned. 'Welcome back, maestro. Care to give us the benefit of your genius?' She saw Nash's puzzled expression, 'You've been toying with your food so long, poor Gino's quite worried.'

'I was thinking about something,' Nash said feebly.

'We know,' Becky gestured to the diners at the surrounding tables, 'we could all hear the cogs grinding. So what was it you were thinking about so deeply?'

Nash hesitated for a moment, 'OK, let me ask you something. What does the word pharmaceutical, suggest to you.'

'Medicines,' she replied promptly. 'Drugs, tablets, injections' – she screwed her face up – 'and cough mixture.'

Nash smiled. 'Exactly, that's just what I thought. So, answer me this. What use would the military have for a pharmaceutical company? I don't just mean as a supplier of aspirin, or any of the proprietary medicines. But something that is cloaked in secrecy and attracts such a high level of security that anything connected to that company is handled by Military Intelligence?'

Becky frowned. She thought for a few moments before shaking her head. 'I've no idea. Why do you ask?'

Nash glanced round; then began to explain the background to the Adam North murder. Or rather, what little he knew. He concentrated on his frustrated attempts to speak to the dead man's father. 'None of it makes sense. If the company was an electronics firm, or involved in the design or manufacture of weapons systems I could understand the military's involvement, but a drugs company....' His voice trailed off into silence.

A second later he looked across the table, his face animated. 'Do you recall me telling you about the time when I was having really vivid nightmares? Almost hallucinations?'

Becky nodded. 'At the time I just thought it was part of your weird mind.'

'Takes one to know one. Anyway, the doctor at Netherdale General said they were due to a mixture of the medication I was taking, combined with alcohol. His exact words were, "Taking either of them on their own wouldn't be a problem. Put them together, and they act like a mood altering drug. Take them for long enough and they'll not only be hallucinogenic, they'll start to affect your behaviour."'

'Like LSD you mean?'

'Something of the sort, although the stuff I was on wasn't anywhere near as powerful as LSD. But, given what he told me, suppose Helm Pharm is researching and developing similar sorts of drugs for military use.'

'This is beginning to sound like something from an American spy film. Or could it be you're back on the medication?'

'The American connection might not be too far from the truth.' Nash ignored the insult. 'Remember I said Dr North spent a long time working in America? Well, I read something a while back about a project called MKULTRA. It was a CIA experiment that involved them feeding drugs to GIs, right through from the 1950s to the 1970s. Unfortunately, much of what is known about it can't be ratified, because the director of the CIA ordered all the files to be destroyed following the Watergate scandal. But if you think about it, it makes sense. It would explain why those serving in Vietnam had such easy access to drugs.'

'That sounds really cruel and horrible. From what I've heard about drugs like that, the effects can last for years. If not for a lifetime.'

'Tell me about it,' Nash said with feeling. 'We come across it all too often at work. I can't prove any of this, but to be honest I can't come up with any other logical explanation for the military being so paranoid about protecting Helm Pharm and their employees. It might be sinister in one sense, but fortunately, it doesn't seem to be sinister with regard to my investigation.' He paused and frowned. 'On the other hand, it could be within my jurisdiction.'

'I don't get you.'

'It would be within my jurisdiction if the murders were committed by someone who'd been fed those drugs.'

'It all seems a bit far-fetched to me.'

Nash sighed. 'I suppose it is. I guess I'm just clutching at straws because I'm unable to make any headway in solving the case.'

CHAPTER ELEVEN

The days passed in a whirl of activity. Jessica had been running, pumping weights and doing circuit training like she'd never dreamed of. Once he'd explained a little of what had happened to his family and hers, Jessica plunged into the routine with heightened enthusiasm. She still wasn't sure what he had in mind, although she'd asked more than once. 'All in good time,' was all he would say.

The training was having an effect on her. For the first couple of days she'd had to work hard to relieve the stiffness and exhaustion brought about by the exercise. Now she felt fitter and stronger, more alive than at any time she could remember. He'd told her about the drugs too. Once he'd explained their purpose, there seemed no point in disguising them in her food or drinks. They took them together, making a small ritual of it, almost like toasting one another.

A couple of days before, they'd returned to his house to top up the motorhome's supply of water and recharge its batteries.

'I don't know how you can bear to go inside, knowing what happened here.'

'I'm here because I have to be, no other reason.'

She saw the grim expression on his face and put her hand on his shoulder. A comradely gesture; nothing more. It worked, he smiled at her.

'Besides the water and batteries, I need to visit the supermarket. There's not all that much room in the van's fridge and the way you trough, it won't last us much longer.'

'It's the exercise. It gives me an appetite.'

They'd been to the supermarket, but for safety, he'd made her remain inside the motorhome. 'I need food, milk and tea bags, plus one or two other items. I've also to visit a couple of other shops. Then we're off back into the wilds.'

Inside, he was so intent on his purchases he failed to notice the man who'd been so kind to him standing at the next checkout queue. Nash watched the soldier's purchases going down the conveyor belt. He thought it seemed a lot for a man on his own. Then he noticed a large number of packets of the same item. What on earth, Nash wondered, could he want all those packets of marzipan for? It's a bit late for Christmas cakes.

Next they went to a DIY store; then to a shop specializing in fishing tackle. Finally, they pulled up outside a mobile phone shop. 'Last call,' he said over his shoulder. 'This time, you go in.' He handed her a wad of £20 notes. 'Here's what I want.'

Back inside the van, Jessica stared at the array of purchases in bewilderment. She'd be fascinated to hear what the items would be used for.

The beds converted into couches. They sat together, watching the small TV. 'I want to catch the late night local news bulletin,' he explained.

'Anything in particular?'

'There was a demo by animal rights activists outside Helm Pharm. It'll have been a shambles, but it might give us a few pointers for what we have to do.'

'What are we going to do, Steve?' He'd told her his name when he was telling her about Melanie and his daughters.

He explained what he had planned. Told her this was the first stage of the operation. It was then that she understood what the purpose of the training was. But she still couldn't work out where the marzipan came into his plans. Or the paint and the five mobile phones. And despite trying to wheedle the information out of him, all he would say was, 'You'll see soon enough.'

When the bulletin ended he flicked the remote to turn the TV off. 'Time for bed.'

'Before that, I want to know something,' Jessica said.

He looked at her.

'You've told me twice that you killed Mother and Adam. I only have your word for it they're dead. How do I know you're not lying? Show me some proof. Or tell me how you killed them.'

He reached across to one of the storage units and pulled open the drawer. He took out two newspaper cuttings and passed them to her. She read them with mounting horror. Now she believed him. With heart and soul she wished she didn't, wished he'd been lying, but he hadn't. He saw the tears trickle down her cheeks. He knew he ought to console her. But that wasn't in his nature. Killers don't do that.

When the girl was asleep, Steve took out his laptop. The volume had been set to mute, so he was able to check his mail without disturbing her. He felt sorry for Jessica, but knew what he had to do; sympathy was a luxury he could not afford.

He read the e-mail from Eco Sounder with quiet amusement. There was something disarming about the campaigner's naïveté when it came to planning an event like that evening's. He hastened to reply. The instructions in his message were clear, concise and detailed. Anyone reading them would have recognized their similarity to a military operation. Which of course it was. He now had a week to make his own preparations. As he closed his e-mail folder he was aware of movement opposite him. He glanced up. Jessica had raised herself on one elbow and was looking at him. 'What are you doing?'

Her voice was drowsy, heavy with sleep.

'Just checking my e-mails. Things are moving. We go to phase one tomorrow. Now get some sleep.'

She sat upright. In doing so the duvet fell clear, exposing her breasts. 'You tell me that, and expect me to sleep. What's happening tomorrow? Why won't you give me any details.'

'Briefing at 0800 hours; after training. Now, cover your gorgeous tits up and go back to sleep.'

Despite her fear, anticipation and the excitement his news had aroused, Jessica fell asleep within minutes. Steve waited until her breathing changed into a regular pattern then settled down. He'd manage a few hours kip himself. The mental image of her breasts delayed his plans somewhat.

She couldn't be sure how long she'd been asleep when his hand shook her shoulder. 'Think yourself lucky,' he told her in answer to the sleepy protest from under the duvet. 'At least you haven't a demented bugler sounding reveille three feet away from your bed.'

Dawn was nowhere near breaking when she stumbled from the motorhome. 'It's still dark.'

'That's the idea. You don't imagine we're going to do this in daylight, do you?'

The run was a nightmare. They went across moorland at seemingly breakneck pace, stumbling and falling, tripping over stones, gorse and heather roots. She lost count of the times he helped her back to her feet. On two occasions, much to her satisfaction, she had to do the same for him when he slipped on ice.

They were back at the motorhome before sunrise. 'Right, quick shower, breakfast, then the briefing. Oh, and don't forget, as of today, we move to the next stage of our treatment. That's essential before we go into action.'

There was no doubt that whatever the training was doing to the rest of her body, her taste buds were benefitting enormously. She devoured the bacon, eggs, sausage and tomatoes he put on her plate, wolfed down several rounds of toast and gulped three mugs of tea without seeming to notice his amusement. 'Good, now that's out of the way, I'll do the washing up. It's your turn to do latrine duty.'

'Thanks a bunch,' Jessica snorted. 'Why couldn't I have done it before breakfast?'

'Didn't want to put you off your food. You've such a picky appetite at the best of times.'

He passed her the keys to the outside lockers. She collected a spade from one; then opened the compartment euphemistically labelled 'waste'. She eased the unit free and strode off up the moor. The sooner this was done the better.

She returned to the van.

'Sit down and listen,' Steve ordered. He began telling her what they were to do. She listened in silence until he finished.

'Won't there be guards?' she objected.

'No, with all the spending cutbacks over the past few years, they can't afford them. They're relying on secrecy and the remote location to deter anyone wanting to break in. Which of course it does. Except to someone who knows where the place is and what's inside. Now, here's what I want you to do. Grab that can of paint' – he pointed to the kitchen worktop – 'and get a tablespoon from the drawer. Stir the paint and bring it across here.'

She did as he ordered. As she was stirring the paint to a uniform shade, literally, for the colour was as near to khaki as could be, she glanced over her shoulder. Steve had spread a newspaper over the table and was busy cutting open packet after packet of marzipan. 'The paint's ready,' she told him.

'Right, bring it here.'

He donned a pair of surgical gloves and pushed one thumb into the centre of a block of the almond paste. 'Put a couple of spoonfuls of paint in the well,' he instructed.

He formed the marzipan round the paint and started to mould it between his hands. When he was sure the paint had been distributed evenly, he picked up the next block. 'Same again.'

Eventually the job was done. 'Open the oven and pass me one of the trays out. Switch the oven to a low heat. Just enough to warm this lot through.'

He placed the blocks on the tray, peeled the gloves off and slid the tray into the oven bottom. 'Now we leave them to cook. By lunchtime it'll smell like Christmas.'

'How long before they're done?'

'No idea, could be three or four hours. Who do you think I am, Gordon F—ing Ramsey?' He grinned. 'It doesn't matter. As long as they're cool enough to handle when we leave.'

'What do we do until then?'

'Not much of anything. We'll need to set off about eight o'clock to be in position in good time. We'll grab a kip later, because we won't get much tonight. When we wake up, we'll take our pills.'

'Couldn't we take them before?'

'Not if you want to get any sleep. You've no idea the effect those things have. That's another reason we won't sleep tonight. It's like the biggest adrenaline rush you've ever had. Only it doesn't wear off until you make it go. As soon as we get back here, we're out on the moor for training. With the effect of that stuff inside you, this morning's run will seem like a stroll. You'll fly across the ground like a sprinter.'

'Do we take them nonstop until this is over?'

'Not unless you want to give yourself a heart attack. No more than one every seventy-two hours. That's the instruction. I saw a bloke take two by accident once. Within hours he was damn near walking on the ceiling. The red caps had to lock him in a padded room for three days. When he came out he'd scratched most of the skin from his arms and legs, more off his face. He was in sick bay for weeks.'

'All this is very encouraging.'

He grinned. 'Just follow the instructions and you'll be fine.'

By the time they set off for their destination Jessica was aware of the change the medication was bringing. Everything seemed in clearer focus, her eagerness to get on with the operation was stronger; she knew she could do her part. She was confident in her leader too. The miles seemed to crawl by, although she knew Steve was driving as fast as he could, in safety. 'How are you feeling?'

She smiled at him. 'Fine, ready for action. How about you?'

'Top form. Now, remember, the stuff we're going to be handling is quite safe. You can't do any harm, even if you drop it, or hit it with a hammer.'

It was unusual for Smith to be nervous. In fact it was almost unheard of. But meeting his boss could be relied upon to make him edgy.

'Give me an update.'

Smith could tell by the tone of his boss's opening question that he wasn't the only one feeling the strain of the situation.

'We've tried everything we know to locate the girl, but with no success. We've had Dr North's new location under surveillance, all his phone calls, text messages and e-mails are monitored, but whoever abducted Jessica North hasn't attempted to contact her father either directly, or via Helm Pharm. To make matters more complicated, that detective, Nash, has been asking some very pertinent questions about the girl and North's family as a whole. One or two of which it was extremely difficult to answer.'

'He has that reputation. All you can do is continue to fend him off. On no account can you allow him access to North. That could be disastrous. But we must find the girl. North is so worried about her safety, and upset at what happened to his wife and son, he's unable to work, which is no good for any of us.'

'Do we need him? I mean, I understand he's supposed to be brilliant, but surely there must be other chemists who could do the work he does equally well, especially as we're so far down the road.'

'You must be joking. North is irreplaceable; for the time being at least. There's an old saying that no one is indispensable, but North's pretty close to it. He's the only scientist capable of understanding these drugs, and more important, predicting their effect. The trial samples we've been using before, the ones that originated from his laboratory have worked really well. We're aware that they needed fine tuning, and North had just prepared a batch he was convinced would be the finished article. But they were destroyed by that intruder at Helm Pharm. We've tried to get other chemists to conduct similar experiments. We were aware that if anything happened to North it would have meant writing off millions. In addition to which there were the difficulties surrounding North's private life which I'm sure you're aware of.'

'What happened? To the other experiments I mean?'

'They were a total disaster. Only one batch got as far as a field trial. The volunteer who'd taken the drugs ran amok and damned near killed three of his colleagues before he could be restrained. After they secured him, the red caps had to keep him locked in a soft room for three days. When they took him out his skin was a mess of scratches which turned into a major infection. He was in a military hospital for almost three months. It was due to an allergic reaction to the cocktail of drugs. We certainly can't afford anything like that to happen again.'

'OK, so we can't dispense with North, or his services. In that case, what do you want me to do next?'

'We have to find the girl. Equally important, we have to find the man who abducted her. Above all we must recover the stolen files. Especially the encrypted ones.'

'You're not worried that he might have succeeded in breaking the encryption, surely.'

'I bloody hope not! And so should you. Actually, I don't think there's a cat in hell's chance. Not unless he either had inside knowledge of the file contents, or a key to the cipher. Or he'd been trained in the sophisticated decoding techniques necessary to crack such a complicated code. Despite that, I shan't be happy until those files are back in our possession, and the longer they stay missing, the more nervous I'll be. And that should apply to you, even more than me. There are things within those encrypted files that neither of us would want to become known.'

'I haven't seen them, but I can imagine.' Smith recalled some of the things his job had called on him to do. No, he definitely wouldn't want them to be seen by anyone else.

His boss continued. 'What if this wretched girl's been abducted by the same man who got into the laboratory? Could it be that she's being held by that animal rights group who were demonstrating the other night? Could they be responsible for both incidents?'

Smith shook his head. 'Not a chance. They're a bunch of amateurs. Not one of them has the know-how to conduct an operation like that. Added to which, the way they chatter amongst themselves on e-mail, their security's about as much use as a bottomless bucket.'

'Nevertheless, there could be one within their ranks capable of more than you think. It's dangerous to judge every member of an organization by the overall appearance. I think you should check them out individually. Failing that, have you drawn up a list of other possible suspects?'

Smith laughed, but it was a laugh with little evidence of humour in it. 'There is no list. As far as we can see there's nobody with the knowledge and skill. Not unless you believe in ghosts.'

'You're absolutely certain? No one? Because if that's the case, explain how it happened?'

There was a long silence.

'There has to be somebody, so I'll ask you again. Are you sure you've checked every possible suspect?'

The silence this time was even longer. Eventually, Smith shifted uncomfortably in his chair. 'Well, I suppose there is one man who might have the know-how. But I've discounted him because of his circumstances.'

'Tell me about him.'

Smith explained, but before long he was interrupted.

'I remember him. He was on a certain overseas mission with you, right?'

Smith nodded, his discomfort patently heightened.

'I think the circumstances make him a more likely candidate, rather than the other way round. As for how he got the knowledge, no security is perfect. Otherwise the intruder wouldn't have been able to gain access to the laboratory, or the kidnapper to manage the abduction of the girl so easily. I definitely think this man warrants a second look. Unless you're reluctant to go near him?'

Smith said nothing.

'Very well, he goes top of your list. And whatever you do, make sure you get to him before the police do. And deal with him. Find him, get the girl back and retrieve those files. We're talking damage limitation, remember.'

'What if we can't find him? As I know only too well, he's always been very good at survival, and escaping capture.'

Smith's boss laughed. 'I take it you're referring to the time you left him for dead? After you flew off in the rescue helicopter, telling the crew you were the only member of the unit still alive. You were lucky I intervened. Otherwise you'd have been court-martialled for that. Even if they didn't find out what else you did on that mission.'

'I was acting on orders,' Smith protested. 'Your orders, let me remind you.'

'I can't remember giving you a written order to shoot one of your unit members in the back. But maybe we're getting a bit paranoid. For one thing, we're only speculating that he's the one who has the girl. If he had her, I'd have thought he'd have contacted North by now. Made some sort of demand. And even if he has got her, and the files, I doubt if he has the ability to decode them. And, even if he does both, what's he going to do about it?'

'I'll check him out anyway, when I've had a look at the animal rights people. Is there anything else?'

'Just find the girl.'

'You understand what you've to do?'

'I run as fast as I can at you. When I reach you, I put one foot into your hand and push off as hard as I can with the other leg.'

'Got it.'

'But it's pitch black. How will I see your hands?'

He fumbled in the backpack and produced a pair of gloves. They glowed luminously in the dark. 'I see, very clever. But how will you get over the fence? I don't fancy being penned up inside an army compound when they open up tomorrow morning.'

'Leave that to me. Just be sure and move well to one side after you land.'

'Why can't you pick the lock on the gates or something?'

'They're on an alarm system. They can only be opened with the right keys.'

She turned and walked reluctantly away from him. She counted thirty paces, as he'd instructed, before she turned. In the darkness she could just make out the silhouette of the ten foot high fence, a slightly darker shape in front of it. Fortunately the ground seemed fairly level. It would be an inglorious end to the adventure if she turned an ankle on the run up. She got into a sprinter's stance and waited a moment, taking deep breaths. 'Ready,' she called as softly as she could. She peered into the gloom. She couldn't see the gloves.

'Ready,' she heard, and at the same time the luminous glow came into view. He must have had his hands in his pockets. She pushed off and accelerated forward, gaining speed with every stride. Her eyes were fixed on that bright spot of light that was getting nearer and nearer and—

'Now!' She heard him shout.

She lifted her left foot high, felt it gripped, and pushed hard with her right leg. She felt him thrust her left leg up and then she was soaring, her momentum carrying her forward. In a split second, her vault had carried her over the fence with its razor wire topping. She put her feet together as he'd taught her, spread her arms to fully outstretched and waited for the impact. She felt an initial shock as she touched down, bent her knees and went down into a crouch. As her palms touched the wet grass she pushed hard down on the turf.

'I'm over,' she called as she straightened up.

'Well done. Just like a gymnast. Watch out, I'm throwing the bag over now.'

She felt, rather than saw the bag looming against the night sky. It dropped a few paces to her left. She located it and slipped the straps over her shoulders. 'I've got it.'

'Good, stay right where you are. I'll be with you in a couple of minutes.'

Was he always this confident, she wondered? Or, was it the effects of the drug? In that case, was his confidence justified? She waited. Time dragged. A couple of minutes, he'd said. Surely by now it must have been five minutes, maybe longer? She peered into the darkness and spotted a luminous patch on the ground a couple of feet or so to the far side of the fence. Had he taken his gloves off and left them on the ground? And where was he? Why was he taking so long? 'Steve,' she called out, as loudly as she dared.

There was no reply, but in the next second, even as her call was dying into silence, she heard the sound of something heavy landing close to her. 'Steve,' she whispered again and held her breath.

'I'm here.'

She let out a long, shuddering sigh of relief. 'But how? How did you get over the fence?'

She could make out his outline now, her night vision improving all the time. He was crouching close to the wire, his arms moving backwards and forwards. He was pulling at something. But what? Then she saw it. She began to laugh. It was a long thin pole. So that was how he'd cleared the fence – he'd pole vaulted it. And the luminous spot she'd seen on the grass? The one he was now retrieving via the string he'd attached to it? It was a take-off cup, painted to glow in the dark. So simple, so effective.

He laid the pole down alongside the cup. 'Come on, we've a fair hike ahead. The building we want is right at the back of the compound, towards the far side. Unfortunately this is the only level bit of ground, so we've had to come in about as far away from our target as possible.'

He took her hand and they ran in silence past row upon row of dark, shuttered buildings. After a few minutes he steered her towards a gap. 'Through there,' he gestured with his free hand.

She reckoned they'd run for almost ten minutes before he slowed. 'Next on the right.'

They came to a halt and stood for a few moments, gathering breath.

'The way we got in was ingenious,' she said, 'but can I ask you one thing? Why not just cut a hole in the fence?'

'I would have done,' he told her, 'but the whole idea is that nobody should know we've been inside.' The patience in his voice was like a schoolmaster with a particularly dense pupil, or a sergeant with a raw recruit.

'Of course. Stupid question. Forget I asked.'

She couldn't see his grin in the darkness, but somehow knew he was laughing at her. 'Turn round.'

She swivelled so her back was to him. His fingers fumbled for the zips on the rucksack. She heard the soft grating sound as he opened it. 'Hand,' he told her.

She stretched her hand behind her, palm up, and felt the coldness of steel against it. Her fingers closed around it. She was surprised how heavy it felt. 'Hand,' he said again. She put her other hand back and clutched at another steel object. She hefted the torch in her left hand, the fingers of her right hand curling round the butt of the pistol he'd handed her. 'You're on guard duty. It's highly unlikely anything will happen, but if it all goes pear-shaped, shoot anybody who comes near. Got it?'

'No problem.' Did she really feel that confident?

'Aim at their feet. With the recoil you'll probably blow their head off. Now, shine the torch on that door.'

She looked at the beam, marvelling at how steady it was. Wondered briefly if her nerves were really that strong; or if it was the effect of the drugs. Before she could dwell on it, she heard a click and saw the door open. 'Pass the bag and the torch.' She did as he ordered. 'OK, you're on your own for a while. Ten minutes should be long enough, unless I have problems inside. The stuff we want is locked in a strong room. I'll need to pick that lock as well.'

She watched him slip through the door, saw it close. Was there no end to his skills, or his ingenuity?

Never had ten minutes passed so slowly. Or had it been far longer? Suddenly, the deep silence of the night was broken by the hooting of an owl. Her nerves, already stretched, were almost at breaking point when she heard the faintest whisper of sound behind her. She looked round, to see the door opening. She let out a deep breath, her heart rate slowing. 'Got it?' she asked.

'No problem.'

They made their way back to the fence and cleared it with no more problem than on the way in. He collected the vaulting pole and cup, unscrewed the sections of the pole and stored everything in one of the motorhome's compartments. A few minutes later they began their return journey. From the passenger seat Jessica could see the clock on the dashboard display. She was surprised to see the whole operation had taken less than an hour.

Several miles down the road, Jessica opened the rucksack at her feet and took out one of the blocks. It looked identical to the marzipan he'd substituted it with. 'What is it?' she asked.

'They call it C4. Plastic explosive. Very powerful, very safe.'

'Is there enough?'

He laughed. 'Those five blocks you're nursing would be enough to blow up half of Helmsdale. They'll certainly be enough to destroy the laboratory at Helm Pharm.'

'When are we going to do it?'

'Next Saturday night.'

'And these?' She held up a handful of disc-shaped objects.

'They were a bonus. You'll see.'

It was three hours later when he pulled the van off the road. He thought she was asleep. She hadn't spoken for the last half hour, and whenever he'd glanced across the cab she'd been sitting, head resting on the window as she was now. 'Jessica,' he said softly.

She straightened. As she sat up he looked across and down. She was holding the pistol he'd given her. The muzzle was pointing directly at his chest. 'Now, I want the truth from you, Steve.' Her voice was cold, demanding. 'I know my mother and brother are dead. I want you to tell me exactly what happened and why. If not, I'll shoot you here and now.'

He believed her. Even without the aggression the drugs gave her, he thought she was capable of it. She'd certainly got the guts for such an act. He knew she'd shoot him as soon as look at him because that was one of the effects of the medication: it removed all inhibitions, all remorse, any sense of guilt.

So he told her. It took a long time. By the time he finished, it was almost dawn. They were still seated in the cab. She looked across at him. The story was incredible, yet she believed it. Every word of it. As he recognized her acceptance of what she'd heard, he reached across and took the gun from her. He pointed it at her. She saw his finger tighten on the trigger and closed her eyes. This couldn't be it, surely? He wasn't going to kill her now? Not after what she'd just learned? And what they had to do? She heard a loud click and opened her eyes.

'You bastard!' She swung her fist and connected with his right eye.

'Ouch!'

'You evil swine. You left me alone out there with an empty gun.'

'You weren't in any danger. Nobody was going to interrupt us. They don't even have security patrols any more.

That's how severe the cutbacks have been. Bugger all security, but that doesn't matter if they can save a few bob.'

'I didn't know that. As far as I knew we could have been interrupted at any time. Standing there like an idiot with an empty gun. I don't see what use I was. For all the good it did, me being there, I might as well have stayed in the van. You could have done it all on your own.'

'I realize that, but you're missing the point. Tonight was a training exercise. Next Saturday's operation will be the real thing. That will be the main event.'

'And I suppose you'll want me to stand lookout again. Well I hope you remember to load the gun. Or, do you want me to walk up behind anybody who gets in our way and shout, "Bang", loudly?'

He grinned. 'No, next week will be completely different. Next week you'll be the star of the show.'

CHAPTER TWELVE

The training had been a different experience for Jessica that morning. For one thing she still felt exhilarated by the night's adventure. But the main reason was her knowledge of what had actually happened, rather than vague hints and suggestions. Ever since she'd been abducted, Jessica had been in fear of her life. That fear still existed, but she knew the threat came from a different source. She recalled the confession she'd got from him.

'After I found out about Melanie and the kids, and after I had to go through the rigmarole of identifying the bodies, filling forms in, arranging the funerals, I got so depressed. I don't think it helped that I was coming off the drugs at the time. So I sat there, in that ghastly house of death, drank a whole bottle of scotch and took a full cocktail of the tablets. And, you know what? At the end, I was stone cold sober. That was when I started planning. At the time, all I knew about was the laboratory. I'd seen the name on some paperwork sent with one of the consignments. It would have been meaningless to anyone else, but with me being from Helmsdale, I recognized it straight away. So that became my target. And I thought, if I could find out something about the people behind the drugs programme, I'd take my revenge on them.'

He saw Jessica was about to protest and held up his hand. 'I know it was crazy, but like I said, I wasn't thinking straight. I read about the fire, and your brother's death, but until I studied the files from the laboratory I didn't make the connection.'

Jessica tried to interrupt again but he shook his head. 'Let me finish. For a while I thought your father was dead as well. So I reckoned you must be in danger. I knew whoever was responsible for the murders must be after you, so I thought if I got to you first I might be able to protect you. After I got you away from that safe house I hung around. That was when I saw your father. I recognized him from his photo in one of the files. That really threw me. So I started to read the files in more detail. What I saw in them horrified me. I couldn't believe most of it.'

Jessica look confused. 'Were you still on the drugs?'

'No, by then I'd got them out of my system.'

'Then, why did you tell me you killed my mother and Adam?'

'Because I reckon what is in those files is so damaging, the people responsible knew they'd have to get rid of anyone who could point the finger at what was going on. I said I murdered them. Well, I did, or as good as. When I took the files from the laboratory, I signed their death warrants. The moment the files went missing, they knew whoever had them would work out what was going on. So you, your father and your family became targets. It's a simple military strategy – destroy the lines of intelligence communication of the enemy and you're halfway to winning the battle.'

'But you still don't know who's behind it.'

'No, I reckon the only way to find that out is via those encrypted disks. And so far I've had no success cracking them. I will though, sooner or later. All I've to do is learn a bit more about computer software.'

Jessica smiled enigmatically. 'How do you know the information you're after is on those disks?'

'It has to be. I can't think of any other reason for hiding the information so well, can you?'

'It might not be what you're after. It could be the design of a new type of gun, or a tank.'

'Not in a chemical laboratory. Look at it this way. There's a hell of a lot of confidential stuff in the open files. The encrypted disks must contain far more secret information.'

He paused, and was silent so long, Jessica asked, 'What is it? What have you thought of?'

'Why were they there? I mean, why were they at Helm Pharm?'

'Sorry, you've lost me.'

'The open files and the personnel files contained all the information about the people connected with the laboratory as well as the project itself. So, why store any other information there? It doesn't make sense. Nor will it, unless I can decipher the contents.'

'This case is bloody frustrating,' Nash grumbled to Superintendent Edwards. 'Every time I try to get some information, I'm being blocked. The worst part is I don't know what's superfluous and what might be relevant. That means I can't follow a specific line of inquiry.'

'Do you think Adam North's murder might be drugs related?'

'One way or the other, yes.'

Ruth frowned. 'What do you mean by "one way or the other"?'

'I can't understand why the military wants to keep Dr North incommunicado, or prevent us talking to anyone at Helm Pharm. That makes me wonder what Helm Pharm is doing that's so important.' He saw Edwards's frown and continued. 'Can you think of a valid reason for a drug manufacturer to receive such a high level of protection and security from the army?'

'I take your point, but how does that tie in with Adam North, and where does it leave us?'

'It could, if he was killed, not because of his addiction, but by someone affected by the drugs, or because he found out something he shouldn't. As to where it leaves us, I'm afraid the answer to that is, groping in the dark.'

Ruth grinned. 'Groping in the dark can be fun,' she murmured, 'but not in the middle of a murder inquiry. Just be patient, Mike, and keep the file open. Something will break, sooner or later. With your cases, something always does.'

The first thing Smith noticed was the closed curtains. It was early afternoon, the sun was out, why keep the house in darkness? He got out of his car and started up the path to the front door. The short drive was empty; it looked as if no one was home. Despite this, Smith leaned on the bell. It was one of those that played a melody. As he waited, his free hand hovered close to his jacket pocket. Getting no response to his doorbell concerto, Smith hammered on the wooden surround. The timpani yielded no better result. He tried the back door. Nothing. He attempted to peer past the blinds, without success.

He looked round, the street was empty. He knocked on the doors of the two neighbouring houses, but with no response. As he turned from the second, he noticed a car in the drive of the house opposite. He walked slowly across the road, his eyes scanning the street all the way.

This time he did get a positive response. By then he was impatient. He hammered loudly on the door, keeping the barrage going for several minutes. The woman who answered was holding an infant in her arms. The child was wailing, noisily.

'Who are you? What do you want? It's taken me over an hour to get this one to sleep. And ten minutes later you come hammering on the door and wake her up.'

'I'm trying to contact the man who lives over there,' Smith pointed to the house across the street. 'It's important I speak to him.'

Sonya knew an army officer when she saw one; she'd worked at the local garrison before she was married. It was there she'd met her husband. Now he'd been dead for months; the bitterness was as keen as on the day she got the news. And she knew how devastated Steve had been when Mel and his girls died. Now this character was snooping round. Why? She didn't like the look of him, didn't like the sound of his voice. It made every request a demand, every statement an order. 'Like I said, who wants to know?'

'I'm afraid that's confidential. Do you know where he is?'

If I did, I wouldn't tell you, she thought. 'He's gone away. He's trying to recover from a bereavement.'

'Yes, yes, I know all about that.' The man waved a dismissive hand.

You callous bastard, Sonya thought.

'Have you any idea where he's gone?'

The baby was crying. Sonya could feel a damp patch on her arm. And the stranger was getting right up her nose. She remembered something Mel had told her. About a holiday disaster they'd had. After which Steve had vowed never to set foot in France again. 'As a matter of fact I do.'

'So?'

'He's gone to France for a couple of weeks. He went at the weekend. Or was it last week? I can't quite remember exactly when. He said he couldn't bear to be in the house any longer, so he was off to get right away.'

'Did he go on his own? Or did you see anyone else at the house? A young woman? Late teens, long dark hair?'

'You must be joking.' There was no mistaking the anger in Sonya's voice, and the look in her eyes was so hostile Smith actually backed away a pace. 'The poor man's wife and children died less than three months ago. And you come around insinuating he's got some girl in tow. Off on a dirty weekend. What sort of animal do you take him for?'

'I'm sorry,' Smith didn't sound very apologetic. 'France, you said, any idea which part?'

'He said something about hiring a car and touring round. Said he'd just point it down the road and see where he ended up.'

'Would you do me a favour?' Smith smiled ingratiatingly. Sonya felt vaguely sick. 'If you see him, or hear from him, would you mind calling this number?'

Sonya took the proffered card. It had no name on it, no address, merely a telephone number. 'Who do I ask for? I assume you do have a name?'

'Smith,' he told her reluctantly.

She nodded and watched him return to his car. After he drove off, she waited on the doorstep to make sure he didn't return, then went inside. She was about to tear the card up, when she changed her mind. She found a piece of paper and a pencil and scribbled a short note. After she changed the baby's nappy, she cradled her in the crook of her arm and opened the front door. She glanced up and down the street, before crossing the road to stuff the note through Steve's letter box. When she was certain the street was empty of cars she returned home.

Jessica was bored. After their morning run and training session, Steve had made breakfast. Immediately afterwards he sat down on the couch and opened his laptop. She sat opposite him and watched for a while. His brow was furrowed in concentration. Eventually, she asked, 'What are you doing?'

He looked up. 'Apart from giving myself a headache and wishing I knew more about computer programming? I'm trying to find some software to decode those encrypted disks.'

'Can I help?'

'Do you know much about encryption?'

'Quite a bit, yes.' She smiled at the surprise on his face. 'I'm studying programming. I was intending to do computer studies at university. That was until I became a burglar.'

He beckoned her over and turned the laptop towards her. 'There you are. See what you make of that.'

She peered at the screen. After a few minutes she looked up. 'You're right; this isn't going to be easy. The whole thing's an alpha-numerical code, but you've probably already worked that out. It's one where numbers have been substituted for letters and vice versa. They're the hardest type to crack.'

'So, we're no further forward.'

'I said it was difficult. I didn't say it was impossible. Any code can be broken, given time. Let me have some paper and I'll make a start.'

The task took three long, frustrating days of concentrated effort. It involved both of them, the laptop, and a seemingly endless supply of paper. When they finished, they had a series of numbers and letters arranged in columns. The tables that provided the answer to the encryption covered both sides of two A4 pages. 'I had lots of theories for the reason behind my abduction,' Jessica said, 'ranging from rape downwards, but writing a software program and applying it to a code breaking exercise never entered my mind. Do you want to start converting the content of these files into English?'

Steve shook his head. 'We need to go back to Helmsdale. With the computer and the lights on, the battery's getting low. Apart from that I need to collect some new gas cylinders and top up the water.'

'Is that why you've banned us from showering for the last three days?'

He nodded. 'Thank goodness for that. I was beginning to think you were developing a fetish for sweaty girls.'

They pulled up outside the house late that evening. He told Jessica to stay in the van. 'I'm going to check the house.'

He went inside and reappeared at the back door a couple of minutes later. After he looked round, he beckoned her inside. She scrambled out of the van, clutching the bag containing the files. She dived through the kitchen door. She wasn't sure why, there was nobody in sight. It was something about his look that conveyed urgency. Or that something was wrong.

'What's matter?' she asked as he closed the door.

He passed her a small piece of paper. 'Steve', she read. 'I'd a bloke snooping round asking questions about you.

Looked like a red cap to me. Said his name was Smith. Didn't like him, or his attitude. Wanted me to ring him when I'd seen you or spoken to you. Are you in trouble? Sonya'.

When she'd finished reading, Jessica asked, 'Who's Sonya?'

'She lives over the road. Her husband was killed on a tour a few months ago. She and Mel were mates.'

'What does it mean? Who is this man Smith? Do you know him? Are you in some sort of trouble?'

He shook his head. 'Apart from kidnapping, imprisonment, breaking and entering, criminal damage and being in possession of explosives, I can't think of anything I've done wrong. But if this guy Smith is who I think he is, I'm in trouble: big trouble. Either I am, or he is,' he added reflectively.

He looked up, saw her puzzled expression and explained. 'I served with a Captain Smith.' He told her about the failed mission.

'It was the first time we'd taken MAD. It stands for Modified Amphetamine Dependency, or Mood Altering Drugs if you prefer it. They were the prototype of the performance enhancing drugs we're taking now. The ones I stole from Helm Pharm laboratory. The ones your father is responsible for developing.'

'What happened? On the mission?'

'There was a hell of an argument. Smith ordered us to attack an insurgent controlled village. Four of us against over two hundred. One of the guys, Johnny, refused. They had a blazing row, but Smith was in command.

'When I met up with Smith after it was over, he told me the insurgents had killed Johnny. He told me to cover him whilst he went to call down the rescue helicopter.

'I came under fire from about half a dozen rebels. I shot a couple, including their headman. The rest took off.' His face darkened with anger. 'That's when I heard the chopper do the same. Take off, I mean. The bastard didn't even wait to see if I'd got away. At the time I thought it was cowardice, pure and simple. I should have known with Smith, nothing's simple and certainly not pure. But I soon learned the truth.'

'How do you mean?'

'I'd taken a round. Just a flesh wound, but it was bleeding a bit. I'd lost my kit in the firefight, so I went back to where Johnny was lying. I knew he'd got dressings in his pack. His body was in the middle of a ring of boulders. His wound was a through and through.'

'What's a through and through?'

'The bullet went into his body and came out again. You can always tell where a bloke's been shot. The entry wound's small, about the size of the bullet. The exit wound's a lot bigger, and far messier. Johnny was lying face up. I had to turn him over to get at his pack. That was when I saw he'd been shot in the back. As I turned him, my left hand was on his chest. This dropped into my palm.'

He placed a small lump of distorted metal on the table. 'I couldn't work out how two guys as smart as Johnny and Smith got outflanked. They'd never allow a bunch of insurgents to come up on them from behind. Then I looked at this and realized the horror of it. And knew that it wasn't cowardice made Smith abandon me. You see, that casing comes from a British army rifle. The Taliban use nothing but Kalashnikovs. Smith shot Johnny in the back and left me to the tender mercies of the insurgents in case I started asking questions when I got back to base.'

'Did you? Ask questions I mean?'

'No, I didn't. I suppose I should have, but I'd no proof. Apart from that bullet, and there's nothing to say Smith fired it. I'd three days walking to think it through. By which time the drugs had worn off. So I decided to keep quiet.'

'That really is horrible. I don't think I can imagine anything more wicked.'

'I'm not sure I can either,' he agreed.

But that was because neither of them had read the encrypted disks.

'What are we going to do?'

He looked at her, pleased by the word 'we'. 'One thing's for certain, we can't be seen here. First thing I'm going to do is move the van. There are some lock-up garages at the end of the street. I rent one. I'll park up behind it, run an extension cable out and charge the batteries. Whilst I'm there I'll replace the gas cylinders and put a couple more in. We might have to stay in the wilds for a while.'

'What about the water?'

'There's a tap in the garage. I've a couple of containers I can use to top the tank up with. It'll take an hour or so. I want you to stay here, out of sight whilst I'm away. That means no lights on.'

He reached into his pocket and took out the pistol. 'This time it is loaded. That's the safety catch. Make sure you leave it on, unless you have to fire it. When I get back, don't open the door until you're absolutely sure it's me on the other side. And just because whoever's there says they're me, don't believe them. Make sure and get proof.'

Jessica had become used to silence. She couldn't believe an empty house could be capable of producing so many noises. The central heating gasped and gurgled, the immersion cylinder bubbled and spluttered and the fabric of the building produced more creaks and groans than an arthritic old man. To begin with, she found herself checking the luminous display on her watch every couple of minutes.

She forced herself to relax, to try different methods to distract her attention from the slow passage of time. She told herself Steve was a professional soldier. He wouldn't put her in harm's way. He knew what he was doing. Nobody could possibly guess she was inside this house. Except that it was his house. And Smith had been round looking for him. She forced herself to patrol the ground floor of the house, moving slowly from room to room, gun raised, ready to confront homicidal intruders capable of shooting people in the back. That served to increase the tension. It didn't help that every other stride provoked the floorboards to provide a new sound to go with the rest.

She returned to the kitchen and sat back to try some deep breathing exercise. The chair creaked alarmingly. She found a position where she could relax without causing it to protest and waited. She glanced at her watch. Fifty-five minutes had passed. He should be back shortly. She hoped. Was it her imagination, or had she heard a sound outside. She listened, waited, heard it again. Someone coming up the path. A shadow passed across the window blind. Jessica raised the pistol. Her thumb felt for the safety catch.

There was a tapping sound on the glass panel of the door. 'Jessica?' She heard the voice. Was it Steve? 'Jessica, it's me, Steve.'

'Prove it,' she said, remembering his instructions. 'Tell me something nobody else could know.'

Without a pause he said, 'You've a mole on the underside of your right breast. And another on the left cheek of your backside.'

She unlocked the door. 'Pervert,' she muttered as she let him in. She saw the gleam of his teeth in the darkness and knew he was laughing at her.

'How did you get on?' Change the subject. Fast.

'Water's topped up. Battery's on charge. And I've replaced the gas cylinders. Battery should have enough in it by morning.'

'Do we stay here tonight? Or in the van?'

'Neither,' he said, to her surprise. 'We've got work to do. The fact that Smith's been snooping round makes it even more urgent. But we can't do it here. The van's too vulnerable as well, whilst it's here. Give me a minute. I need to collect something. Then we're going visiting.'

'We can't visit someone. Not at this hour of the night. People will be in bed, asleep. Normal people that is, not nutcases like you.'

'There's nothing abnormal about Sonya. She doesn't sleep very well, she told me. And I've just passed her house. The lounge light's on.'

'And what's she going to make of me? Turning up with you in the middle of the night, I mean? Won't she think it a bit, well, you know?'

'I'll soon put her right. I'll explain that I kidnapped you.'

'You're going to tell her that?'

'I have to, can't avoid it. Not if we're going to convince her what we're going to tell her isn't a fairy story. Now, hang on there a couple of minutes.'

He disappeared, but was back in no time. 'Bring the gun, and be ready to use it.' He slipped the strap of the laptop case over his shoulder and let them out of the house. When they reached the front wall he held up a hand to detain her. He peered round the end of the building, looking both up and down the street. 'Walk, don't run,' he told her. 'And, arm in arm. Pretend we're a courting couple.'

'The things you have to do in the army,' she muttered.

CHAPTER THIRTEEN

Smith's visit had unsettled Sonya more than she'd have thought possible. Concern over Steve coupled with her continuing grief meant that for the past three nights she'd hardly slept a wink. She'd prowled the house throughout the early hours, unable to settle to anything. Hot baths, hot chocolate, camomile tea; nothing helped.

The knock was little more than a gentle tap, but in the silence it sounded thunderous. Sonya jumped; her heart racing. The shock was compounded by the knowledge that the knock was on the window, not the door. She crossed the lounge swiftly, before whoever was out there could knock again. She didn't want the kids waking. She flung back the curtains, saw it was Steve and sighed with relief. He pointed towards the door and signalled to her to close the curtains. She nodded and hurried to let him in.

She unlocked the front door and opened it wide. 'Steve, what's going on?' She started to ask, but the words died in her throat. Partly at the sight of the girl standing behind him, but mostly because of the gun.

'Tell you inside,' he brushed past her. The girl followed. Sonya closed the door, locked it and turned. The hallway was empty. She went into the lounge. Her visitors were standing in the middle of the room. Steve saw the tension in her face. 'Relax, Sonya.'

'What's going on?' She looked at Jessica. 'Smith asked me if you had a girl with you. He even described her,' she said slowly.

'Did Smith tell you her name?'

'No, just the description. Are you and her…? Is she your…?'

'No, nothing like that. Sonya, this is Jessica North. I kidnapped her a couple of weeks ago.'

'What! Did you say kidnapped?'

'That's right.'

Sonya looked from Steve to Jessica then back again. 'This must seem a silly question. But if you kidnapped her, how come she's carrying the gun?'

'It isn't a silly question,' Jessica answered for him. 'If Steve hadn't kidnapped me, I'd have been dead by now. Just like my mother and brother. Murdered!'

Sonya shook her head, not in denial, but to try and make sense of what she'd heard. 'Let's sit down, try to relax,' Steve told her. 'I'll explain what's been happening.' He looked across at Jessica and coughed gently. 'I think Sonya might feel a little easier if you put that away.' He pointed to the gun.

Jessica looked down. 'Oops, sorry, force of habit.' She stuffed the pistol into her coat pocket.

The story took almost an hour, not least because of the regular need to convince Sonya she hadn't wandered into an episode of *Spooks*. It was the final piece of evidence that proved conclusive. Steve produced a photograph and passed it to her. 'See if you recognize anyone on there.'

The image was of four men, pictured outside a camouflage tent in the desert. 'That's you, on the right,' Sonya said immediately. She looked closely. 'And that one, the one in the centre, that's the bloke who came here. The one who called himself Smith.'

'That's probably the only thing he's said in the last couple of years that isn't a lie,' Steve told her.

'What do you intend to do?'

'We need a safe house until morning. I left the van behind the lock-ups, charging the batteries. We can't stay over the road for obvious reasons.'

'I haven't a bed spare, unless you take mine. I can doss down on the settee,' Sonya offered.

Jessica went scarlet. Steve smiled. 'I told you, it isn't like that. What we need is a table to work at. We need to decipher the files I stole from the laboratory.'

'Use the dining room.' She pointed through the archway. 'I'll go put the kettle on.' She led the way, pausing to lift a basketful of ironing and a small collection of soft toys from the table. 'I've a fold-up table in the kitchen if you need extra space.'

'No, this will do fine.'

When she returned with coffee, Sonya said, 'I've been thinking. Ever since Smith came, there have been cars driving past at all hours of the night. I didn't notice at first, but after a couple of nights I started listening for them. About three times a night a car would go past, driving slowly, turn at the end of the street and come back. I wondered if it was revellers who'd been out clubbing, but when it happened again and again I began to think it was something more sinister. Or am I being paranoid?'

'No, I don't think so,' Steve told her.

'Before you get started, do you want something to eat? I cook a mean egg banjo,' she added.

Steve looked at Jessica. 'Great idea,' he said. 'We haven't eaten since lunchtime and Jessica's got an appetite like a horse.'

It took over three hours, with all three of them working at it, before they finished breaking the coded files down into English. They sat round the oval table, their faces a grim reminder of what they'd learned. 'I can't believe anyone could be so evil,' Sonya said at last. She leaned across and put her hand on Jessica's. 'I'm sorry I behaved like a cow when you came in, love. This must have come as a hell of a shock, and my attitude didn't help.'

Jessica's eyes were bright with tears. She gripped Sonya's hand, and Steve knew she was close to breaking point.

'Listen to this.' He turned a page. 'This is an extract from the personnel file on me. "Subject, Hirst, Steven. Rank: Sergeant. Training report summary. This man is perfect for infiltration and assassination work. A natural born killer. Description: Tall, black hair, dark brown eyes, swarthy/sun-burnt complexion. Would easily pass for a rag-head, especially after period in heat. Touch of tar-brush in ancestry? Personal Notes: Wife and daughters killed in carbon mon-oxide poisoning. How will this affect performance? Monitor carefully on return to active service."'

'How absolutely cold-blooded and heartless,' Jessica exclaimed.

Hirst turned another page. 'You think that's bad, listen to this. "North, Jessica. Student, intelligent, pretty. Boarding school, final year. TBW. Smith to deal when product available. Acc. Preferred."'

'What does that mean? What's TBW? And what do they mean by product?'

'Product means you,' Hirst told her grimly, 'and the rest is short for: to be wasted. Accident preferred.'

He saw Jessica's jaw tighten, her shoulders straighten and realized the strength he'd seen before was going to help her through this ordeal. 'What are we going to do?' she asked.

'First of all, I need a photocopier. You can bet these will be the only copies of the disks in existence. That's why they're so desperate to find me. They want to retrieve them before they're deciphered. They also want to kill us both. I'm going to make damned certain they fail at that as well.'

'There's a copier in my room,' Sonya said. 'It's one of those all in one things that's attached to my computer. Will that do?'

'Perfect, I hope you've got plenty of paper. I'm going to need to make two copies of each file. That's going to need about a hundred and fifty sheets.'

'No problem,' Sonya paused and listened. They heard a soft cry. 'That's the baby, she'll want her feed. Come with me, I'll show you where the copier is.'

'Show Jessica, I'm going to get the van. It should have enough charge in the batteries by now. I'll park in the alley behind your house. We should be finished in an hour or so, with luck.'

True to Steve's estimate, they were on their way before 7 a.m. Sonya hugged Jessica before they left. 'Good luck,' she said. 'If anybody can look after you, Steve will. He's a good man, and he's been through a lot. You both have. Don't forget, if you need anything, at any time, even when this is all over, just let me know.' She looked at Hirst. 'Have you any idea what you're going to do with that?' Sonya pointed towards the table, and the documents and disks on it.

'Not yet.'

'You want retribution, don't you?'

Hirst nodded. 'Why, what have you got in mind?'

'What about Mr Nash?'

'Who's he?' Jessica asked.

Steve stared at Sonya, taking in the implications of what she'd suggested. Whilst he was thinking, Sonya explained. 'Mr Nash is the policeman who dealt with Steve. He was very nice, and sympathetic. I think he'd be ideal.'

'A policeman,' Jessica sounded alarmed. 'Won't that get Steve in trouble? Get all of us in trouble?'

'Do you care? Do either of you care? Knowing what's in there? Knowing if their plans had run smoothly both of you would be dead?'

'Sonya's right,' Hirst said at last. 'It doesn't matter about us. Not compared to stopping what they're doing. And I think her idea's a good one.'

Jessica shrugged. 'OK, I'll go along with it.'

'Will you ring him?' Hirst asked. 'As soon as you can? The sooner he sees that stuff, the better.'

'No problem,' Sonya reassured him.

Jessica got into the passenger seat, pulled her seatbelt on and draped her coat over her lap. She wasn't cold, but it concealed the pistol she was gripping. 'Sonya's nice,' she remarked after Steve cleared the outskirts of town. 'Although I thought we were going to have trouble with her at first.'

'That was before she knew the truth.'

'Do you think it was fair, leaving that stuff with her? What if she gets found out? You know, Official Secrets Act stuff?'

'That wouldn't apply, not with the crimes they've committed. In any case, they have no reason to suspect she's involved.'

'What next?'

'We know Smith's after me, or at least suspects I'm responsible for the laboratory break in and kidnapping you. We need to take the heat off, give ourselves a few days' breathing space. It'll also give Nash time to act on those files, if he can do anything.'

'How do we go about that?'

'By getting Smith to look in another direction.'

'Stop talking in riddles and explain. What are you going to do?'

'Nothing. You are, using your computer skills.'

'It seems we were wrong after all,' Smith hesitated. 'It is the animal rights people who are behind this after all.'

'How do you know?'

'We put an intercept on Dr North's phone calls, text messages and e-mails. He received an e-mail late this afternoon. It came via a character who goes by the name of Eco Sounder. But we know the message didn't originate from him.'

He glanced down at the paper in his hand. 'The message reads, "Dr North, you are torturing animals. This must stop at once. You may not care about the creatures you are inflicting such suffering on so we've taken something you might be concerned about. We are holding your daughter prisoner, as a hostage for your future behaviour. She has not been harmed, YET."' Smith looked up. 'The word, yet, is in capital letters.

'"You will make a public statement confessing your crimes and stop this barbarous activity immediately. If you fail to do this we cannot guarantee Jessica's continued good health or her survival even. She is a very pretty girl. It would be a shame to see her scarred for life. But there are other scars that can be inflicted. Particularly on pretty, defenceless girls. These are not threats. They are promises. And they are the very least of the pain we will inflict on her if you fail to comply. And comply with immediate effect."'

'Are you certain that message is genuine? Could it be a hoax?'

Smith shook his head. 'It definitely isn't a hoax. For one thing, nobody but the kidnapper knows Jessica's missing. And if I still had any doubts, this removed them.' He held up the sheet of paper. The photograph on it showed a young girl, definitely Jessica North, seated on a stool. The background was out of focus but there appeared to be trees in the far distance. Her wrists and ankles were bound with tape. Alongside her was a man, his face obscured by a balaclava. Although his appearance was frightening enough, it was by no means as scary as the pistol he was holding against Jessica's temple.

'What do you suggest we do?'

Smith looked from his boss to the photo and back again. 'I've ordered our IT people to trace the origin of the e-mail. Once we have the sender's IP details, we can pay him a visit. That should enable us to retrieve the North girl and continue with our original plan.' He stopped and looked at his boss. 'You still intend to dispose of her?'

'Of course. It's even more important than before. Once North's usefulness is over, he can go too. A clean sweep. His disposal will be easy. An overdose, brought on by grief after losing his family. Then nothing can be traced back to us.'

Smith's mobile rang. He glanced at the screen. 'This will be the IT report. Now we're in business.' He listened to the caller, his expression a mixture of bewilderment and anger. It changed to disappointment as he spoke. 'Very well. No, but thank you for trying.'

He disconnected and looked at his boss. 'They identified the sender's e-mail account.'

'And?'

'According to them, the message originated from Dr North.'

'That's impossible.'

Smith vented his exasperation. 'I know that, you know that, but they're convinced that's what happened.'

'Somebody's playing games with us.'

'Yes, and at the moment they're winning, hands down.'

There was a message waiting for Nash at the station next morning. He glanced at the number, but didn't recognize it. 'Did the caller leave a name?'

The receptionist shook her head. 'She refused to give it. But she said it was vitally important and urgent. She did say,' the woman paused, 'something strange. She said you'd know her when you spoke to her.'

Nash dialled the number when he reached his office.

'Hello.' The answer was cautious, to put it mildly.

'This is Mike Nash. You left me a message.'

'Thank you for ringing. We met recently. After you'd been escorting someone to the mortuary. Do you remember? If so, please don't use any names. I'm sorry if this sounds mysterious, but I really don't trust the phone.'

Sonya Williams, Nash thought. 'I remember. How can I help?'

'Would you come straight round? I need to speak to you urgently. Very urgently.'

'When you say straight round, how soon do you mean?'

'I mean, now.'

'I'll have to leave a message for my sergeant to explain why I'm out.'

'Please don't say where you've gone.' Nash caught the note of panic in her voice.

'No problem, she's used to me being vague.'

Nash arrived twenty minutes later. Sonya Williams opened the door as soon as he got out of the car. 'Now, what's the urgency?' he asked once he was inside her hall.

'I've been entrusted with some information,' Sonya chose her words carefully. 'I'm not at liberty to say how, or from whom, but it's most important that you see it straight away. The person who gave me it was doubtful, but I persuaded them you were completely trustworthy.'

She smiled. 'I know that sounds odd, you being a policeman, but this information is very sensitive. I think the best thing would be to show you it. Once you've seen it, I think you'll understand.'

'Very well.' Nash prided himself on being able to second guess people most of the time, but Sonya's remarks completely mystified him.

She led the way into the lounge and indicated a chair by the dining table. Nash noticed a collection of papers and some CDs on the table. 'Sit there and I'll show you the stuff. Would you like a coffee before you start?'

Nash smiled. 'That would be nice.'

Once they were seated, Sonya opened the first of the files and passed it across. He started reading, his curiosity increasing with every line. When he'd finished the files, Sonya passed him a set of loose papers. 'These are transcripts of what's on those disks. They've been decoded. There's also a sheet that gives details of the encryption.'

Nash had only read a few lines when he looked up. Sonya could see the effect in his face. Stunned, barely covered the expression. 'Where did you get these?'

Sonya shook her head. 'I can't tell you that.'

'You're sure they're genuine?'

'If you've any doubts, keep reading. There are things in there that prove it. Things only a few people know. I believe some of it refers to an event you've been investigating. And it couldn't have been known, except by the person responsible.'

Nash read through to the end. By the time he'd finished, he was convinced. But despite his pleas, Sonya refused to divulge the source. 'Now you know why I wanted you to see them straight away. And why I want them out of this house. I know it sounds paranoid, but I'm afraid the people behind this might be watching me. I've already had a visit from one of them.'

'Why was that?' Nash asked, innocently.

'He wanted to know....' Sonya's voice tailed off as she realized how close she'd come to giving Hirst's identity away. 'He wanted some information from me,' she ended lamely.

'The information in here's dynamite, right enough,' Nash agreed, 'but at present, I'm not sure how to handle it. First things first though, I'm going to take this stuff with me. Once I get it to the station I'll lock it in my safe until I can see how to use it.'

The failure to penetrate the laboratory's defences had left Paul Farley feeling angry and humiliated. The e-mail from his mystery informant hadn't offered much in the way of comfort. But at least it had offered a solution. As he checked his messages and saw a new one from the sender's address, Paul hoped the contents would fulfil that promise.

He opened it up and started to read. His interest sharpened and by the end of the first paragraph, his attention was well and truly hooked. What the sender was proposing was far more radical than anything Paul had envisaged. But it was a great idea. The more he thought about it, the better he liked it. Apart from achieving their original objective, it would restore Paul's credibility and send an unmistakeable message that they were a force to be reckoned with.

He noted the passage containing a warning about the potential danger, but paid little heed to it. He made careful notes regarding the set up process; he was quite content to obey the instructions to the letter. Yielding overall control didn't worry him. He was more concerned with the success of the venture. After all, he'd ignored the sender's advice last time. Jumped the gun through eagerness, the result had been humiliation. This time he'd do as he was told. This time they'd get it right.

As he finished reading the message for a third time, Paul was struck by a random thought. The tone of the message, the instructions and the detailed and careful planning, made it sound almost like a military operation. Paul wondered if the sender had been in the forces at some stage. He returned to the task in hand, dismissing the idea as a fleeting fancy. He was going to be too busy for idle speculation. There were messages to send, people to contact, purchases to be made.

By Friday evening, everything was ready. He'd received confirmation that the equipment would be there. He'd made the booking suggested in the e-mail and paid the rental. Tomorrow evening, St Wilfred's Church Hall on the outskirts of Helmsdale would act as the meeting place for the activists. Well away from the prying eyes of Nash and any other police officers. Activists would be travelling from all over the north of England. Four of them would be driving the vans they'd hired.

When they were gathered in the hall he'd finally get to meet their new colleague. Paul was looking forward to seeing their benefactor face to face.

Following the incursion into the laboratory and the foiled demonstration by the animal rights group, security at Helm Pharm had been tightened. The area close to the power lines had been cleared of trees that might be used to sabotage the power supply, much to the anger of several landowners whose protests had gone unheeded. The number of guards on site had been increased. With these measures, the security people felt at ease. Four guards patrolled the grounds; two were on duty in the gatehouse, two monitoring events on the CCTV screens in the control room. A further four were on call in the rest room, where they were drinking coffee and watching *Match of the Day*. Confidence was high that there was no possibility of a repeat of the break in. If anyone tried, the guards were sure they had more than sufficient power to repulse such an attack.

CHAPTER FOURTEEN

Steve and Jessica were sitting at the table in the motorhome. Each had a glass of water and a small blue capsule in front of them. 'Before we take these, I've got to warn you what they do to you. This pill heightens the effect of the others you've been taking. It will sharpen your reflexes; make you feel stronger, fitter, more able to tackle any physical task. It will also make you feel invulnerable. That's the danger. It will give you a bigger high than anything you could buy from a drug dealer. Any of them would pay a fortune for it if they knew what the effects are. You'll get to think you can tackle anything or anybody, that there's nothing you can't achieve. To a certain extent, you'll be right, but there are limitations. The limitations imposed by your own physique. So, don't think you can go tackle an eighteen stone judo black belt. It makes you stronger – it doesn't make you invincible.

'The effect of the drug will stay in your system for twenty-four hours. Be prepared for that. There's another pill that prolongs the effect, but we won't need that. Nor will you need to sleep. Your stamina will be increased phenomenally. In fact you'll be hyper until the medication is completely out of your system. That's why you've got to take plenty of fluids. Flush it away. All right?'

They raised their glasses, toasting the success of the venture, swallowed the capsules and drank the water.

St Wilfred's was like many church halls around the county. A large main hall contained a stage capable of producing small amateur concerts and shows, with a couple of large side rooms and a kitchen.

The group that gathered in the main hall that Saturday was as different from the Women's Institute meeting the previous night as could be imagined. They weren't seated, the chairs having been stacked around the walls. Instead they were standing in small groups, chattering and speculating about the possible outcome of that night's adventure.

A fair number expressed reservations, citing the inglorious end to their previous attempt at the laboratory. Others were telling colleagues of the purchases they'd been asked to make, the purpose of which seemed evident. The method was what they couldn't understand. They knew they had the means to get in, but how would security be overcome?

Paul hovered close to the stage, his anxiety increasing as the minutes passed and the time of the meeting got closer. Doubts crept in. He'd only the e-mailer's word that this wasn't a hoax. If they had been set up…. His brain whirled with the horrendous possibility of such a scenario. His eyes searched the crowd, for the umpteenth time. He knew everyone in the hall. No sign of their mystery informant yet. Every time the door opened, Paul looked across, his hopes increasing. Seconds later, as he recognized the new arrival, his disappointment was visible.

He glanced at the clock above the stage. It was time for the meeting to start. Where was their new colleague? It wouldn't be a good start if he was late. As he was fretting, the hall lights went out and the stage curtains opened. A spotlight illuminated the figure standing at the back, centre stage, dressed from head to toe in black, his face obscured by a balaclava. Several female activists clutched at the arm of their nearest companion, in momentary panic at this terrifying sight. The figure on the stage stepped forward.

'The plan is simple.' The voice was male, strong enough to be heard clearly by the silent crowd. 'When the lights at Helm Pharm go out, the four of you with bolt cutters will attack the fences where you were instructed. As soon as you've created a big enough gap, the team that go in should head straight for the laboratory. Your task is to get there without coming into contact with the security staff. Avoid them where you can. The doors to the laboratory are electronic; they will have been disabled long before you reach them. From the time you get to the laboratory you have fifteen minutes to remove all the animals. After that I cannot guarantee your survival, let alone your safety. That means you do not have time to release the animals. What you must do is pick up the cages with the animals still inside. Take one in each hand, go back to the fence where the other team will be waiting to take them from you and store them in the vans. We estimate you'll have time for two, possibly three trips each.'

'We,' Paul wondered, who did he mean by 'we'?

'What about the guards?' one of the activists called out.

'They'll be running around in the dark like headless chickens. They'll have plenty to worry about, believe me. I should warn you, there will be several loud explosions whilst you're carrying out your task. Ignore them; they're designed to divert attention away from you. Now, did everyone make the purchases you were asked to?'

There was a confused babble of sound. The man on stage held up one hand. 'Show me.'

The activists held up their hands. The man on stage scanned them. He pointed to one man. 'Where's your balaclava?'

'Didn't get one. I'm not hiding my face. I want them to see me. I want them to recognize me. I'm proud of who I am, of what I do.'

There was a mutter of sound from those around him, not unsympathetic. 'If you're not prepared to cover your face, you don't go in,' the man on stage told him calmly.

'Oh yes, and who do you think is going to stop me?' the objector sneered.

The man on stage didn't reply, but the dissenter felt a sharp dig in his ribs and looked round. Another figure clad all in black was standing alongside him, proffering a tin of shoe polish and a soft cloth.

The objector looked down and his face drained of colour. He'd been prepared to argue the point, eager almost: but not with someone holding a gun. As more and more of the activists realized what the intruder was holding, they backed away, leaving a widening circle of space. As all attention was on the gun, nobody noticed that the man on the stage had disappeared. Seconds later, the hall was plunged into darkness. The blackout lasted a few seconds. When the lights came back on the activists looked round. Of the man on stage and the gunman in the hall, there was no sign.

'How did you know? About the shoe polish, I mean?' Jessica asked as they drove away.

'Stands to reason. They're a bolshie lot, otherwise they wouldn't be involved in this sort of activity. I knew someone wouldn't kow-tow. I was surprised it was only one. But he soon toed the line when he saw you waving the gun around.'

He pulled to a halt at the end of a quiet lane. There were no houses within a hundred yards. They waited for a second. 'Ideal spot,' he told her. 'Very little chance of being disturbed.'

'Won't it look suspicious? I mean, if anyone did see us? A man walking his dog for instance.'

Steve laughed. 'I doubt it. They'd think it was a courting couple.' He glanced at his watch. 'Come on.'

They got out of the van and looked at their target. The small building looked impregnable behind a heavy duty steel fence. The gate was secured by three locks, any of which would have kept a burglar busy for the best part of an hour. 'Ready?'

'Let's do it.' Excitement bubbled in Jessica's voice.

She watched him walk to the gate. A few seconds later he returned. They went back to the van and climbed in. Steve saw the expression on her face before the courtesy light went out and suppressed a smile. He knew that look. 'Make the call.'

She pressed Short Code 1 on her mobile. A second later they heard a sharp crack, followed instantly by a bright flash of light. What remained of the gate was lying on the ground, a twisted heap of scrap metal. 'That's one mobile phone gone,' Steve observed as they stepped over the wreckage.

'You should have seen the salesman's face when I bought them,' Jessica laughed. 'I told him they were Christmas presents for next year.'

'Naturally, doesn't everyone go Christmas shopping in January?' He was inspecting the door as he spoke. 'No need for plastic on this, they obviously thought the gate was a strong enough deterrent. Shine the torch on the lock. I'll have it open in a couple of minutes.'

True to his word, they were soon inside. She played the torch beam over the interior. 'So that's what one of these looks like.'

He moved closer, there was very little room. 'Shine the torch over there.' He pointed to the corner. 'I'm going to have to squeeze past. I need to be in there.'

As he pushed against her, Jessica could smell his scent, clean and masculine. It was as if all her senses were heightened, whether by the excitement, the drug, or both, she wasn't sure.

He strapped a larger block of explosive to a heavy steel structure, attached another mobile phone to it and stood up. 'Job done,' he told her. 'Let's get clear. Douse the light as soon as you get hold of the door handle.'

As they climbed back into the van she looked at the clock on the dashboard. 'Ten minutes to get to the laboratory,' she said.

Steve started the engine. 'Plenty of time.'

When they were on the approach road leading to Helm Pharm, he said, 'Make the call.'

She pressed Short Code 2 on the mobile. Seconds later she saw a brilliant flash of light in her wing mirror. Almost immediately, the street lights went out. Taking out the electricity substation would black out Helm Pharm and neutralize the electronic lock controls, leaving the doors open. The laboratory that had seemed secure, was again a soft target.

After the strangers left, the activists had indulged in an agonizing, short and, at times, vicious debate as to whether to continue the attempt. Paul had settled the matter. 'What do we care if one of them has a gun? Better to have someone like that on our side than against us. What matters most to you, the fact that somebody's got a weapon, or what we came for? To liberate the creatures those bastards are tormenting.'

That effectively ended any opposition. Even as Paul spoke, the leading objector, the one who'd refused to buy a balaclava was opening the tin of shoe polish. When the others saw him begin to smear his face, that was that.

At exactly the time specified in the e-mail, Paul heard an explosion in the distance. The night sky to the north was illuminated by a bright flash. Seconds later, the security lights on the Helm Pharm buildings died out, the bulbs waning to a dull glow, before disappearing completely. The street lights went out at the same instant, leaving total darkness. Exactly as promised.

Paul put on his balaclava and fixed the night vision goggles over his eyes. 'Bolt cutters, off you go,' he spoke in an urgent whisper, restraining the impulse to shout.

Unseen in the darkness, a vehicle, lights out, pulled up nearby. Before Steve and Jessica got out, he flicked a switch in the panel over the rear view mirror. 'What's that?' Jessica asked.

'Turning off the courtesy light,' he explained briefly.

They stood for a moment in front of the van. 'I'm going to deal with the gatehouse,' he told her. 'You know what to do.'

When the lights went out the two men in the gatehouse contacted the control room via their radios. 'Hold your position,' they were told. 'The fence will keep intruders at bay. Wait for further orders. It may be nothing more than a power cut.'

They waited. The night was silent. Time passed. Nothing moved. 'I don't like this,' one of the guards said. 'Without lights we're helpless. There could be an army out there for all we know.'

Seconds later, they heard a noise. The merest whisper of sound. Like someone scratching. 'Is that you?' one of the guards asked his colleague.

'No, I thought it was you.'

As he spoke they felt a sudden chill and the sound of the hatch window opening. This was followed by a thud, and the sound of the window closing. Before the guards could work out that someone had slipped a screwdriver under the sill and prised the window open, there was a sudden flash of light followed by a deafening thunderclap. As the sound died away the kiosk was filled with thick, choking smoke.

Blinded, disorientated, their hearing gone and their breathing laboured, the guards stumbled from their prison, reeling in dizzy gyrations as they sucked greedily at the clean, cold night air.

Steve was halfway to his destination by then, having dived through the nearest hole cut in the fence. He sprinted towards the office block. As he reached the front door, he heard a loud explosion from the rear. He grinned, it sounded as if Jessica was enjoying herself. He plunged into the dark building.

As Steve was attacking the gatehouse, Jessica had slipped through the fence unnoticed – just another balaclava-clad figure waiting to rescue the caged animals. Once inside the perimeter, she peeled away from the others and headed for the rear of the office block. She flicked her torch on for a brief moment, locating her target. She doused the light, waited a second, then replaced her goggles. She dropped to her knees and felt along the hard metal surface of the manhole cover. She found the lifting plate and slid a screwdriver through it. She placed the block of C4 alongside the tap and replaced the cover before running round the corner of the building. She took the mobile from her pocket and pressed Short Code 3. The explosion was followed by a few seconds of silence. Jessica had put her gloved hands over her ears, anticipating the blast. She heard the patter of water, like a fountain playing on leaves. Steve had explained that they needed to cut off the water so the sprinkler systems wouldn't work. 'Why not turn the stop tap off?' she'd asked.

He'd shaken his head. 'Too much of a gamble. It's no good getting to it and finding the tap's rusted up, or too stiff to move.'

Any doubt that the loss of the lights might be accidental was dispelled by the explosion at the gatehouse and the blast to the rear of the offices. As the guards patrolling the grounds reported intrusions from all four sides of the compound, the head of security lifted the phone to summon assistance. Neither man in the control room heard the door open. As quietly as it had opened, it closed a split second later. In the corridor, Steve counted to five, hands over his ears. Then he watched as the men stumbled out, suffering as their colleagues in the gatehouse had done. He remembered Jessica's face when he displayed the trophies he'd lifted in the raid on the munitions store. 'What are they?' she'd asked.

'Flash bangs.' He'd laughed at her mystified expression. 'That's what we call them anyway. Stun grenades. They give off a big flash of light, a loud bang, then a thick cloud of smoke. Designed to frighten and disorientate rather than kill. Rumour is they were designed for the SAS.'

'Won't they be missed?'

'Probably not. That amount of C4 would be obvious. But a couple of flash bangs, what harm could they do? In any case, do you care? I certainly don't.'

By the time the men reeled out of the front door, Jessica had finished planting further charges at each corner of the office block and the laboratory. As she jogged towards the back corner of the compound, she heard the sound of someone running behind her. So high was her confidence that she didn't bother to look round, merely calling over her shoulder, 'What kept you?'

'Cheeky bitch. Everything OK?'

'No problem.' He could hear the excitement, stronger than ever in her voice.

'Now for the main event. Glasses back on.'

They lowered their goggles and watched for a moment. Jessica saw figures moving through the grounds. The activists were almost clear of the compound. The security guards had regrouped close to the gatehouse and it looked as if they were discussing the situation. There was certainly no move being made to re-enter the offices, or the gatehouse.

'Go plant the big one,' Steve told her. 'I'll keep an eye on those characters.'

She walked up to the oil tank that fed the central heating systems and taped a large block of explosive on the side. She attached the mobile phone and stepped back. The process took little more than twenty seconds, but then she'd been practising it all week, night after night, against the side panel of the motorhome. 'Isn't this dangerous?' she'd asked early on.

Steve had grinned. 'Only if you develop a craving for almond paste. That's marzipan you're using.'

She rejoined Steve. 'Hit the phone,' he told her. 'They look as if they're about to go back inside. And for God's sake don't press the wrong button. If you do, we'll be in orbit.'

She pressed Short Code 4, and the small charges she'd placed against the brickwork of the two buildings exploded in a series of dramatic sounding and looking blasts, that in fact did little damage.

They watched as the guards retreated to the safety of the perimeter. The explosions had ensured no one was close to the buildings, Steve took Jessica's hand and they sprinted for the hole in the fence. They dived through and reached the van. 'Go for it,' he told her.

'Are we clear? Is this far enough away?'

'Press the button and we'll find out. We can't afford to wait for them to go back. The whole idea is to destroy the buildings without harming anybody.'

Short Code 5 provided the biggest explosion of all as the gas tank ignited. They held their breath, counting the seconds as Steve had calculated. Then they heard a second blast as the boiler in the laboratory exploded, followed a split second later by another from the office block. As they continued to watch, flames appeared in both buildings, visible even through the non-reflective glass of the windows. Jessica gripped Steve's hand, her eyes shining, reflecting the glow of a dozen fires. Within seconds they heard the sound of breaking glass as the heat shattered window after window in a succession of smaller explosions, like aftershocks following an earthquake.

'Time to go,' Steve told her. 'Back to the lock-up for the motorhome.'

They climbed in the van, and as they drove away, Jessica could see the reflection of the fires dancing in her wing mirror.

It was shortly after 3 a.m. when they reached the retreat that had been their hiding place for the past three weeks. As they entered the living quarters, Jessica asked, 'What do you do when you come back from a mission? Or operation, or whatever you call it?'

Steve grinned. 'We call it a lot worse than that, especially if it hasn't gone well. We usually have a few beers, relax, phone home if we can. Some of the single lads go clubbing, try to get laid. Usually with far less success than they brag about.'

'So, where's the beer?'

The lager was strong; neither of them was a seasoned drinker. After a couple of tins, Jessica felt as if she was floating. She was sitting on the couch, with Steve alongside her. There wasn't much room on the seat, not for two of them, so they were close together. They'd relived the thrill of the night's activities, chattering excitedly as they remembered the total success. Jessica felt strong, still ready for action. 'So what do we do next?' she asked.

'I'm not sure. I hadn't thought about much beyond tonight.'

'That's not what I meant, Steve.'

He looked at her, startled. Jessica stood up and began to unbutton her jeans. She slipped them off, and her panties came with them. Before he could guess her intention she'd taken her T-shirt and bra off. She stood in front of him, naked, her head tilted, a smile on her lips. 'What was it you said the single lads do?'

He felt the blood pounding in his head, his arousal painful. 'And we're both single, Steve,' she bent over him, her breasts tantalisingly close to his face. He fought against the desire, but as if it was no longer part of him, his right hand moved to cup her breast. As he felt the smooth warmth of her skin against his palm, she unzipped his combat trousers and reached inside. He gave a soft moan, a mixture of pain and pleasure as her hand located its target. Then they were scrabbling, tearing and tugging at his clothing until he too was naked.

They stood for a moment facing one another, panting slightly, more with anticipation than the exertion. Then he reached out and wrestled with the couches, pulling them together until they formed a bed. As he straightened, Jessica was upon him, forcing him down onto the mattress, her lithe body astride him. He felt her moan and writhe briefly before he pulled her to him. Only then did they kiss.

CHAPTER FIFTEEN

Nash stared at the charred ruins, the smoke still rising in a lazy plume in the clear morning air. He'd been called out in the early hours, but the fires were raging too fiercely for anyone to get near. As nothing meaningful could be done he'd arranged for them to return in daylight. Satisfied that everyone had been accounted for, he'd returned to the flat. Becky had complained about his cold feet. That was until he'd reminded her she wouldn't have to suffer them much longer. After that, he smiled a little sadly, there had been no complaints. But it proved how much he'd miss her.

On their return he'd interviewed all of the guards. Not that it had done much good. Their evidence, what little there was of it, told him little he either didn't know or couldn't have worked out.

Ruth Edwards called him on his mobile to tell him she was on her way over. As he finished the call he saw his sergeant walking across the drive from the gatehouse. She was carrying an evidence bag, with what looked like an ice hockey puck clearly visible through the clear plastic. His eyes widened with surprise. 'No wonder the guards scarpered out of that box sharpish,' he said.

'Do you know what this is?'

He nodded. 'So should you. Didn't you go on an explosives course last year?'

She shook her head. 'It was cancelled, if you remember.'

'Well, that's a stun grenade. Did you find it in the gatehouse?'

'I did, and I've just had a word with Doug Curran. Their forensics people have identified the accelerant used in the explosion that blew up the oil tank: C4, plastic explosive.'

Nash whistled. 'Somebody wasn't messing about.'

Clara looked over his shoulder. 'Ruth's here.'

'The guards can't tell us anything. All they said is the lights went out and there were a lot of explosions. Like I didn't already know that. All they said that I didn't know, was that they caught glimpses of people rushing to and from the laboratory shifting cages. That tallies, because we found a load of empty cages a mile or so down the road. My first guess would be that was down to the animal rights lot, but I'm not convinced they acted alone. Or that it was them who torched the buildings.'

'Why do you say that?'

'The fire service identified the accelerant as C4. Distribution of C4 is strictly controlled. You need to be licensed to buy it, and it's strictly for military or civil engineering work – demolition, quarrying, that sort of thing. Not the sort of activities you associate with animal rights groups. So, if the bombers couldn't buy it legally, they'd have to steal it. And that amount of C4 would be missed, surely. So, how come nobody's reported any C4 being stolen. Then there are the stun grenades.'

He saw Ruth's look of surprise. 'Clara found one in the gatehouse, and if you look over your shoulder you'll see DC Pearce with what looks like another.'

Pearce joined them. 'This was in the control room,' he told them.

'Thanks, Viv. Give it to the boffins.' Nash pointed to the forensics team. 'Although I doubt very much if they'll find anything.'

'Why do you say that?' Ruth asked as Pearce walked away.

'Look at it this way. The electrics were disabled first, by blowing up the substation. That knocked out the lights and opened the doors. The fences were cut in four places, to allow access and to give escape routes if the guards managed to get near any of the intruders. The two places where the guards could have summoned help were put out of action. Then the water main was fractured. That meant the sprinkler system was useless.'

'What about those small explosions round the building that the guards told you about?'

'Scare tactics, designed to keep anyone out of harm's way. The buildings were the target. The whole raid was intended to destroy the premises without causing injury. That's my guess. Finally, they hit the oil tank, knowing the fire would travel down the oil lines to the boilers inside the building. Bang, instant inferno. A very smooth, well planned, professionally executed operation. Almost military, you might say.'

'Are you suggesting soldiers carried out this raid? If so, why?'

'Why, is certainly the big question, but the way the raid was carried out and the materials used points towards somebody with military experience.'

'It still doesn't explain how they got hold of such a large quantity of C4 without someone noticing it was missing,' Ruth paused, 'unless they replaced it with something that could easily be mistaken for C4.'

'That could be anything, from plasticine to....' Nash's words died away. 'Marzipan blocks,' he finished lamely. His mind was filled with a vision of a soldier in Good Buys supermarket. He'd wondered what use the man had for so many blocks of marzipan. Now, Nash thought, he knew. And at the same time, guessed who'd supplied the files and disks Sonya Williams had given him. He kept these ideas to himself. Better to wait until he'd seen him. After he'd spoken to Steve Hirst, looked into his eyes, he might have a better idea of what was going on.

In the meantime he'd another task to perform. A personal one. And one he wasn't looking forward to. 'Would you take over for a few hours, Ruth?'

'Of course, any particular reason?'

'I promised Becky I'd take her to the station. She leaves for London this morning.'

'Is she going for long?'

Nash explained about the new job. Ruth's eyes sparkled with interest. 'No problem, I'll mind the shop. Is there anything I should be aware of?'

Nash glanced at his watch. 'The Director of Helm Pharm is due here in half an hour. The rest of the workforce isn't due in until tomorrow, I guess. Although I wouldn't be surprised if one or two turn up if they've heard the news on the radio, even though it's Sunday. I've lined Clara and Viv up to interview them in the morning. I'd be particularly interested to see if Dr Richard North is amongst them.'

'Mike, I want to talk to you. About us, I mean.'

Nash's expression was wary. He could guess what was coming. He'd been expecting it. He wasn't about to make it easy for her though. 'Go on.'

Becky cleared her throat nervously. 'Look, Mike, I've no idea how long I'm going to be away, and we've both got our careers to think about. For the time being I think we should call it quits, go our separate ways. Let's not descend to long distance telephone bickering. At least we'll be going out on a high note. What do you say?'

Nash didn't rush to reply, he knew that would be taken the wrong way. 'If that's what you want, Becky, I won't stand in your way. I've already told you that.'

The train was pulling out of the station. Becky looked out of the window. Nash was standing on the platform. Her last view of him was the figure receding into the distance, into her past, a rather forlorn sight. With a shock, Becky realized that he hadn't actually answered her final question, the all important one. The knowledge bothered her for a long time.

Nash walked thoughtfully back to his car. He'd miss Becky; that was true. Miss her a lot. On the other hand, there were plenty of good looking women around. And if all else failed, there was always the beer in The Horse and Jockey. Nash grinned to himself. He could even join the darts team. His natural optimism fought its way through the sadness of Becky's departure.

Instead of returning to Helm Pharm, he headed for the far side of town. He drove slowly down the street. He was going to interview Steve Hirst; the man he suspected had been responsible for destroying the laboratory.

He noticed the closed curtains, the absence of a vehicle on the drive. His knock at the door provoked no response. He turned away and decided to seek information nearby. Sonya Williams had just put the baby down for her nap when she noticed the car and saw Nash outside Steve's house. She frowned, what was Nash doing there? Had something gone wrong?

She watched him walk across the street and opened the door. 'Do you want me?'

Nash grinned. 'Now there's a leading question, if ever I heard one.'

'I didn't mean that,' Sonya blushed slightly. 'I meant, do you want to speak to me.' She tried to inject some severity into her voice, but failed.

'I'd much rather talk to you, but I was hoping to have a word with Steve Hirst. Do you know where he is?'

'No, I'm sorry, I've no idea.' Not a lie.

'That's a shame.' He paused, 'Didn't he say where he was going?'

'Would you like to come in, Inspector Nash? It's not exactly the weather for standing on the doorstep.'

'That would be nice. And please, call me Mike.'

'Can I get you a drink? Coffee, perhaps?'

'Only if you'll join me.'

When Sonya returned, Nash was sitting on the sofa. She passed him a mug and sat alongside him. 'Now, why do you want to see Steve?'

'I want to know how good he is with a saw.'

Sonya blinked in astonishment. 'A saw? Why?'

Nash explained about the raids on the laboratory. 'Then we have the kidnapping of Jessica North. Although perhaps kidnapping is the wrong term. Rescue would be more accurate, I guess, seeing she'd already been kidnapped.'

Sonya gasped. 'How did you find all that out?'

Nash grinned. 'Thank you for confirming it. I was only guessing until now.'

'You devious so and so! You tricked me.'

'Sorry, Sonya.' Nash reached across and put his hand on hers. A reassuring gesture. 'But, I've no proof. Nor am I particularly interested in getting any. Knowing what's been happening at that laboratory, I'm more concerned in bringing them to justice than persecuting Steve.'

Nash's words comforted her, as did his hand still resting on hers. She rather liked it, which came as something of a shock. 'So tell me,' Nash continued. 'Has Steve got Jessica safe? And, was it Jessica who took part in last night's raid with him?'

After some moments Sonya said, 'If I tell you, I'll deny I ever said it. But every guess you've made is right.'

'She must be quite a girl,' Nash commented. 'What about her father?'

'We don't know where he is.' Sonya abandoned the last pretence of ignorance. 'Jessica's very worried about him. He's not strong, like she is. What you read in those files came as a dreadful shock to her, but I think she'll be able to withstand it. Her fear is, it would break her father.'

'Understandable,' Nash agreed, 'but more important than anything, we need to get him out of their clutches.' He squeezed her hand encouragingly. 'That's where you come in, Sonya. I need you to contact Steve. There are things I need to know. I take it they're somewhere out in the wilds, in that camper van of his?'

'I'm not going to say any more.' Sonya patted the back of Nash's hand as she disengaged her own. 'But I'll tell you when you've guessed wrong. What do you want me to say to Steve, if and when I can get hold of him?'

When Nash was leaving, he turned and put his hand on Sonya's arm. They were standing in the hall. 'I want you to take care. Be on your guard. If what we suspect is true, those people will know you're a friend of Steve's. And, if I've worked out that he's behind what happened at the laboratory, they will too. That means anyone close to him is in danger. If you need me, call me, anytime, day or night. OK, Sonya?'

'You really think they might come after me?' Her eyes widened in alarm.

'If they can't track Steve down they'll be desperate to get that stuff back.'

'I'll be on my guard. But it's a comfort knowing I can call you.'

Nash passed her his card. 'That's got my home and mobile numbers on it. I've also put Sergeant Mironova's details on the back. Her name's Clara. If you can't get hold of me for any reason, speak to her. When I go back to the station, I'll fill her in with all the details.'

She watched him walk across to the car. As he drove away, Sonya felt concerned by what he'd said, but the thought that he was only a phone call away was some comfort. As she collected the empty mugs from the lounge, the house seemed quiet, empty. It came as a surprise to her that Mike's visit had affected her like that. She'd not felt lonely or alone since her husband's death – having the kids around helped. Now, for the first time, Sonya realized how much she missed the company of a man.

She did the washing up, daydreaming as she stared out of the kitchen window. Imagining the touch of his hand on her arm; remembering the warmth of his contact when he's squeezed her hand. She sighed, wondering about Mike. She knew he wasn't married, but was he spoken for? With a start, she realized her thoughts were wandering into dangerous territory. But then, what was life without a little danger, a little excitement.

She laughed and turned to put the kettle on. She was slightly shaken by her attitude. She hadn't been one for looking at other men. Not before, and not since. So why was this one any different?

Next morning brought guilt, which in turn caused awkwardness. They dressed in silence. Jessica watched as Steve folded the couches back, hiding the scene of what had happened. As she watched, she thought about what they'd done. From the moment he'd abducted her, he'd not attempted to take advantage. And last night, she'd more or less forced herself on him. He was certainly not to blame. He was still grieving for his wife and children. Her thoughts were a jumble of emotions: she was worried about her father, ashamed of her behaviour and thoroughly miserable.

Steve concentrated on the task. It was only the work of minutes to put it straight, yet he stretched the job out as long as he could. He dared not look at Jessica. She'd been willing enough, more than willing in fact. But he should have been stronger, should have had the willpower to resist; might have done too, if she hadn't been so damned attractive. He thought of Mel. A bit late for that, but he knew she wouldn't have minded; wouldn't have expected him to remain celibate the rest of his life. She'd have said, 'Get on with it, and good luck'. He knew Jessica wasn't a virgin; at least he hadn't that guilt to bear. Better face it, get it over with. He looked up. 'Any regrets?'

She'd been about to ask him the same question. 'Not for me,' she told him. 'But what about you?'

'Not for a minute. I was worrying about you.'

She laughed. 'And I was worrying about you. With it being so soon, I mean.' They looked at each other and the awkwardness fell away. 'That's really good news,' she told him.

'Why do you say that?'

She pointed to the couches. 'Because that bed's a damned sight more comfortable to sleep on than those things.'

'We'd better start thinking about our next move.'

She looked at him, teasing. 'I thought you'd have had it planned by now. You're the master tactician.'

'I might have done,' he retorted, 'but I got distracted.'

By mid-afternoon they were no nearer the solution. 'We know what we want, the problem is, how to go about it,' Steve said.

He was interrupted by the bleeping of his mobile. He read the text with mounting interest, before passing the phone to Jessica. 'I think Sonya's just shown us the way forward.'

'This policeman, Nash, you're sure you trust him?'

'Yes,' Steve explained. 'When I met him I was in a real state, as you can imagine. He was very kind. Understanding, if you know what I mean. And genuine. I think I'd be prepared to trust him.'

'It's a big risk though, after what we've done.'

'It's a question of weighing risk against reward. In any case, if what Sonya says is accurate, he's worked it all out by now. I vote we go for it. What have we got to lose?'

As soon as he returned to the CID suite, Nash called Clara into his office. As she walked in, he was standing by the door. He called Viv across. 'I'm going to show Clara something. Before I start, I'm going to lock this door. Don't let anyone near until I open it. Then I'll show you. Ring down to reception, get them to transfer any calls to you. Clear?'

'OK, Mike.' Pearce was obviously puzzled but knew Nash well enough to know this must be serious.

Nash locked the door and signalled to Mironova to sit down. He opened the safe and passed her the documents he'd stashed there. 'Read those,' he told her.

One glance at his face should have warned her that the contents would make grim reading. But nothing in his expression prepared her for the enormity of the crimes described in those pages.

When she'd finished, Clara looked up. 'Are you sure this stuff's genuine? And how did you come by it?'

'I'm certain it's kosher.' He explained how he'd got the files.

'What is this Hirst bloke, a one-man army?'

'More or less. I reckon he's probably been dosing himself with those drugs' – Nash indicated the files – 'and for the last effort, he had help.'

'Who from? Not this Mrs Williams, surely?'

'Hardly,' Nash laughed. 'Sonya's got enough on her plate with three youngsters to look after. No, I think Jessica North was his assistant.'

Clara noted Nash's use of Sonya's Christian name, but for once refrained from making a sarcastic comment.

'That is absolutely disgusting,' Clara indicated the paperwork.

'I agree. It's a catalogue of cold-blooded evil. What I find incredible is how they got away with it.'

'I wondered that, too. Any ideas?'

Nash thought for a moment. 'Well, for one thing, it's easy enough to hide behind the Official Secrets Act. And it looks as if nobody questioned it, because it was such a rogue operation, nobody had proper control.'

'It's so callous.'

'Which bit? Giving Lara North drugs that turned her into a nymphomaniac? Or making Adam into a drug addict and feeding that addiction? All to keep Dr North in line. I bet they threatened to sell photos to the tabloids of some of the raunchiest images of his wife. Or told him they'd feed Adam with some adulterated heroin. In his state, by the time he knew it, the poison would be in his system.'

Nash paused, brow furrowed. 'What is it, Mike?'

'I'm worried about how we're going to prove any of this. Particularly if we can't get any fingerprints off the files or disks. We've no idea of the identity of the person behind it all: apart from this Smith character. And I'm very concerned about Dr North. I just hope Hirst's as good as we think, because we're hamstrung by procedures. Without some unorthodox tactics,

I don't think we'll get anywhere, even if we know who's responsible.'

'There's been a development.'

'What sort of development?' Smith's boss demanded.

'I ordered our surveillance teams to monitor all communications from Mrs Williams, her landline, mobile, e-mail. Hirst's neighbour,' he added by way of explanation.

'I know who you're talking about,' the tone was waspish, irritable. 'Can I take it you've met with some success for a change?'

Smith winced at the sarcasm. 'Among the phone calls she made and received from her mobile were two to the detective, Nash.' Smith paused. 'And two from Hirst.'

'You think she's acting as a go-between?'

'I don't think we can afford to take the chance.'

'What do you suggest?'

'A search of her house. Hold her, and use her to bring Hirst to us.'

'Go for it. Use whatever means you need. We must have closure, at all costs. Understand?'

Smith didn't answer. There didn't seem to be any need.

CHAPTER SIXTEEN

Shortly after Nash had briefed Pearce, who was equally shocked by the revelation, his mobile rang. 'Mike, it's Sonya.'

'Are you all right? No trouble, is there?'

'No, but I've been in contact with the person you asked me to. I don't want to say any more over the phone. Can you pop round this evening?'

'No problem, any particular time?'

'Whenever you like. The kids are at my mother's, so we won't be disturbed.'

'OK, I'll make it as soon as I can.'

Sonya put the phone down. Telephone security was important, but she was aware that was only part of the reason for asking Nash to come round. The other should have worried her. But it didn't.

Nash thought it sensible to go through to Netherdale and brief Ruth Edwards on developments. The superintendent was as horrified by the news as Mironova and Pearce had been. She too saw the need for secrecy and less than orthodox tactics. It was after 7.30 when Nash left, having received assurances from Ruth of her full backup, and a promise to brief the chief constable on developments.

He called in his flat, where he dined on a takeaway pizza, before driving across town to Sonya's house. She was obviously on the lookout for him, because the door opened when he was only halfway down the path. Her figure was silhouetted by the hall light behind her. Nash was so intent on admiring it that he tripped over the corner of a paving slab. He stumbled and looked up in time to see her giggle.

'I sent Steve a text as you asked.' They were seated on the settee again. Nash guessed she'd showered because he could smell her perfume, fresh and clean, intermingled with the scent of a shampoo. He sipped his coffee, waiting for her to continue. 'I got him to ask the questions you wanted.'

'And what was the reply?'

'Jessica said Caroline Dunning was a frequent visitor to their house. From the time they returned to England.' Sonya's expression was one of distaste. 'She thought Dr Dunning was one of her mother's lovers. And that she suspected the woman was conducting an affair with her father at the same time.'

'Good Lord! The woman must be totally amoral.'

Sonya nodded. 'I think evil's the word you're looking for, Mike. Anyway, Jessica can't swear to it that Dunning was the one got Adam hooked on drugs, but from what we've read, that sounds likely, don't you think?'

Nash nodded. 'Anyway,' Sonya continued, 'one thing Jessica can remember, is Dr Dunning supplying her mother with some sort of inhaler. To help as a decongestant, or so Jessica was told.'

Sonya saw Nash grimace. 'What is it?'

'I found an inhaler at the scene of the fire. The contents could be mistaken for a decongestant, to the uninitiated.'

'What was in it?'

'The technical name is methylamphetamine.' Nash saw Sonya's puzzled frown. 'Better known as crystal meth. At least that was the main ingredient.'

'I've heard of that. I thought it was banned. What does it do?'

'It is banned. As of 2007 it was reclassified as a Class A drug. As to what it does, crystal meth is probably the most powerful aphrodisiac around. It heightens the libido to such an extent that it will cause women to behave like nymphomaniacs, and has a similar effect as Viagra on men, with one added exception. It makes ejaculation difficult, thus prolonging sexual activity. I think we can now see where Jessica's description of her mother's behaviour stems from. The forensic tests on the body suggest she'd been a user for a long time. I think we can safely say we've identified the villain of the piece. Thank you for that, Sonya. I'd better be going. It's getting late.'

As Nash was about to walk out into the hallway, they heard the sound of a car outside. Sonya put her hand on his arm. 'Don't go yet, please.'

She'd no sooner said it than there was a knock on the front door. It was loud, demanding. Nash looked at Sonya. 'Are you expecting anyone?'

She shook her head. 'I'll wait in here,' he told her. 'If it's Smith, cough loudly as you open the door. Whatever you do, whatever he says, don't let him in.'

He waited, heard the sound of the front door being opened, heard Sonya cough.

'Mrs Williams, you lied to us. You said Hirst had gone to France. We believe you not only know where he really is, you're holding some classified documents that he passed to you. That's an offence under the Official Secrets Act. We are going to conduct a search of your house, and if we find them you'll be placed under arrest.'

'No you're not, and no I won't,' Nash heard Sonya reply. There was no trace of fear or hesitation in her voice now. He marvelled at the change. 'Not without a warrant. And I know you won't have one, because you've no jurisdiction on civil premises.'

'Is this jurisdiction enough?'

'Put that gun away.'

Nash had heard enough. He stepped forward. 'Is there a problem here?'

He could barely see the man standing beyond the pool of light from the outside lamp.

'Who are you?'

'Detective Inspector Nash, Helmsdale CID. Mrs Williams is right. You have no jurisdiction here. Furthermore, I've already searched this house and I can state categorically that she is not in possession of any documents, classified or otherwise, that would be of the slightest interest to you. Unless you read *Cosmopolitan* magazine,' he added sarcastically. 'Unless you want me to arrest you, I suggest you clear off: now.'

He nodded to Sonya, who needed little encouragement to slam the door shut. She slid the bolts and chain across and leant against it. She was breathing heavily, as if she'd been running, and Nash knew she wasn't far from tears.

'That was very brave.'

'I couldn't have done it if you hadn't been here.'

'I think that's the last we've seen of him,' he smiled comfortingly.

'He scares me, Mike. What if he comes back, when you're not here? I know you've taken the disks and files away, but he won't know that.'

'He's obviously desperate to get them back. The fact that I was here might put him off,' he paused and thought. 'But knowing the devious way people like him think; it might make him more suspicious.'

He looked at her, realized how near to tears she was. 'It's all right, Sonya. I can arrange for officers to drive past if you want, make sure you're OK?'

'You wouldn't stay? Please, Mike. I'm really scared. Knowing what's in those files. And knowing what they've done already.'

'I suppose I could kip down on the sofa.' Nash glanced at it.

'You wouldn't need to, Mike.'

He looked up, surprised.

'I told you the children are at my mother's. You could have a bed upstairs.'

After they checked all the doors and windows to make sure the house was secure, Nash followed Sonya up the steep flight of stairs. At the top she gestured to the first bedroom. Nash opened the door and looked at the room in dismay. Beds there were, but they were children's bunk beds. He might just fit half of his frame into one of them. 'Perhaps not,' Sonya murmured. She opened another door. 'There's this one.'

'Oh, very funny.' Nash gazed at the baby's cot.

'Or then again,' her voice was husky, nervous, as she opened a third door. 'There's this.'

The double bed was definitely big enough for one. 'But if I had that, where would you sleep?' Nash turned to look at Sonya. She was beginning to unbutton her blouse.

'I'm sure I'll find somewhere,' she told him.

As he climbed into bed alongside her, she said, 'To serve and protect, isn't that a police motto?'

'I think that's in America,' he said. 'But I'll do my best.'

Much later, as they were drifting off to sleep, Nash heard Sonya murmur, 'Who needs crystal meth…?'

Nash woke early. He could feel Sonya's breath warm on his cheek. It felt mildly erotic. His eyes became accustomed to the half light. His mind was filled with one thought: Smith would try and get those files; they contained far too much damning information. Nash was sure he wouldn't give up.

Sonya stirred, her arm reached out for him. That distracted him. 'What are you thinking about?' she said sleepily.

'I was just thinking how we could have a bit of fun.'

Her hand slid down his body. 'Good.' Her thigh pressed closer completing his arousal. 'I was just thinking the same.'

Later, as they held each other close, she asked, 'What was your idea?'

He smiled. 'You don't miss much. You did say you had another copy of that stuff?'

Sonya nodded, then listened. 'It could be dangerous,' she protested.

'I don't think so. I'll make sure I'm well protected. The main thing is, if it works, they'll have to show their hand.'

'If you're determined to go ahead with it, we'd better make a start.'

As Sonya was making toast and coffee, Nash got on his mobile. He explained what he wanted. It took a while, not least because of several sarcastic comments from Clara. When he finished he looked up. Sonya was watching him. 'Sorted,' he told her.

'Sounded as if you were getting a bit of grief; the sort of conversation an unfaithful husband might have.'

Nash laughed. 'Clara wouldn't take that as a compliment. My sergeant loves taking the piss out of me. Particularly, well, on certain subjects.'

'Your love life? You must have a good working relationship. She sounds the sort of woman I'd like.'

'You can judge for yourself. You'll be meeting her soon.'

As Nash was finishing his toast, his mobile rang. 'All ready?' he asked after glancing at the caller display. 'Any sign of the opposition?' He listened. 'Good, I'll be coming out in about five minutes.'

He stood up and reached for the carrier bag containing the documents. 'Showtime,' he said. He smiled at Sonya.

She was looking nervous. 'Be careful, Mike. These people are dangerous.' She gestured to the carrier bag. 'You know what they're capable of.'

'Don't worry, this is my town. I've all the help I need within shouting distance.'

'That's all very well, but what if you can't shout.'

'Let's not think that way. I'll be all right, I promise.'

He paused before opening the front door. 'Ready to give me the big send off?'

She nodded. 'Before you open that, I want to thank you for last night.'

She reached forward to kiss him.

'Think nothing of it.' He grinned as she released him. 'It was my pleasure.'

She blushed. 'That wasn't what I meant.'

He opened the door and walked down the path, seemingly oblivious to the van that was pulling to a halt behind his car. He fumbled his car keys from his pocket and turned to wave goodbye. Sonya waved back, before closing the door. As he reached his car, Nash felt something cold pressed against his neck. 'Don't turn round. Don't move.'

As the man spoke, a cloth dropped over Nash's head. Unseen hands pushed him to his left, towards where the van was parked. Within seconds he was bundled into the back, the door slammed behind him and the vehicle moved off. Unable to see, Nash felt his arms being dragged behind his back, then taped together. His ankles were secured the same way. The carrier bag with its precious contents was ripped from his grasp. No words were spoken, but Nash felt the pace accelerate as the vehicle sped onto the main road from the estate.

They travelled for what seemed a long time before Nash felt the vehicle slow down. Seconds later he was rolled across the back of the van as it made a sharp left turn. A further five minutes or so passed before the van came to a rest. Nash heard the handbrake being applied, then the sound of doors opening. A moment later he registered a draught of cold air. As he did so, he was pushed, none too gently, from the back of the vehicle. Hands grabbed him, hauled him to his feet; then he was punched repeatedly about the body and head. Nash sank to his knees, semi-conscious and in considerable pain from the beating. Next came the feet. Boots, he guessed, as blow after blow thudded into his already bruised body. One of his captors muttered something and the kicking ceased. Nash was by this time beginning to drift off. He heard the engine of the van start up, through a mist of sound. He thought it had pulled away. Was that it coming back? He heard a door slam, footsteps running towards him. The next second the hood was lifted from his head and he stared into a pair of beautiful blue eyes, eyes that he knew well. 'You took your time,' he muttered. 'What kept you?'

'Mike!' Clara's voice was sharp with distress. 'Are you badly hurt? I'll have to get you to hospital.'

'No,' he was starting to come round, but speech and mustering his thoughts weren't easy. 'Sonya's house. More important,' he gasped.

Clara slit the tape and removed it. He struggled to his feet, Clara's arms supporting him. He stood for a minute; the road swaying in time with him. They were on a moorland road with no vehicles or buildings in sight. 'Where are we?'

'Half way to Bishop's Cross. On the back road.'

'Viv?'

'As far as I know he's on station. I was more concerned about you. Still am.'

'I'll be all right. Help me to the car, let's get moving.'

As soon as they were in the car, Clara called Pearce on the radio. By the time they reached the outskirts of Helmsdale, the DC had reported that he'd followed the van to a house in Netherdale. 'Get Viv to alert Binns. We'll need a warrant to search that place,' Nash told Mironova.

They pulled up outside Sonya's house and Clara hurried round to help Nash out of his seat. He winced as he stood up. 'Are you sure you're OK?'

'Stiffening up, that's all.'

The door opened as Clara helped Nash down the path. 'Mike,' Sonya exclaimed; shock and distress apparent. 'What have they done to you?'

'Bit of a beating, that's all.' Nash tried a reassuring smile. It didn't seem to have worked.

'Sonya, this is DS Mironova, Clara.' Nash introduced her.

'Come on in; let's get those cuts seen to.'

'What's she mean? What cuts?'

'You've half a dozen on your face.'

Between them, the two women manoeuvred Nash inside the house and into the dining room, where he was pushed onto one of the dining chairs and told to sit still. A few minutes later they reappeared from the kitchen. Sonya had a washing up bowl, flannel and towels, whilst Clara was carrying three mugs of coffee. 'This is going to sting a bit,' Sonya warned him.

Nash winced as the warm liquid stung his battered face. 'Ouch!'

'It's only diluted disinfectant. Know something, Clara? I've three youngsters, all under the age of seven. None of them make this much fuss.'

'Men,' Clara joined in disparagingly. 'They're just big babies.'

'Oy, they're my cuts. I know how much they hurt,' Nash protested.

Sonya finished mopping his face. 'There's no fresh blood oozing out, so that's a good thing.' She winked at Clara. 'Mind you, his face is an awful mess.'

'Difficult to say how much of that's down to the beating though,' Clara pointed out. 'It wasn't much to look at to start with.'

'Come on, Mike, on your feet,' Sonya said. 'Get your kit off. Let's see what they've done to the rest of you.'

'I don't fancy a threesome,' Nash gasped as he struggled to get off the chair.

'State you're in, you couldn't even manage a twosome,' Sonya retorted.

They helped him off with his shirt. Both women gasped as they saw the extent of the bruising on his ribs, his arms and his stomach. 'They worked you over good and proper,' Clara said. 'I only hope you think it was worthwhile.'

'Drop your trousers, let's see what they did to the lower end,' Sonya ordered.

Nash undid his belt and allowed his trousers to drop. 'Bloody hell, Mike.' Clara stared in horror at the bruised state of his legs and thighs. 'What a mess.'

'At least they left the crown jewels alone,' Nash muttered.

'Probably couldn't find them,' Sonya chimed in. 'Clara, will you mop any blood up with that flannel. I'm going to get some witch hazel from the kitchen. It'll help lessen the bruising.'

'Sit down again, Mike. Before you fall over,' Clara instructed.

Nash submitted to their ministrations and allowed them to help him dress. 'You really need a long soak in a hot bath,' Sonya told him. 'But no doubt you'll ignore anything that sounds like sensible advice.'

'How long did you say you've known him?' Clara asked.

'Only a few days, why?'

'Sounds as if it was longer.'

'Come on, Clara; let's get off to the station.'

'What was in the carrier bag they took from Mike?' Mironova asked.

'A load of CDs and a copy of the personnel files.' Sonya paused. 'I hope they won't be too disappointed by the CDs. Not everybody's a fan of Abba and Queen.'

As they drove back to the station, Clara asked, 'What's happening with you and Becky?'

'It's all over,' Nash told her. 'Becky seemed to want it that way. She told me when I took her to the train.'

'I see,' Clara thought for a moment. 'It was good of you to stay and protect Mrs Williams last night. It must have been uncomfortable sleeping on that sofa though.'

'I didn't—' Nash stopped as he realized his blunder.

'Of course you didn't,' Clara laughed. 'I'd have been disappointed in you if you had. But I was teasing you, I already knew.'

Nash was surprised. 'Did Sonya tell you?'

'She didn't have to. I could tell by the way she looked at you. She seems nice.'

Nash shrugged; then wished he hadn't. 'She was lonely, I was lonely. That's all it was.'

When they reached the station, the CID suite was empty, but Clara froze as she entered the outer office. 'Mike,' she said softly. 'Somebody's been in here.'

He beckoned her out into the corridor and made sure the door was closed. 'How do you know?'

183

'Last night, I had to leave in a hurry. There was a fight at the Cock and Bottle. Nothing serious, handbags at dawn, you know the sort of thing. Anyway, when I went out, I left a mug of coffee on my desk. Just now, when I looked, it had been moved to the centre table.'

'You're sure about that?'

'Absolutely positive.'

'It couldn't have been moved by the cleaners?'

'They'd already left.'

'What about Viv?'

'He'd gone too. He'd another date.'

'I'd better ring Jimmy Johnson, get him to do a sweep for bugs.'

'It can't have happened a second time, surely.'

'Probably not, but better safe than sorry. For the time being we'll go foist ourselves on Curran.'

The bug hunt yielded no unpleasant surprises, but when Nash entered his own office he noticed one or two items were out of place. 'You weren't being paranoid,' he told Clara. 'There has been an intruder, what's more it was someone with the know-how to bypass our security. I want you to study those transcripts. I'll field any phone calls. I don't want you disturbed whilst you're reading. First of all though, we should check how Viv's surveillance is working out.'

Pearce had little to report. 'The van pulled up and half a dozen blokes got out. They looked like army types – short haircuts, the way they walked. They went inside, and about ten minutes later somebody came out. I wasn't close enough to get a good view, but it could have been a woman. They got into a car that was parked next to the van and drove off. Unfortunately they went the other way, so I couldn't see the number plate. Apart from that, nothing's happened.'

'We've managed to retrieve the disks and the files.' Smith looked triumphant. 'Nash had them at the Williams woman's house. We collared him as he left.'

'You didn't kill him, I hope?'

'No, the lads roughed him up a bit. Payback for him having them arrested. We left him out on the moors, took the battery from his mobile phone. He was trussed up, bag over his head. With any luck' – Smith laughed – 'he'll have fallen into a bog or is still stranded there. Anyway, the main point is we have the data back.'

'You'd better check it though, just to be on the safe side. Let me know. Send me a text or whatever. I've a train to catch. I'm due in Whitehall later today.'

Smith checked the documents first; finding them in order was a relief in itself. But the most crucial information was loaded on the disks. He slid the first of these into the PC on his boss's desk and waited. Seconds later, those of Smith's men who were in earshot stopped, as the opening bars of *Bohemian Rhapsody* came from the speakers.

'Oh, shit!' Smith scrabbled at the pile of disks. He stuffed another into the CD slot. The Swedish superstars strived to entertain him – *Waterloo* seemed almost prophetic. 'Nash, you bastard.' Smith knew he'd been duped, knew the information they were desperate to protect was beyond their reach. But could it be deciphered? That was the least of his problems. First, he had to break the news to his boss.

CHAPTER SEVENTEEN

'You think this is where Dad is?'

Hirst looked at Jessica, not knowing what to tell her. They'd swapped the motorhome for Hirst's small van. 'I'm not sure,' he told her after a pause.

Jessica stared at him for a second. 'You mean you're not sure if he's still alive.' Her voice was little more than a whisper.

'I'm sorry, Jessica, but it's a possibility. It all depends on how far along they are with their research. If they've finished developing the drug, your father may have no further use. And if they're capable of getting rid of your mother and brother, they wouldn't hesitate to do the same with him. For one thing, he knows too much. These people are military, don't forget. The reason for not taking prisoners is that they've to be guarded. That takes manpower. Cold, hard logic. The sooner we get to your father, the better.'

'What if he isn't here? What if they're holding him somewhere else?'

Hirst thought about it. 'In that case, we need something to bargain with.'

'Sorry, I don't understand.'

'We need to get hold of something to exchange for your father's safe release. We could have used the disks, but that

186

would have meant them getting away with everything. So we need something else. Your father might well be in that building, in which case he'll be a free man in an hour or two. What we've to do is get hold of something to bargain with in case he's elsewhere.'

'How do you know he'll be free if he's in there?'

Hirst pointed. 'See that car? It's been parked there since we arrived. Pulled up just in front of us. Unless I read Nash totally wrong, that'll be one of his men.'

'If Nash knows they're here, why hasn't he gone in yet?'

'He's a policeman. He has to do everything by the book. He'll be waiting for a search warrant.'

'Hang on, Steve, there's somebody coming out.'

'Let's get a bit closer.'

Hirst started the engine and they drove slowly down the road. He glanced sideways at the figure opening the car door alongside them, then accelerated away.

'Did you see who that was?' Jessica asked, her voice excited.

'I did indeed, it was our bargaining tool.'

He stopped the van abruptly, reached across and grabbed the collar of Jessica's shirt. He gave a sharp tug and the garment ripped. 'Out of the van, now,' he ordered. 'Smear some mud on your face and arms. Quick, we've only got seconds.'

As he was speaking, Hirst dived out, slammed the door and climbed into the back of the van and opened the rear door a fraction of an inch. Jessica got out of the passenger side and began scrabbling in the verge, smearing mud as he'd told her. She'd no idea what Steve had in mind. He shouted through the open door. 'Stand in the road, right by the driver's door. Try to look distressed. Cry if you can. When the car stops, back away. I need the driver out of the vehicle.'

Hirst had only just finished speaking when he heard a car approaching. 'Is it the right one?' he asked.

Jessica nodded. He saw the brief flash of blue as the car passed him, heard the squeal of brakes as it pulled to an abrupt halt. He pushed the door a couple more inches, as far as he dare. He heard a voice above the car engine. Loud, excited, and elated. 'Jessica, thank God you're safe. What's happened to you?'

Hirst could see the car driver now. As he watched, Jessica turned towards the back of the van. The driver faced her. Hirst slid the door fully open, thankful the hinges had been greased. He crept out and round behind the car driver. Seconds later it was all over. Hirst bundled the driver into the back of the van. 'Duct tape, in the glove compartment,' he told Jessica. In a matter of minutes their captive was bound hand and foot, gagged into the bargain.

'Now what?' Jessica asked. 'It's going to be a bit crowded in the motorhome with three of us.'

'Don't worry about that.' Hirst looked up from their squirming prisoner, who was attempting to remonstrate through the gag. 'I've somewhere else in mind for this one, later. None of the luxuries of caravan life, I'm afraid. Let's go.'

As they were driving, Hirst passed Jessica his mobile. 'Send Sonya a text. Ask her to phone Nash,' he grinned. 'She'll enjoy that, I reckon. We need to know if they've got your father out of that house. If so, we can turn this one' – he jerked his thumb towards the back of the van – 'over to Nash. Then we can let the law take its course. Our part of it will be over.'

Jessica felt a vague sense of disappointment at the last phrase. But, if it meant her father was safe, that's all she really needed. A thought struck her. She lifted her head from composing the text. 'Why did you say Sonya would enjoy phoning Nash?'

'She sounded so cheerful when she rang this morning. She told me Nash had stayed to guard her overnight.' He grinned. 'Make what you want of that.'

After she'd sent the message, Jessica closed the phone. 'What will you do once this is over?' Her tone was casual, enquiring, but no more.

'Report back for duty.' Out of the corner of his eye, Hirst saw the girl's look of surprise. 'I'm still a serving soldier, don't forget. I'm only on extended compassionate leave. I'm due back soon.'

'After all this, will they want you back?'

'Why not? There's only a handful of people have the slightest inkling of what I've been up to. Apart from you and Sonya, there's Nash and his colleagues. I don't think any of them will give the game away. As for the others, they dare not say anything.'

Sonya had just put her third load of washing into the tumble dryer when she heard the message alert tone on her phone. She smiled as she read it, then punched in the number of Helmsdale police station. 'Is Mr Nash available please? Or Sergeant Mironova.'

She waited; then heard Clara's voice. 'It's Sonya. Is Mike there? I've a message for him.'

'Hang on, Sonya.'

She heard Clara's voice. 'Mike, your girlfriend's on line one.'

There was a pause, then she heard Clara again. 'Sonya. Why? How many have you got?'

She wasn't sure what Nash's reply was, but it sounded like, 'Cheeky devil'.

'Hi, Sonya, what's up?'

She explained the text she'd got from Hirst. 'Obviously Jessica's keen to know if her father's safe.'

'That's interesting. It means they were watching this morning's little charade. How did they get to know about that, I wonder?'

Sonya was glad Nash couldn't see her face. 'Because I told him what you were planning,' she confessed. 'You may have treated the danger lightly, but I wasn't prepared to take the chance. So I made sure Steve and Jessica were on hand in case of trouble. He nearly intervened too, when he saw you getting roughed up.'

She waited, was she in trouble? Would Nash be angry? When he spoke, his voice was gentle as a caress. 'That was extremely thoughtful of you, Sonya. As to the other, we haven't got hold of a warrant yet. It'll be another couple of hours at least. Obviously I'll let you know if we do find Dr North, for Jessica's peace of mind.'

'What's happening outside?'

The guard turned from his survey of the street. 'Nothing much. Some idle bastard of a salesman reading a paper, that's all. How's the boffin?'

'Going to pieces, I reckon. Keeps mumbling away to himself and scribbling little notes on scraps of paper. I sneaked a look at one earlier; meaningless drivel about his wife and family. How he needed to contact her.' He laughed. 'The only way he'll contact her is with a ouija board. I tell you, he'll do himself an injury or something like that if we're not careful. I'm surprised Smithy doesn't just finish him off. I can't see he'll ever be any good to the project again, for all they say he's brilliant.'

'Do you think he needs watching? If he injures himself on our watch we'll get it in the neck.'

'Not at the minute. He's fast asleep. I looked in quarter of an hour ago, he was snoring fit to bring the house down.'

Need time alone. Need to fool them. Must get out of here. Warn Lara; danger, danger to Jessica. Something about Jessica, she's disappeared; kidnapped. That's it. I was away, you see. Sorry, Lara. I'd have looked after her if I'd been home. But I wasn't. Where was I? Can't remember. But I do know I wasn't here. Must get out of this place. Those men are watching me. Got to fool them. They think I'm going mad. I'm not though. You don't think I'm going mad, do you? Perhaps I am. But I must get out. It's dangerous here. I know that. Get out and find Jessica. Warn her, before it's too late. Warn her of what though? Danger, yes. But what sort of danger? I … wish … I … could … remember.

Here comes one of them now. Pull the blankets over and start snoring. Long, deep breaths, release the air slowly. Again.... Again.... Again.... That's it, he's gone. Now, if he goes and talks to the other one, I might be able to sneak out of the back. I saw where they hid the key. Right, come on Richard. Let's go. Careful down the stairs. The next one creaks. Listen. Good, they're in the lounge, talking. Past the door. Hope they don't spot me. Hope there isn't a third man. There is sometimes; usually at night. Into the kitchen. Phew, nobody there. Find the key. Got it. Back door next. Then away. Ease it open: don't let it creak. Now, out and close. Lock it back up. I'm out. Now, where do I go from here? I still can't find Jessica. I don't know where to look.

DC Pearce saw the approaching figure. A dishevelled old man with greying hair and stooped posture muttering to himself. Viv thought, I hope I never get like that. He wondered briefly where he'd come from. Had he come out of one of the houses, or was he a tramp? He looked and acted like a tramp. Certainly not like a distinguished scientist. But then, Pearce had never met Dr North.

As he watched the old man shuffling along the street, Pearce's mobile rang. He glanced at the caller display before answering. 'Hi, Mike.'

'We've got the warrant at last. We'll be with you in ten minutes or so. Any more activity?'

'Nothing. I'm glad you're coming soon. This job's hardly the most exciting I've ever had. I'm reduced to watching old tramps.'

'We'll soon put you out of your misery,' Nash promised.

The raid went according to plan. The two men occupying the house were cautioned. 'Where's Dr North?' Nash asked.

'Who?' One of the men replied, but Nash saw the involuntary glance the other made towards the stairs.

Nash signalled to Mironova. She took the steps two at a time and was gone less than five minutes. She returned, shaking her head. 'There's nobody up there,' she reported.

Nash's disappointment was obvious, but not half as patent as the astonishment on the two detained men's faces.

'Take them to the station for questioning,' he instructed Binns, who was in charge of the uniformed contingent. 'I want a sweep doing of the gardens and all the surrounding area. This is the man we're looking for.'

He gestured to Mironova, who pulled out a set of photos of North. They were taken from his passport renewal. It's a well-known fact that passport photos never do the subject justice. North's aged him considerably.

Pearce looked over Clara's shoulder. 'Oh shit!' he exclaimed.

Nash looked up. 'What's wrong, Viv?'

'That man I told you I'd seen in the street. The one I thought was a tramp. I reckon it might have been Dr North. He can't have gone far.'

One mistake was compounded by another. Nash called in patrol cars to help in the search. Despite scouring the streets surrounding the house, they found no trace of the missing scientist. If they'd thought to look on the bus that passed three of the patrol cars, they might have spotted him. But they didn't.

They weren't to know North would catch the bus. How could they, when he hadn't planned to. He saw the bus approaching. Saw the destination board. The name was familiar. He was close enough to a stop for the driver to brake and let him on. North fumbled in his pocket and found some change. 'Single to Gorton, please.'

He took the ticket and walked down the aisle. The single-decker bus was all but empty – only a fat, middle-aged woman and an extremely elderly man, who appeared to be asleep. North took a seat near the back. Why had he got on the bus? He wasn't sure, but the name sounded familiar. Gorton, he felt sure he ought to know it. But he couldn't think why. Maybe it would come back to him when he got there.

Nash waited with Mironova and Binns for reports. The team of uniformed officers had left the van parked outside the house, together with the CID officers' cars. As they were waiting, none of them paid any attention to the car that drove slowly past. Smith swore as he saw the collection of vehicles. How had they found this place? He turned the corner and headed towards town. No point in wasting time. His boss had to know the latest setback. He pressed the short code on his mobile and waited. It went straight to voicemail. He'd been trying the number for a couple of hours now, with no success. His concern was mounting, almost to panic level now.

'Anything from forensics on that house?'

'No, I'll chase them up.'

'Do that, I need to know if North was being held there. If he was, we've an excuse for holding on to those two characters we've got in the cells downstairs.'

'But how will we know? We don't have North's fingerprints.'

'No, but we have an unidentified set from his house at Gorton. The set we couldn't access on the computer, if you remember.'

'I should do,' Mironova eyed her boss with respect. 'I didn't think to make the connection, but you remembered.'

Nash smiled. 'Experience, that's all, Clara. One thing they can't teach on courses. As soon as we know, I'll get a message to his daughter.'

'Via the Merry Widow, I suppose. I don't know, Mike, you get all the worst jobs.'

'Go do some work,' Nash scowled.

Mironova was back within minutes. 'SOCO reckon some of the prints they lifted from that house match that set from Gorton, just as you suggested. So, what's happened to Dr North?'

'If Pearce is right, and the bloke he saw walking down the road was North, we must assume he escaped from the two guards. Although where he's gone, is anybody's guess.'

'I'll leave you to pass the news to your lady friend, shall I? Do you want me to close the door whilst you whisper sweet nothings, or can I listen in on your chat-up line?'

Nash's reply was non-verbal and extremely vulgar. It involved the use of only one finger.

There was no reply from Sonya's house, so Nash tried her mobile. 'Hi, Mike, I'm at my mother's. Tommy, my youngest is down with a cold and a bit of a fever, so I thought it best to leave all three with Mum for a few days, until the other business is sorted out.' Nash could tell by her lowered tone that her mother was within earshot.

'Right, I get you. It's about that I'm ringing, actually.' He gave her a brief outline of what had happened at the house. 'That means that Jessica's father is still on the loose, but so is Smith. That worries me. I need to get to Dr North first. It's the only way I can guarantee to keep him safe. It would help enormously if I knew who this boss of Smith's is. If I could take them out of the equation it would help to neutralize Smith. I'm sure Hirst must have some idea. If not, maybe Jessica can tell me. Will you put it to them, Sonya?'

'I'll see what I can do. Try and find him, Mike. I know Jessica's worried stiff. This news isn't going to help.'

After he rang off, Nash called Mironova into his office. 'Hear all you want, get any good tips?' he enquired sarcastically.

'Not really, it was all rather boring and business-like.'

'Sorry to disappoint you. Now, let's try and work out where to find Dr North.'

'How do we go about it?'

'Something Viv said gave me an idea. He said the bloke he saw looked like an old tramp, and that he was muttering away to himself. Now I know a lot of the winos who wander around behave like that, but as far as we know Dr North isn't one. So I guess he's in the middle of some sort of break-down. Bear in mind he's just heard that his wife and son have been killed, that his daughter's been kidnapped, and that he's been in the hands of some ruthless bastards who have probably been feeding him all sorts of hallucinatory drugs. That seems to be what they're best at – messing with people's heads.'

'OK, I grant you he's probably in a mess. But does that get us any further forward?'

'In that sort of state, where's the most likely place for someone to go?'

'I don't know, somewhere familiar, I suppose. Given that he has any memory left.'

'Agreed. Which gives us two favourite options. The laboratory, or his house.'

As he was speaking, Nash had a fleeting mental image. Of standing in the lounge of the house they'd raided that morning, questioning the two men they'd found there. Over their shoulder, through the lounge window, he'd seen something. Something so familiar his memory had discounted it until now. 'Clara, ask Viv to get his car. We'll check the laboratory, North won't know about the explosion. If we don't find any trace there, we'll go out to Gorton. Whilst he's bringing his car round, get onto Shires Bus Company. Ask them what service passed that house at 1.15 this afternoon.'

'You think North caught a bus. And that was why we couldn't find him?'

'I do, and I'd be very surprised if it doesn't go to Gorton.'

'If North was as confused as you think, would he realize where the bus was headed?'

'He would, if it was showing on the destination board.'

The news Sonya gave them, had Jessica in a frenzy of anxiety. 'If they've harmed him, I'll—'

Steve attempted to reassure her. 'Nash is a good copper. He'll find him, don't worry.'

They were still in the van. Their prisoner was trussed and gagged in the back. Hirst saw Jessica turn to look at the helpless figure lying on the metal floor. 'Don't even think about it,' he advised Jessica.

'Think about what?'

'Revenge. Believe me, it won't help. Let's give Nash the information and turn that one' – he pointed over his shoulder – 'over to him. Let him deal with it from now on. I've to go back tomorrow. Once I'm clear, you can hand this to Nash. By the time anyone can catch up with me, I'll be way out of reach.'

He didn't add that he'd be back in foreign parts, back on duty. Better not to complicate matters. Reluctantly, Jessica agreed.

'That bus does go to Gorton,' Mironova told Nash as they walked downstairs. 'Doesn't it get boring, always being right?'

'I don't always get it right,' Nash protested. 'I make lots of mistakes.'

'I'm talking about work, not your love life.'

There was no sign of the missing scientist at the laboratory, just one or two demolition contractors watching a crane with a ball attachment knocking down what remained of the walls of the building. Nash had a word with their foreman, who confirmed they'd not seen any strangers hanging about the place. 'We're the first people he's seen,' Nash told the others as he got back in the car. 'He said it made a change for them to work without drawing a crowd. Must be the isolated location, I suppose. Right, Viv, head for Gorton, will you?'

The cottage was a forlorn sight. The blackened shell of what had once been a beautiful house was in stark contrast to the beauty of the surrounding countryside. They picked their way carefully through the debris, which remained as it had been after the fire. The brightly coloured incident tape that had cordoned off the building fluttered and danced in the breeze. It did nothing to enhance the beauty of the scene. As they reached what had once been the kitchen, where the blaze had been fiercest, Pearce stopped suddenly and lifted a hand. 'Listen,' he said, 'what's that noise?'

The sound appeared to be coming from the upper floor. As the detectives listened, Nash and Mironova identified the noise at the same time. They looked at one another, realization dawning. It was the sound of someone crying. 'Viv, stay here,' Nash told the DC, his voice barely above a whisper. 'We don't want to crowd him. Clara, with me.'

They walked as quietly as they could up the stairs, wincing slightly as they trod on broken glass and plaster, the sound of their footsteps amplified in the silence. They traced the weeping sound to the largest of the bedrooms. The door had been burned away by the fire, so they were able to see in as they picked their way across the charred floorboards of the landing. A man was standing by the window, half turned away from them. He was holding a picture frame in his hand. Although the glass had been shattered by the heat, they could make out that the photo within the frame was that of a woman and two small children. 'Dr North?' Nash's voice was gentle.

The man turned, and Mironova saw the tracks made by his tears down the soot-grimed cheeks of his face. 'Dr North, I'm a police officer. You're quite safe,' Nash told him, his voice strengthening with the desire to get his message through to the scientist's confused brain. 'Dr North, we've come to take you to Jessica. Your daughter, Jessica,' Nash repeated. 'She's very worried about you. You'd like that, wouldn't you? To see Jessica again. To make sure she's safe?'

North's tears flowed faster and faster. 'Jessica,' he whispered. He looked down at the photograph. 'My little Jessica. What happened to us? Adam, Lara, what….' His voice tailed off as his distress threatened to overwhelm him.

Nash signalled to Mironova. Clara stepped forward and put her arm around the scientist. Gently, murmuring words of encouragement, she led him from the room, coaxed him down the stairs and out of the ruined building. Nash followed, noticing that North was still clutching the picture frame, the last memory he had of his wife and son, the last memory of what he'd lost. Or more correctly, what had been taken from him. Nash's resolve to bring the killers to justice hardened. The acts of violence, the lives ruined as completely as the building they'd just left were bad enough. The cold-blooded way it had been carried it out made the whole thing ten times worse.

CHAPTER EIGHTEEN

Clara sat with Dr North in the back of the car, whilst Nash sat in front alongside Pearce. The journey to Helmsdale was conducted in silence. As soon as Nash's mobile picked up a signal, he sent Sonya a text. 'North safe, tell J' was all it said, all Jessica needed to know.

It was almost dark when they reached the police station. Clara led North from the car. He looked round in bewilderment at the array of police cars, ambulances and fire engines. 'Where am I?' he demanded, suddenly suspicious.

Clara looked at Nash for help. 'It's all right, Dr North. I've sent Jessica a message, she knows you're safe. She knows you're with me. She'll come to you as soon as she can.'

North peered at him. 'What did you say your name is?'

'Nash, Mike Nash. Detective Inspector Nash.'

'Why was Jessica kidnapped?' North's memory was returning in snatches.

'She was taken away from those men who were holding her prisoner. The same men who were holding you. A man she didn't know realized the danger she was in and rescued her, to keep the others from harming her. Like they did to your wife, and to your son.'

North stared at Nash, bewilderment and horror inter-mingled. 'What do you mean? They told me Adam was mur-dered, but I thought Lara died in a fire?'

'I'm sorry, Dr North. They were both murdered.'

Clara led the distressed man into the building. He'd begun muttering to himself; snatches of words, unrecogniz-able to his listeners. Nash drew Pearce to one side. 'Get the police surgeon in. I want him to check Dr North over. In the meantime stick him in a cell, one where we're certain he can't harm himself. When the doctor arrives, tell him I want Dr North's mental state assessing. Also, I want him to take a sample of his blood. Get him to send it for analysis. I want particular attention given to finding any trace of hallucina-tory drugs, or anything that might be used to tamper with his mental state.'

The text message came as an enormous relief. Naturally Jessica wanted to go to her father immediately. 'No way,' Hirst told her firmly. 'Your father's in safe hands. We've a job still to do. Think of your mother and brother; much as you want to be with your father, they deserve justice. The only way we can get that for them is either by handing our prisoner over to Nash, or,' he drew one finger across his throat. 'No matter what they're guilty of, murder is still murder. Let the law deal with them.'

'Very well,' Jessica hid her disappointment, 'but how do we go about it?'

Hirst told her. After he explained, he added, 'By the time you're back with your father, I'll be away. Remember, when you're telling your story, make sure Nash understands I was the one who destroyed the laboratory. Tell him you were a prisoner in the van at the time, tied up with duct tape.'

'What will they do to you?' Jessica protested.

'Nothing, because I won't be around. They can't pros-ecute me unless I'm here. And for the foreseeable future I'll be out of the country. Hopefully, by the time I get back, the fuss will have died down. When the truth about what went on at Helm Pharm comes out, public opinion will be on my side. Who knows, Paul and his eco-warrior friends might even want to claim responsibility for it. Do their credibility the world of good. But you could let Nash know about the marzipan. I don't want our Sappers trying to destroy a target with marzipan instead of C4.'

It was late that evening when they returned to Helmsdale. Hirst pulled up outside the row of lock-up garages and opened the end one. He reversed the motorhome out of the building, where the headlights illuminated the interior. He collected the prisoner from the back of the van and dumped his burden in the far corner of the garage, slammed the up-and-over door shut and locked it. When he returned to the motorhome he handed the key to Jessica. 'Put that somewhere safe until tomorrow,' he told her.

Jessica went to put the key inside her bra. 'No, I said somewhere safe,' Hirst warned her.

She grinned and attached the ring to her jeans belt. 'I'm going to park the van outside the house. I'll be back in five minutes, then we'll go somewhere safe for the night. Tomorrow morning I'll drop you at Sonya's house, park this on my drive and collect my stuff. I'll be away by nine o'clock. Then you can phone Nash.'

There was a reckless abandon about their lovemaking that night. When it was over, and they lay wrapped together, Steve felt the warm salt of her tears, wet against his shoulder. 'Don't take on,' he urged her. 'Soon, all this will be a memory, because you'll have lots more to think about. Taking care of your father for one thing. God knows what they'll have done to him. Forget me, and get on with the rest of your life. You're young; you've got a great future ahead of you.'

'But I don't want to forget you. I won't forget you. How could I?'

'You will. And if not, well, who knows, we might meet again sometime. When you're going where I am, the one thing you avoid at all costs, is making plans for the future.'

As they fell asleep, Steve's words were in Jessica's mind. They seemed almost prophetic.

The first thing Nash noticed as he drove along the street was the motorhome. He ignored it and parked outside Sonya's house. She was obviously on the lookout for him, because the door opened as he was walking up the path. 'Come on in.' Sonya smiled. 'I'll introduce you and pour coffee. I'll have to go buy some more, the rate you drink it.'

'You don't imagine for one minute I'd stop coming to see you if there was no coffee?' Nash teased. 'Because I can assure you, the coffee isn't the attraction.'

Nash had expected to meet a schoolgirl, slightly awkward perhaps, little more than a child. He was unprepared for the poised and attractive young woman who stood waiting for him in the lounge. 'Miss North? I'm Mike Nash.'

She shook hands. 'Jessica,' she prompted. 'Call me Jessica. How's my father? Can I see him?'

'He's at the police station for the time being. I thought it was safer for him there. I got our doctor to have a look at him yesterday. He's not in very good shape, I'm afraid. He doesn't know the full extent of what's been done to your family; I haven't let him read those files. I thought it better to wait until you were with him. He'll need your support. I'm afraid what little he does know has affected him very badly. I got the doctor to take a blood test – I'm fairly sure they'll have been feeding him drugs, but we can't do much until we know what we're fighting against, and how long it'll take to get them out of his system.'

'I've got something to give you,' Jessica held out her hand. 'That's the key to the end one of the lock-up garages round there.' She pointed to the end of the street. 'Inside, you'll find what you're looking for.'

'My sergeant will be here in a few minutes, and my DC. Between us we'll take you and the prisoner back to the station. In separate vehicles,' he added hastily.

'Before they arrive, I assume the man who abducted you is still as much a mystery to you as he is to us?' Nash saw the look of surprise on her face and smiled. 'Of course, we could speculate as to his identity, but without a description, which you are obviously unable to give, as he wore a balaclava all the time, we've no way of identifying him. Or the vehicle either because he just dumped you in the street and drove off. It was sheer chance that you happened to knock on Sonya's door. Sheer fluke that she happens to be a friend of mine.'

Jessica's smile broadened throughout Nash's little speech. 'You know, Mr Nash, S—, my abductor, said you were a nice, kind person. Now I know what he meant. Before your people arrive, I'd better tell you what you'll find in the garage.'

As Jessica finished speaking, Nash heard the sound of cars arriving and glanced outside. 'My sergeant and DC,' he explained.

'I'll let them in.' Sonya hurried to the door.

Nash waited until Clara had driven off with Jessica, before turning to Pearce. 'Drive down to the end of the street, where the garages are and wait for me. 'I'll be about five minutes, no more.'

'OK, Mike.' Pearce hid a smile until he was out of the door.

'Thanks for all your help, Sonya,' Nash turned to leave. 'Sadly, now that this is over, I haven't a good excuse for coming to see you.'

'If you don't, who's going to drink that enormous jar of coffee?'

'Which enormous jar of coffee?'

'The one I'm going to buy as soon as I can get to the shops.' Sonya laid her hand on his arm. 'And, if that isn't excuse enough.' She leaned forward and kissed him.

He wasn't sure if it was seconds or minutes later when he surfaced for air. 'When?' he asked, gasping slightly.

'How about tonight? Unless you're going to be too busy.'

'It might be late,' he warned.

'Better late than not at all, but if I've to wait until then, I'd better have another of those.'

He kissed her once more. 'Now I must go, whilst I still can.'

Pearce was standing by his car. 'Have you got a pen-knife?' Nash asked.

Viv held up a Swiss Army knife.

'Ideal.' Nash slipped the key in the lock and turned the handle. They stared in, and saw the bound figure in the corner, eyes blinking in the glare of the low winter sun that flooded the concrete shell with bright light. 'Good morning, Dr Dunning. Or should I say Colonel Dunning?' Nash smiled. 'Caroline Dunning, you are under arrest for the murder of Lara North, Adam North and one unidentified male. You are also charged….'

Smith parked opposite the entrance to the police station car park. From his vantage point he had a good view of the building and the area alongside it. He saw a car pull up, recognized the young woman who climbed out of the passenger seat: Jessica North. If the police had her, that was very bad news. He maintained his vigil, and saw another car pull in twenty minutes later. He saw the two men get out and relaxed. To his horror, he then saw one of them open the back door and extract a prisoner. At the sight of Dunning, her wrists handcuffed together, his panic became horror. He started the engine and drove away. He needed to get onto military premises as quickly as possible. The nearest barracks was more than half an hour away. He needed to get there fast. Once there, he was safe. The police wouldn't be able to get to him on army premises. But not before he'd made a phone call. One that would ensure not only his safety; but the release of Colonel Dunning.

Nash and Pearce handed Dunning over to Sergeant Binns. The paperwork took about twenty minutes to complete, largely because of the prisoner's complete refusal to cooperate, even to the extent of providing an address. When it was done, Nash told Binns, 'Get a female officer to search her, then

chuck her into a cell until we're ready for her, and, Jack' –
Binns looked up – 'don't stand any nonsense. The woman's
a multi-murderer and worse, despite her cut-glass accent and
high sounding titles. Keep her in seclusion until we're ready
to interview her. No visitors, no phone calls.'

'But, Mike, I can't do that,' Binns protested. 'It's against
the rules.'

'Official Secrets Act,' Nash told him. 'She's in possession of highly sensitive information. Can't risk her passing it
on to a potential enemy.'

'Can you do that?' Pearce asked as they went upstairs.

'I've no idea. But if I don't know, it stands to reason
other people don't.'

Nash walked into the CID suite to find Jessica and her
father sitting with Clara. Both of them were in tears, whilst
Clara also looked upset. 'Dr North, Jessica,' Nash winked at
the girl, a gesture unseen by everyone except Mironova. 'I'm
glad to say we have the person responsible for ordering the
murders of Mrs North and Adam in custody. Unfortunately
the hitman himself is still at large, so for the time being I
think it would be safer for you to remain here until I can
find you suitable accommodation. Please excuse me for a few
minutes, I have some phone calls to make, then I can tell you
both exactly what all this is about.'

Nash went into his office. He was about to pick up the
phone when it rang. He glanced at the number on the display. 'Ruth, I was about to ring you.'

'Good idea, wrong person.' The voice was that of Chief
Constable O'Donnell.

'Sorry, ma'am, I wanted to tell Superintendent
Edwards—'

'That you've just arrested a high ranking army officer,'
she finished for him.

Nash gasped. 'You knew about it? How?'

'I've just had a phone call from the MOD. It would
appear that the excrement has collided with the ventilator:

big style. They're sending a bigwig up by plane to secure your prisoner's release. He'll be here tomorrow.'

'Before you agree to anything, ma'am, I think you ought to hear the case against her. I was going to leave it until later, but I think we should interview her straight away. Before that, I'd like you to look through the evidence. It will take a long time, I'm afraid.'

'Very well, Ruth and I will be over in about an hour. One thing's for sure, life's never boring with you around, Mike.'

When Nash put the phone down he went to the safe and took out the file. He called Pearce in. 'Viv, I want you to make four copies of these transcriptions. Put them in envelopes, marked for Dr North, the chief constable, Superintendent Edwards, and the MOD.'

'What do you want doing with the disks?'

'Nothing. They remain in the safe at all times. Clear?'

'OK, Mike. Speaking of the files and disks, I've got the results back from the forensics people. There are several sets of fingerprints on each.'

'Get me the report, please.'

Whilst he was waiting, Nash ran downstairs. 'Jack, have you got that set of Dunning's fingerprints handy? I'd like to borrow them for a while.'

Binns passed them over. 'She's a cocky bitch, that one. Reckons we can't hold her. Said she'd be walking out of here within forty-eight hours.'

Nash gritted his teeth. 'We'll see about that.'

As he returned to the CID suite, Nash braced himself for the ordeal of interviewing Dr North. He was about to go in when the door opened, and Clara came out. 'I've just got the results of Dr North's blood test,' she handed him a sheet of paper. 'The doctor rang before he faxed it through. He's really angry, and concerned for Dr North's safety, and that of those around him. He believes we ought to consider having him sectioned until they can assess the long term effects of the drugs they've been feeding him.'

Nash read the first part of the report, which was mostly incomprehensible. It contained a list of seven different chemical formulae, which meant nothing to a layman. The conclusion, however, where the doctor had summed up the effects, was dynamite.

'There is little doubt that the person who administered these drugs to Dr North was well aware of the effect they would have. It is a combination no ethically minded physician would prescribe, and no pharmacist would make up. Briefly, the combination is that of a complex variety of hallucinatory drugs, aphrodisiacs, mood suppressants and sedatives. The combined effect would be to render Dr North incapable of decision making, outside of his own sphere of work. He would be compliant to the wishes of others and subservient to the sexual demands of persons close to him to whom he felt attracted. Although it is difficult to judge how the balance of the drugs was arrived at, or the length of time they had been administered, my own examination of the patient would tend to suggest a period of months, if not years, and the resultant state of mind is that Dr North is in urgent need of long term, in-depth psychiatric care.'

Clara watched Nash's face change as he read it. His expression was grim. 'The problem's going to be how we get round this.' He tapped the report.

'Having him sectioned, you mean?'

He nodded. 'Let me have a word with Jessica, alone. Tell Dr North I need to take a statement from her about the kidnapping. Get him another cup of tea or something.'

Nash opened the door. North was still clutching the photograph in one hand, whilst the other was holding Jessica's. 'I'm going to ask my sergeant to get you another drink, whilst I take a statement from Jessica about the man who abducted her. If I was you, I'd opt for tea, her coffee's lousy. Either that or ask DC Pearce to make it. Clara's coffee tastes like something that's been drained out of a car engine.'

North seemed to accept this. He let go of his daughter's hand. 'You won't keep her long, will you?' North asked; his voice tremulous.

'Not a minute longer than necessary,' Nash reassured him. 'And she'll be right next door.' He pointed to his office.

North smiled, a major achievement given the contents of the report in Nash's pocket. Jessica followed the detective into his office; a worried frown on her face. As soon as Nash closed the door she asked, 'What do you need to know. I mean, that you don't know already?'

Nash studied her. Something about Jessica, the way she acted, the way she spoke of the time she'd spent with Hirst made him suspicious. He decided to test her out. 'Nothing you're not prepared to tell me.' He smiled. 'And I guess there could be quite a bit, one way or another.'

'I'm not sure what you mean.' Jessica's blush gave Nash his answer.

'It's all right, I was only teasing you. I only met Steve once, and that was in awful circumstances. But I liked him a lot. Obviously not as much as you did.'

Jessica's face was beetroot. 'Please, don't tell my father. He's in a bad enough state to begin with.'

'What could I tell him? I don't know anything. I might have my suspicions, but that's probably my dirty mind. And in any case that wasn't the reason I asked you in here. I don't want to know anything about your abduction; or your relationship with Steve Hirst. That's your private business. What I wanted to get you on your own for was this.' He fished the report from his pocket. 'Sit down before you read it. Along with everything else you've learned it proves what evil bastards they are. And when I tell you about the phone call I've just had, you'll realize how dangerous they still are.'

She wouldn't sit. She was too strong for that. Nash realized the core of steel within her, much as Hirst had done. She read the report, her face whitening with anger. At the end she was ashen; her lip trembled as she fought with her tears. 'Is there no end to this?' She turned towards Nash and almost flung herself into his arms, weeping, inconsolable. Nash put an arm round her shoulders, stroking her, soothing her.

The door opened and Clara coughed. Nash looked up. 'Jessica's a bit upset, Clara. Come in, close the door behind you. I don't want Dr North to see her in this state.'

Jessica pulled herself upright, as much a mental act as a physical one. She dried her eyes on her sleeve and managed a watery smile. 'Sorry,' she muttered, 'everything just got to me. I was all right before. I got used to hating Mother and Adam for the way they behaved. But knowing they were being poisoned, that makes it unbearable. Then to find out they've been doing the same to Dad; that was too much. Why didn't they have a go at me, I wonder?'

'I think I can answer that. You were unavailable for two thirds of the year, being away at school. The drugs they used were designed for long term effect. They couldn't get to you. Now, what do you want to do about this?' Nash tapped the paper.

'I don't like the thought of him going into an institution.' Jessica shrugged. 'But you've seen what a state he's in. That man out there' – Nash noticed the girl's hand was trembling. With anger as much as distress, he thought – 'That isn't my father. Not the father I knew. Not the father who cared for us, played games with us when we were little. That's as much a ruined shell as our cottage. So, yes, call your doctor and make the arrangements.' She sighed wearily. 'I'll sign the papers. But what I'll do whilst he's in care, I've no idea.'

'Why don't you have a word with Sonya Williams? She might have some ideas.'

If Nash had any doubt about Jessica's resilience it was resolved by her retort. 'I could do, perhaps. She might let me stay for a while. Then I could always go out for the evening, if she was entertaining someone.'

Clara's laughter and Jessica's smile were the brightest spots of the day so far, Nash thought. Until he remembered Sonya's parting promise.

'Mike, the chief and Ruth are downstairs talking to Jack,' Clara told him.

'Right, stall them when they come up, will you. I'll phone and make these arrangements. Introduce them to Dr North; then bring them in here. I'd like them to meet a very brave young woman.'

CHAPTER NINETEEN

After Pearce left to take North and Jessica to the doctor's surgery, Nash met with the chief constable and Superintendent Edwards. He handed them each a copy of the file transcripts.

'Before you read these, they refer to the people involved in this case, so let me fill you in with the details. Basically, the idea was American in origin. It was a development of the MKULTRA scheme, which was dreamed up by the CIA as early as the 1950s. Incidentally, there are documents to confirm this. They found that if they fed soldiers with certain hallucinogenic drugs, principally LSD, it made them less susceptible to both pain and fear. The experiments continued right through the Vietnam War, up until the administration got spooked by the Watergate affair. The CIA was instructed to stop all trials, and any evidence relating to MKULTRA was destroyed on the orders of Richard Helms, the then Director. Although there was no official involvement or backing, it seems certain pharmaceutical companies took up the baton after the Gulf War, and began experiments using the new generation of drugs that was becoming available. Dr North had already been headhunted to work for one of these companies. The American military was approached, but they were unwilling to commit to the scheme in an official capacity, although they probably kept abreast of developments. However, the British forces were keen to see what was achievable, so they assigned a high ranking scientific officer to set up a small company that would continue work on the project. Helm Pharm was that company. Dr North, who by now was the leading expert, was brought back from America to work on the scheme.

'However, he had serious reservations about the use the drugs were being put to, particularly the use of human guinea pigs in the form of soldiers serving in the front line. To ensure his compliance, the head of the project, who we now know to be Dr, or Colonel Dunning, set about a three-pronged attack that would ensure North's compliance. She fed him mood altering drugs, the main part of these being an aphrodisiac. Then she allowed North to seduce her, ensuring there were plenty of candid photos of his adultery. At the same time she became a "family friend", spending a lot of time at the North household. She fed Lara North a cocktail of drugs that turned her into an uncontrollable nymphomaniac, and at the same time became her lover too. This "treatment" continued on and off for several years, ensuring the deterioration in the marriage. Somewhere along the line, she introduced North's son, Adam, to class A drugs, principally cocaine laced with an additional addiction fixer that ensured he couldn't be weaned off them.'

Nash paused and looked at the two senior officers, noting the look of horror on their faces. 'If you think that's cold blooded and callous, wait until you hear the rest. Recently, Dunning found out that Lara had begun to suspect that she was in effect being poisoned. She might well have threatened Dunning with exposure. Unfortunately for her, there was a break-in at the laboratory, and the disks containing all this information were stolen. That effectively signed the death warrant for Lara and Adam North. For Jessica too, but for the fact that someone guessed what they had in mind for her and removed her from harm's way. Dunning's second in command, a military intelligence officer by the name of

Major Smith, was detailed to carry out the assassinations. You both know what happened. Lara and her lover, a man whose name we don't know, were burned to death in a fire at the North home, one that was rigged to look like an electrical fault. A few weeks later, Adam North was placed in the stocks and suffocated with superglue.

'Smith was probably under the influence of one of Dr North's drug cocktails, a product aptly named MAD. It stands for modified amphetamine dependency. It was first trialled recently by a party led by Smith whilst abroad. Their mission was to attack a far superior Taliban group. Smith was instructed to make sure none of his fellow soldiers returned from that mission. One did, however, and it is thanks to him that this information has come out. He is also responsible for Jessica North being alive today.

'As I see it, Dunning is responsible for the deaths of those soldiers as well as those of Mrs North and her son. In addition, there are countless charges relating to the drugs administered that are down to her. That is the woman in the cells downstairs. The woman whose release the MOD is sending a senior official here to secure.'

There was a long silence. Eventually, O'Donnell spoke. 'I think you've done really well to piece all this together, Mike. If things had been different I feel confident the CPS would have been happy to take the case to court. However, as things stand their hands and ours are tied. If the MOD insists on our releasing Dr Dunning, or Colonel Dunning, or whatever the blasted woman's title really is, then there's nothing whatsoever we can do about it. All I'll be able to do is insist there is no comeback on North or his daughter over this. If I can manage to get them to call their attack dogs off them, at least we'll have achieved something.' She saw Nash about to protest and held up her hand.

'I know it's frustrating for you. Bloody frustrating, and we all feel the same, but I'm afraid you'll have to accept it, Mike. I can't see any way we'll be able to bring the Dunning woman to court unless the MOD agrees. And that isn't going to happen.'

Nash broke the news to Mironova and Pearce, and the CID officers spent the afternoon gloomily tidying up files. The thought that they had a murderer in their cells but would not be able to prosecute her didn't go down well with any of them. After a while, Nash left the other two and went back to his office. He spent half an hour sitting behind his desk, reflecting on the case, before emerging. 'I'm off,' he told the others. 'I've some shopping to do. I'll be out for half an hour or so.'

When he returned, Clara saw that he was in a noticeably more cheerful frame of mind. 'I didn't realize shopping had such a good effect on you,' she commented.

Nash smiled. 'It all depends on what you go shopping for. Besides which, I've got a date tonight.'

'Oh yes, the Merry Widow.'

'You got it,' Nash admitted. He winked at her and went into his office, whistling as he closed the door behind him. Clara stared at the closing door, trying to work out how half an hour could have effected such a change. She turned to Pearce. 'I wonder if he's been taking some of those drugs.'

'If he has, I wouldn't mind some,' Pearce told her morosely.

Nash went to his flat and showered before leaving to go to Sonya's house. He picked up the carrier bag he'd brought from the office, then drove the short distance across town.

'Have you eaten?' Sonya asked after she let him in.

They walked into the lounge, his arm around her waist. 'No, to be honest, I haven't felt hungry. Something happened this afternoon that spoilt my appetite.'

'I'll have to tempt you then.'

'You don't need to cook to do that.'

She looked at him, head on one side. 'Whatever went wrong, you've solved it or you're on the way to putting it right.'

'How do you work that out?'

'Because you made a suggestive remark. You'd only do that if you'd got things sorted. So, what's in the carrier?' She pointed to the bag he'd put down on the settee.

'I'll show you later. What are you going to tempt me with first?'

'I thought chicken casserole would be nice. You don't want anything too heavy.' He watched her move towards him. Her eyes were smoky with desire. 'Not before exercise.'

After they'd eaten, Nash told her what had happened at the station. 'The likelihood is that the MOD will insist that we release Dunning and drop all charges against her. Which sickens me and my colleagues, but on the face of it there's nothing we can do.'

'Have they really got the power to do that?'

'Of course they have. All they need to do is use the "in the interests of national security" line, and there's nothing we can do about it.'

'Even though you've got conclusive evidence that she's guilty of murder, or conspiracy, or whatever the technical name is?'

'That's near enough. And no, we'll have to let her go.'

'And that's it? You're going to leave it at that? I don't believe you're prepared to give in so meekly.'

'Did I say I was giving in? Did I say I was leaving it at that? Do you really believe I'm that spineless?'

'No, of course I don't. But from what you've told me, what else can you do?'

Nash told her what he had in mind. As he did so, Sonya's eyes widened in shock, which turned to admiration, the admiration cloaking her desire. When Nash finished speaking, she reached across the table and caressed his cheek. 'Mike, you're a clever, conniving, cunning bastard. Take me to bed and make love to me.'

Nash hid his reluctance remarkably well. Several times.

Next morning, he wandered into the bathroom and showered in leisurely fashion whilst Sonya went to make breakfast. When he joined her in the kitchen she passed him a coffee, in a mug of considerable dimensions. 'I know you said I'd to drink a jarful,' he joked, 'but I didn't realize I'd to do it all in one go. This mug's more like a young swimming pool.'

'I thought you might be thirsty. Hungry too after last night. So I'm making a full English.'

'Great, that'll set me up for the day ahead.'

Sonya glanced across at him. 'You sound much better this morning.'

'Well, there's nothing like a good night's sleep to set you up for the day. And that was nothing like a good night's sleep.'

Nash put the mug down and went across to where Sonya was attempting to open a packet of bacon. He slipped his arms round her, feeling the curve of her breasts against his arms, through the towelling of her bath robe. She leaned back against him as he began to caress her, moaning slightly in mock protest as she sensed his arousal. Breakfast was delayed for quite some time.

As they were eating, Sonya's mobile rang. She glanced at the display and frowned. She answered the call, relaxed and made the sign of a letter 'J' in the air. Her conversation seemed to be limited to a series of agreements to whatever was being said. She ended the call and put the phone down. 'That was Jessica. Her father's being kept in a clinic in Netherdale until they've got the drugs out of his system. She reckons it'll be two or three weeks. She needs somewhere to stay in the meantime and asked if I could help her out.'

Sonya put her hand on Mike's. 'I'm sorry, but the poor girl sounded so lonely and upset, I hadn't the heart to say no. It'll mean you won't be able to come and stay for a while though.'

Nash smiled. 'Don't worry about me. Who do you think suggested the idea to Jessica in the first place?'

'You did? That was thoughtful of you, Mike.'

'Now, before I go, are you comfortable with our little arrangement?'

'You mean, about the—'

'Yes, because if not, I can always take it on my own. You'll come in for a bit of flak and a considerable amount of publicity.'

Sonya's eyes strayed to the photograph on the dresser. Of her husband in full dress uniform, taken just before he left for the final time. Any doubts she had vanished. 'Of course I'll do it. If only for the sake of Steve and others like him.'

When Nash reached Netherdale HQ, the chief constable was already in a meeting with the official from the MOD. He waited patiently in the outer office until O'Donnell appeared. She introduced Nash to the civil servant. 'I'm afraid I have to leave now. I'm due at the Home Office this afternoon and if I don't get off soon I'll miss my train. Detective Inspector Nash is aware of most of what you're asking for. I'm sure he'll do his best to comply.'

The official's back was turned to the chief constable. Nash, whose eyes were on her, hid a grin as he noticed the crossed fingers.

'So, Nash,' the official started almost before the door closed. 'You'll release Colonel Dunning this morning. All charges against her will be dropped. That has already been agreed.'

The words were issued more as a command than a request. Nash waited for the rest. 'In addition, I'll travel to Helmsdale with you, to take charge of the sensitive information that was stolen from Helm Pharm.'

'That's evidence in a murder inquiry,' Nash protested.

'It is also protected by the Official Secrets Act.' The official did little to disguise his triumph. 'Which outweighs your murder case. Finally, I want all the evidence you have about the person who is responsible for the destruction of Ministry of Defence property, by which I mean the Helm Pharm laboratory.'

'I'm afraid you're asking too much,' Nash told him. 'I will release Colonel Dunning, under protest. I will relinquish the disks and documents in my safe, under protest. But no way will I give you information that might or might not be relevant to the explosion at that laboratory. For one thing, I don't trust you or your department to handle it correctly. For another, much of it is speculation. That wouldn't be good enough for prosecution by the CPS, but I'm far from confident that you'd be as discriminating. In other words, I'm not prepared to give you ammunition for you to indulge in a witch-hunt.'

'You'll do as you're told, Nash. If you value your career in the police force, that is.'

'Sorry, did I get that right? Are you threatening me?'

'Too damned right I am. If you don't do exactly as requested, your career will be over, and all your pension rights will be forfeit.'

'I see,' Nash replied thoughtfully. He gestured towards the third occupant of the room, a young woman sitting quietly in the corner, taking notes. 'You are aware that this conversation is being witnessed and minuted, I trust.'

'I don't care what you and your secretary cook up between you,' the civil servant snarled, without either civility or servility.

Nash smiled sweetly. 'Oh, sorry, didn't I introduce you? This isn't my secretary. This is Chief Superintendent Edwards. She leaves here in two days' time, to take up her new role as a senior officer in Her Majesty's Inspectorate of Constabulary.' Nash paused to let the unpalatable news sink in. 'And that, I think, trumps your ace.'

Nash returned to Helmsdale and asked Binns to prepare the release forms. He took the MOD official to his office and handed over the disks and papers from inside his safe. 'Get a receipt for these,' he told Mironova. 'And don't let him leave without signing it.' He saw little point in indulging in politeness. 'Treat him like one of your drug pushers, not to be trusted. I'll be downstairs seeing to the release of our murderous Colonel.'

Dunning was waiting by the reception desk, with Binns hovering close by when Nash appeared, followed by the civil servant and Mironova. Nash signed the forms and escorted the released prisoner to the door. The MOD official was already outside when Nash caught hold of the woman's sleeve. 'Listen!' he told her.

She frowned. 'Listen to what? I can't hear anything.'

'No, neither can I,' Nash replied. 'Which means the fat lady hasn't started to sing.'

'What was all that about?' Mironova asked as they watched the MOD car leave. 'About it not being over? Surely there's nothing we can do now?'

'Don't be too sure, Clara,' Nash told her cheerfully. 'My father had a few favourite sayings. One of them was, "there's more than one way of skinning a cat". I never understood exactly what he meant until now. He'd another too, which Colonel Dunning might come to regret never hearing. It was "never trust a politician – you'll know when they're lying because their lips move".'

'I'm sorry, Mike, you've lost me completely.'

'Come on, I'll make coffee and explain.'

'I'll make it if you want,' Clara volunteered.

Nash shuddered. 'No thanks, I want coffee, not dishwater.'

Around lunchtime, Nash rang Sonya. 'I hope you're calling to say it's all systems go,' Sonya said. 'I've just got back from the shops. It's cost me a fortune. Do you know how much some of those things cost? Particularly the amounts you asked for.'

'It's go all right,' Nash calmed her. 'When can you make a start?'

'I'm not sure. I can only do it after I've put the children to bed. And I've Jessica coming to stay, bear in mind.'

'Get her to help you,' Nash suggested. 'It might make a welcome distraction from worrying about her father. And she'll enjoy it, especially when she knows what it will achieve.'

'Good idea. I'll put it to her tonight. The only problem is when am I going to see you? It makes things very difficult, with Jessica and the kids here.'

'I'd an idea about that too. You can always ask Jessica to look after the children overnight. Then you can come round to my place. You're not the only one with a double bed you know.'

'Another great idea! Two in five minutes! Mike, you're really on top form.'

Nash was still smiling when he put the phone down.

Four days later, when Becky Pollard reached her office, Helmsdale was far from her thoughts. Her regrets at ending the affair with Mike had been shelved as she plunged into the busy life of an assistant editor for one of the national dailies. There was a large padded envelope on her desk. She frowned, she wasn't expecting anything. She examined the handwriting – it was unfamiliar. The postmark was familiar though; Netherdale. Something from *The Gazette* perhaps? She opened the envelope and slid the contents out. She ignored the other items and went straight to the letter. She began to read, curiosity turning to astonishment, mounting to shock. She put the letter down and picked up the other papers. She read them through once, then a second time, then a third. When she'd finished, she scooped everything up and put it back in the envelope. She set off for the editor's office. Irrational though it was, she couldn't help casting a glance over her shoulder to see if anyone was watching her.

When she reached the editorial suite, her boss was engaged. Becky sat with his secretary for ten anxious minutes until he finished his meeting. 'What is it?' he asked, eyeing the envelope in her hand.

Becky explained. 'This arrived this morning. The fact that it was addressed to me tells me DI Nash has caused it to be sent.'

'How do you know that?'

'Because Mike and I were in a relationship. I ended it when I came down here,' Becky told him. 'The thing is, this woman, Mrs Williams, has written this because she knows the only way to get justice for the victims is to expose what was going on at that laboratory. She says' – Becky pulled the letter out and scanned it – 'she's giving us a forty-eight hour exclusive. Then she's sending it to all the other nationals.'

'Let me have a look.'

Becky passed the envelope across. 'Have you tried the disks?'

She shook her head. 'I brought it straight to you.'

He began reading. After a few minutes he said, 'Bloody hell! This is C4, Semtex and dynamite all rolled into one.' He buzzed his secretary. 'Get the head of legal off his fat arse and down to my office immediately.

'If this is kosher, we go to print the day after tomorrow. We need to check it out and run it past the legal bods first. If they OK it, we run it. Get the senior crime man on it. He can do the interviews and write up. You do the verification. Ring this Nash character first. I take it you're still speaking to one another?'

Becky reassured him.

As she was speaking, a few miles away, an office in the Ministry of Defence was filled with the sound of the overture from *Carmen*. It had seemed appropriate to Nash to substitute the computer disks for an opera about a woman who betrayed her lover.

CHAPTER TWENTY

Most thunderstorms start with a few clouds on the horizon. As the storm builds, the lightning flashes and the rolling thunder become more frequent. So it was with the Dunning case, as the papers began to call it. When first one, then all of the dailies started carrying the story, official denials became less and less convincing. When the intensity increased, and the likelihood of the story losing impetus faded, questions began to be asked in Parliament. Members demanded answers. At first it was radical MPs who took up the baton. Then opposition parties waded in, glad for a chance to embarrass the government. An official inquiry was demanded. Once, twice, three times the Minister of Defence denied the claims, refused the inquiry. An early day motion was tabled, and in the resulting debate, the government only scraped a majority by virtue of a three line whip.

Within a month of Dunning's release from custody, Nash received a phone call. It was from the same MOD official who'd high-handedly demanded her release. When the conversation was over, Nash put the phone down and looked across his desk at Mironova. 'Colonel Dunning will be delivered by the military police into our custody in an hour's time. The MOD will not oppose her being sent for trial on charges of murder and conspiracy.'

'That's terrific news. What about Smith? Do we get him as well?'

'Unfortunately not. At least not at the moment. That will have to come later. Apparently Smith's gone back onto the front line. He's currently serving abroad, I believe.' Nash thought for a moment. 'I guess that means I'll have to go and retrieve the real evidence from Sonya tonight, so we can deliver it to the CPS.'

'Oh dear, poor you,' Clara sympathized. 'You get all the worst jobs, don't you? Speaking of which, how's Dr North?'

'I spoke to Jessica a couple of days ago. They've rented a bungalow on the outskirts of town. She gets the keys tomorrow. She's hoping to move in the day after, and bring her father home then. Apparently he's much better now the drugs are out of his system. It'll take a long time for him to make a full recovery of course, but there is hope. Jessica said the worst thing is coping with the shattering of his faith, by the betrayal of people he trusted.

'The other thing that bloke from the MOD told me is that any further experiments along the lines of the one at Helm Pharm wouldn't be sanctioned. He said there might even be legislation against it, which is another good thing to come out of this mess.'

It was exactly an hour later when the receptionist rang through to tell Nash the prisoner had arrived. Nash and Mironova hurried downstairs. As Clara was completing the formalities of the handover with the military policewomen, Nash spoke to Dunning. 'You know what, Colonel? Now I can hear the fat lady singing.'

three months later

The man dressed in Taliban fighter's distinctive clothing glared at his captives. The two men were seated, the rocks hot and uncomfortable under them, their backs hunched away from the searing heat given off by the panels of the scout car. Their wrists were bound tightly, their uniforms, once neat and clean as was expected of British soldiers, now dusty, sweat bedraggled and bloodstained.

They stared back, dumb defiance all they could manage in the face of their captor's obvious and implacable hatred, and the rough cloth gags stuffed into their mouths.

The fighter bent over his prisoners, rummaging through their pockets. He removed a small bottle and looked at it for a few moments, examining the tablets and capsules inside. He shrugged and tossed it into their vehicle, before resuming his search. There was little of interest, although he smiled as he pocketed a cigarette packet. When he'd completed his search, he gestured with his Kalashnikov. He didn't need to speak; he knew one of his prisoners wouldn't have understood him if he had. Besides, the weapon in his hands and the hostility in his eyes said all that was needed.

They stumbled to their feet, awkward from their bonds, and the length of time since they'd been allowed to move freely. He gestured again, pointing towards their vehicle. They climbed in; the cab was like a furnace. The gunman stepped forward, up to the man in the passenger seat. He placed the rifle against the soldier's temple and pulled the trigger.

The man's companion recoiled, as a pulpy mass of brain and blood spattered across his already soiled uniform. The second shot came as the first was still ringing, the echoes reverberating round the empty, barren landscape. The fighter regarded his victims for a moment before stepping well clear of the vehicle. He raised the Kalashnikov and fired a third shot. It punctured the fuel tank.

A devout Muslim is denied the sinful pleasure of alcohol. In its place, tobacco rates highly. He lit a cigarette from the packet he'd liberated from one of the dead men, his nose wrinkling momentarily at the unfamiliar taste. He let the match burn down for a second, before tossing it into the widening pool of diesel.

He turned away, using his shaal to shield his head from the blast. He watched the vehicle burn for a few minutes.

Then he turned his eyes to the distant hills. He sighed, before he began to move. It was a long walk home.

Jessica was sitting at the breakfast table. Her father was seated across from her. The small bungalow they'd rented on the outskirts of Helmsdale was a far cry from their last house, but it would do, certainly until her father recovered. He was staring into his bowl as she watched him, pushing the cornflakes around without making much effort to eat them. His breakdown had been severe, a retreat from the harsh realities of the shock upon shock his brain had finally refused to cope with.

Jessica's thoughts were interrupted by the click of the letter box. She got up and walked through to the hall. As she returned to the kitchen, she was already scanning the paper. She found the item she was looking for inside the front page. She began to read:

> 'The names of two British soldiers, missing in Afghanistan for over a week were released by the Ministry of Defence yesterday, 24 hours after their bodies were found in the burnt out scoutcar they had been using on patrol. The two men were Major Anthony Smith and Sergeant Steven Hirst.'

Jessica's eyes filled with tears, she felt nausea rising in her stomach. What had Steve been doing, what had he been thinking of, going on patrol with Smith? And what had happened between them, out there in that arid wasteland? She tasted bile in her throat and stumbled out of the room, vision blurred as she headed for the toilet.

Dr North picked up the paper his daughter had left open. He scanned the page, without seeing anything that might have upset her. But Jessica was distressed, and that was something he couldn't cope with. He began to tremble, tears coursing down his cheeks. Then Jessica was back. She cradled his head in her arms and began to rock him, gently as with a baby. 'It's all right, Daddy,' she told him, her tone as soft and loving as a mother's. 'Don't be upset, Daddy, everything's all right.' She smoothed his hair with her hand. 'You'll see. Everything's going to be all right now. We've got each other, haven't we?'

But she was lying. To herself as well as to her father. It wasn't all right. How could it be after news like that? She felt the tears well up again, and dashed them away angrily. Tears were a weakness she could not afford.

Nash read the news as he was sitting in his office. Mironova walked in as he finished. She saw the look of sadness on his face. 'Something wrong, Mike?'

He passed her the paper. 'I don't think Smith's much of a loss, but that's bad news about Hirst,' he said as she read the article. 'He was a really decent bloke. We'd never have brought Dunning to trial, let alone stopped that vile experimentation, if it hadn't been for him.

'What I can't understand is what he was doing anywhere near Smith. He knew what Smith was capable of. Would you go out on patrol with someone you knew was a cold-blooded killer? One who you knew had already shot one of your mates in the back? Makes you wonder what exactly went on out in that desert, doesn't it? One thing's for sure, we'll never prosecute Smith now.'

'At least we've got his boss. Dunning was the architect of the evil. Putting her on trial will do a lot to help those such as Dr North, to say nothing of the servicemen's families who were affected by that wicked bitch.'

'That reminds me, I didn't get chance to tell you, with you being off yesterday. CPS rang. Dunning's changed her plea to guilty. The trial starts next week, but it's a formality now. With a bit of luck sentencing will take place before the end of the month. As you said, it'll give closure to some people.' Nash glanced down at the paper. 'Unfortunately, not for everyone.'

eighteen months later

Jessica was alone when Sonya phoned. Her father had just left for work. In the year and a half since their ordeal, Jessica had matured even more. There was a depth of character in her features that marked her out from others of her age.

Part of this had been due to what she'd been through, but mostly it was from having to nurse her father through his break-down and back to some semblance of recovery. It had been a slow, painful process, with many relapses along the way. He was better now, but his health was fragile. Going back to work had helped; Richard North had been hesitant about accepting a teaching post, but he'd taken to it well enough for Jessica to hope it marked a turning point in his fight to recover.

'Hi, Jessica, how's things?'

They'd become friends after Steve's return to active ser-vice. The bond between them had been strengthened further after the news of his death. 'Not too bad. I've just seen Dad off to work, and I was thinking about taking a bath.'

Sonya sighed. 'Talk about the idle rich. Listen, do you fancy coming for coffee this morning? If you can delay your ablutions, that is.'

'OK, give me an hour.'

Sonya looked well, better than Jessica had seen her for a long time. 'You're looking good. What's that down to? Don't tell me, let me guess. The long arm of the law?'

Sonya grinned. 'Mike only pops in now and again.'

Jessica laughed. 'Pops what in?'

Sonya blushed slightly. 'I mean, he comes to keep me company occasionally. He only stays for a bit.'

'A bit of what?'

'Oh, all right, so Mike and I spend a night together now and again. It isn't serious, with either of us; just a bit of harm-less fun. There, now I've confessed my sins, are you satisfied?'

'You certainly seem to be. He must be doing you good.'

Sonya's eyes were dreamy. 'Oh yes, he sure is.'

'Sonya!' Jessica pretended to be shocked, but spoilt the effect by giggling. 'So what's the panic this morning? I can tell you're up to something.'

Her friend's eyes sparkled. 'You know that motorhome? The one Steve left to you? You haven't sold it or anything have you?'

'No, why?'

'I had this great idea. Came to me this morning. How do you fancy going on holiday? You and me, I mean, together? If we take the motorhome it wouldn't be wildly expensive.'

'That's totally weird. I was only thinking last night that I ought to use it. And I reckon a holiday's what I need. But what about the kids?'

'Well, I suppose we'd have to take them as well.'

'It'd be a bit cramped, but I suppose we could manage. Have you got anywhere in mind?'

'Not really, I thought we could just point it and go. We could take it in turns to drive, that'd make it much easier.'

Jessica was watching the children playing. She bent down and scooped the youngest up, swinging him onto her hip like a veteran. Sonya smiled. 'Your little Stevie's really growing, isn't he?'

Jessica laughed. 'Growing into a little monster, aren't you, nuisance face?' The infant chuckled with glee as his mother tickled him. 'So, come on, give me some clue about this holiday. Where do you fancy?'

'Have you ever been to the Lake District?'

Jessica swung her son to cradle him. 'No, never. You?'

'No, we'd planned to, but then….'

'Let's give it a go then.'

The hotel was part of a leisure complex, more of a clubhouse really. All summer long, campers, caravanners and fell walkers thronged the site. Now, as the season was nearing the end, the place was quieter.

It was that dead hour after the lunchtime trade had ended. A time for leisurely tidying, washing glasses, and other small chores before the first customers of the evening. The barman was polishing glasses, staring out of the window. The bar overlooked the lake; the water rippled in the warm autumn sunshine. Around the shores, the belt of woodland was beginning to take on a golden hue as the leaves turned colour. Above the tree line, the majestic Cumbrian hills towered, splendid in their gaunt, dark livery.

A motorhome drove slowly past on the service road, breaking his reverie and stirring up memories. It was a similar colour and shape to the one....

He frowned and set the glass down before taking out his wallet. Flicking it open, he stared again at the photo in the clear plastic window.

He'd taken it surreptitiously, using the camera on his mobile phone. It was the act of taking the photo that had caused him to realize how much the girl had come to mean to him. Much more than a mere comrade in arms, a colleague on a mission. He looked at her face, eyes aglow with the satisfaction of what they'd achieved, excited by what they still had to do.

He reached for his phone, as he'd reached for it a dozen times before. He'd brought her number up on the screen before he paused. He took a long, deep, shuddering breath. No, better not go there. To all intents and purposes he was dead; had died that day in the blazing Afghan heat. Buried, with full military honours.

Better to remain dead. Better not to go back, to change things. She had the rest of her life before her. So much to do and see: so much to achieve. The last thing she needed was a permanent reminder of the past. He sighed and switched off the phone, stuffed the wallet back in his pocket, picked up the towel and another glass.

THE END

The D.I. Mike Nash Series

Book 1: WHAT LIES BENEATH
Book 2: VANISH WITHOUT TRACE
Book 3: PLAYING WITH FIRE
Book 4: KILLING CHRISTMAS

Please join our mailing list for updates on D. I. Mike Nash,
free Kindle crime thriller, detective, mystery books
and new releases.

www.joffebooks.com

FREE KINDLE BOOKS

Please join our mailing list for free Kindle books and new releases, including crime thrillers, mysteries, romance and more, as well as news on the next book by Bill Kitson! www.joffebooks.com

Thank you for reading this book. If you enjoyed it please leave feedback on Amazon or Goodreads, and if there is anything we missed or you have a question about then please get in touch. The author and publishing team appreciate your feedback and time reading this book.

We're very grateful to eagle-eyed readers who take the time to contact us. Please send any errors you find to corrections@joffebooks.com